Tam-sin knew dreams; she had been able to
summon and dismiss them at her own will; they
and the people in them had been but toys with
which she could play at desire. Until she had
dreamed for Lord Starrex and plunged them
both into such a venture as she could not control.
Somehow she had brought them here, to new
identities, new adventures, and doubtless,
new dangers.

But there was Kas, who had striven to put
an end to both in two times, two worlds, and who
must also have been wrenched with them into
this, though not in her company?

She was to find out, and the doing was to
bring her into the alien laws and unmapped
lands of yet a third world, and eventually
a fourth and a fifth. . . .

For Tamisan, or Tam-sin, or whatever her
name in whatever world, dreamed true—and in
so doing altered continually the writing of
the histories of the stars.

PERILOUS DREAMS

Andre Norton

DAW BOOKS, INC.
DONALD A. WOLLHEIM, PUBLISHER

1301 Avenue of the Americas
New York, N. Y.   10019

FIRST PRINTING, JUNE 1976

1 2 3 4 5 6 7 8 9

PRINTED IN U.S.A.

CONTENTS

PERILOUS
DREAMS

PART ONE

TOYS
OF
TAMISAN

Toys of Tamisan

I

"She is certified by the Foostmam, Lord Starrex, a true action dreamer to the tenth power!"

Jabis was being too eager, or almost so; he was pushing too much. Tamisan sneered mentally, keeping her face carefully blank, though she took quick glances about from beneath half-closed eyelids. This sale very much concerned herself, since she was the product being discussed, but she had nothing to say in the matter.

She supposed this was a typical sky tower. It seemed to float, since its supports were so slender and well concealed, lifting it high above Ty-Kry. However, none of the windows gave on real sky. Each framed a very different landscape, illustrating, she guessed, other planet scenes; perhaps some were dream remembered or inspired.

There was a living lambil-grass carpet around the easirest on which the owner half lay and half sat. But Jabis had not even been offered a pull-down wall seat, and the two other men in attendance on Lord Starrex stood also. They were real men and not androids, which placed the owner in the multi-credit class. One, Tamisan thought, was a bodyguard, and the other, who was younger and thinner, with a dissatisfied mouth, had on clothing nearly equal to that of the man

3

on the easirest, but with a shade of difference which meant a
lesser place in the household.

Tamisan catalogued what she could see and filed it away
for future reference. Most dreamers did not observe much of
the world about them, they were too enmeshed in their own
creations to care for reality. Tamisan frowned. She *was* a
dreamer. Jabis, and the Foostmam could prove that. The
lounger on the easirest could prove it if he paid Jabis's price.
But she was also something more; Tamisan herself was not
quite sure what. That there was a differçnce in her she had
had mother wit enough to conceal since she had first been
aware that the others in the Foostmam's Hive were not able
to come cleanly out of their dreams into the here and now.
Why, some of them had to be fed, clothed, cared for as if
they were not aware they had any bodies!

"Action dreamer." Lord Starrex shifted his shoulders
against the padding which immediately accommodated itself
to his stirring to give him maximum comfort. "Action dreaming is a little childish."

Tamisan's control held. She felt inside her a small flare of
anger. Childish was it? She would like to show him just how
childish a dream she could spin to enmesh a client. But Jabis
was not in the least moved by that derogatory remark from a
possible purchaser, it was in his eyes only a logical bargaining
move.

"If you wish an E dreamer . . ." He shrugged. "But your
demand to the Hive specified an A."

He was daring to be a little abrupt. Was he so sure of this
lord as all that, Tamisan wondered. He must have some inside information which allowed him to be so confident, for
Jabis could cringe and belly-down in awe as the lowest beg-
gar if he thought such a gesture needful to gain a credit or
two.

"Kas, this is your idea; what is she worth?" Starrex asked
indifferently.

The younger of his companions moved forward a step or
two; he was the reason for her being here. He was Lord Kas,
cousin to the owner of all this magnificence, though certainly
not, Tamisan had already deduced, with any authority in the
household. But the fact that Starrex lay in the easirest was
not dictated by indolence, but rather by what was hidden by
the fas-silk lap robe concealing half his body. A man who

might not walk straight again could find pleasure in the abilities of an action dreamer.

"She has a ten-point rating," Kas reminded the other.

The black brows which gave a stern set to Starrex's features arose a trifle. "Is that so?"

Jabis was quick to take advantage. "It is so, Lord Starrex. Of all this year's swarm, she rated the highest. It was ... is ... the reason why we make this offer to your lordship."

"I do not pay for reports only," returned Starrex.

Jabis was not to be ruffled. "A point ten, my lord, does not give demonstrations. As you know, the Hive accrediting can not be forged. It is only that I have urgent business in Brok and must leave for there, that I am selling her at all. I have had an offer from the Foostmam herself to retain this one for lease outs."

Tamisan, had she had anything to wager, or someone with whom to wager it, would have set this winning of this bout with her uncle. Uncle? To Tamisan's thinking she had no blood tie with this small insect of a man, with his wrinkled face, his never-still eyes and his thin hands with their half-crooked fingers always reminding her of claws outstretched to grab. Surely her mother must have been very unlike Uncle Jabis, or else how could her father ever have seen aught worth bedding (not for just one night but for half a year) in her.

Not for the first time her thoughts were on the riddle of her parents. Her mother had not been a dreamer, though she had had a sister who had regrettably (for the sake of the family fortune) died in the Hive during adolescent stimulation as an E dreamer. Her father had been from off world—an alien, though humanoid enough to crossbreed. He had disappeared again off world when his desire for star roving had become too strong to master. Had it not been that she had early shown dreamer talent Uncle Jabis and the rest of the greedy Yeska clan would never have taken any thought of her after her mother had died of the blue plague.

She was crossbred and had intelligence enough to guess early that that had given her the difference between her powers and those of others in the Hive. The ability to dream was an inborn talent. For those of low power it was a withdrawal from the world, and those dreamers were largely useless. But the others, who could project dreams to include others through linkage, brought high prices, according to the strength and stability of their creations. E dreamers, who created erotic and lascivious otherworlds once were rated more highly than action dreamers. But of late years the swing had been in the opposite direction, though how long that might hold no one could guess. Those lucky enough to have an A dreamer to sell were pushing their wares speedily lest the market decline.

Tamisan's hidden talent was that she herself was never as completely lost in the dream world as those she conveyed to it. Also, (and this she had discovered very recently and hugged that discovery to her) she could in a measure control the linkage so she was not a powerless prisoner forced to dream at another's desire.

She considered what she knew concerning Lord Starrex. That Jabis would sell her to the owner of one of the sky towers had been clear from the first, and naturally he would select what he thought would be the best bargain. But, though rumors wafted through the Hive, Tamisan believed that much of their news of the outer worlds was inaccurate and garbled. Dreamers were roofed and walled from any real meeting with everyday life, their talents feverishly fed and fostered by long sessions with tri-dee projectors and information tapes.

Starrex, unlike most of his class, had been a doer. He had broken the pattern of caste by going off world on lengthy trips. It was only after some mysterious accident had crippled him that he became a recluse, supposedly hiding a maimed body. He did not seem like the others who had come to the Hive seeking wares. Of course, it had been Lord Kas who had summoned them here.

Stretched out on the easirest with that cover of fabulous silk across most of his body, he was hard to judge. She thought that standing he would top Jabis, and he seemed to be well muscled, more like his guard than his cousin.

He had a face unusual in its planes, broad across the forehead and cheek bones, then slimming to a strong chin which narrowed to give his head a vaguely wedge-shaped line. He was dark skinned, almost as dark as a space crewman. His black hair was cut very short so that it was a tight velvet cap, in contrast to the longer strands of his cousin.

His lutrax tunic of a coppery rust shade, was of rich material but less ornamented than that of the younger man. Its sleeves were wide and loose, and now and then he ran his hands up his arms, pushing the fabric away from his skin. He wore only a single jewel, a koros stone set in an earring as a drop which dangled forward against his jawline.

Tamisan did not consider him handsome, but there was something arresting about him. Perhaps it was his air of arrogant assurance, as if in all his life he had never had his wishes crossed. But he had not met Jabis before, and perhaps now even Lord Starrex would have something to learn.

Twisting and turning, indignant and persuasive, using every trick in a very considerable training for dealing and under-dealing, Jabis bargained. He appealed to gods and demons to witness his disinterested desire to please, his despair at being misunderstood. It was quite a notable act and Tamisan stored up some of the choicer bits in her mental reservoir for the making of dreams. It was far more stimulating to watch than a tri-dee, and she wondered why this living drama material was not made available to the Hive. Perhaps, the Foostmam and her assistants feared it, along with any other shred of reality, which might awaken the dreamers from their conditioned absorption in their own creations.

For an instant or two she wondered if Lord Starrex was not enjoying it, too. There was a kind of weariness in his face which suggested boredom, though that was normal for anyone wanting a personal dreamer. Then, suddenly, as if he were tired of it all, he interrupted one of Jabis's more impassioned pleas for celestial understanding of his need for receiving just dues with a single sentence.

"I tire, fellow; take your price and go." He closed his eyes in dismissal.

It was the guard who drew a credit plaque from his belt, swung a long arm over the back of the easirest for Lord Starrex to plant a thumb on its surface to certify payment, and then tossed it to Jabis. It fell to the floor, so the small man had to scrabble for it with his fingers. Tamisan saw the look in his darting eyes. Jabis had little liking for Lord Starrex, which did not mean, of course, that he disdained the credit plaque he had to stoop to catch up.

He did not give a glance to Tamisan as he bowed himself out. She was left standing as if she were an android. It was Lord Kas who stepped forward and touched her lightly on the arm as if he thought she needed guidance.

"Come," he said, and his fingers about her wrist drew her after him. The Lord Starrex took no notice of his new possession.

"What is your name?" Lord Kas spoke slowly, emphasizing each word, as if he needed to do so to pierce some veil between them. Tamisan guessed that he had had contact with a lower-rated dreamer, one who was always bemused in the real world. Caution suggested that she allow him to believe she was in a similar daze. So she raised her head slowly and looked at him, trying to give the appearance of one finding it difficult to focus.

"Tamisan," she answered after a lengthy pause. "I be Tamisan."

"Tamisan, that is a pretty name," he said as one would address a dull-minded child. "I am Lord Kas. I am your friend."

But Tamisan, sensitive to shades of voice, thought she had done well in playing bemused. Whatever Kas might be, he was not her friend, at least not unless it served his purpose.

"These rooms are yours." He had escorted her down a hall to a far door where he passed his hand over the surface in a pattern to break a light lock. Then his grip on her wrist brought her into a high-ceilinged room. There were no windows to interrupt its curve of wall; the place was oval in shape. The center descended in a series of wide, shallow steps to a pool where a small fountain raised a perfumed mist to patter back into a bone-white basin. On the steps were a number of cushions and soft lie-ons, of many delicate shades of blue and green. The oval walls were draped with a shimmer of zidex webbing of pale gray covered with whirls and lines of the palest green.

A great deal of care had gone into the making and furnishing of the room. Perhaps Tamisan was only the latest in a series of dreamers, for this was truly the rest place, raised to a point of luxury unknown even in the Hive, for a dreamer.

A strip of the web tapestry along the wall was raised and a personal-care android entered. The head was only an oval ball with faceted eye-plates and hearing sensors to break its surface; its unclothed, humanoid form was ivory-white.

"This is Porpae," Kas told her. "She will watch over you."

My guard, Tamisan thought. That the care the andriod would give her would be unceasing and of the best, she did not doubt, any more than that ivory being would stand between her and any hope of freedom.

"If you have any wish, tell it to Porpae." Kas dropped his

hold on her arm and turned to the door. "When Lord Starrex wishes to dream, he will send for you."

"I am at his command," she mumbled; it was the proper response.

She watched Kas leave and then looked to Porpae. Tamisan had cause to believe that the android was programmed to record her every move. But would anyone here believe that a dreamer had any desire to be free? A dreamer wished only to dream; it was her life, her entire life. To leave a place which did all to foster such a life, that would be akin to self-killing, something a certified dreamer could not think on.

"I hunger," she told the android. "I would eat."

"Food comes." Porpae went to the wall, swept aside the web once more, to display a series of buttons she pressed in a complicated manner.

When the food did arrive in a closed tray with the viands each in their own hot or cold compartment, Tamisan ate. She recognized the usual dishes of a dreamer's diet, but they were better cooked and more tastily served than in the Hive. She ate, she made use of the bathing place Porpae guided her to behind another wall web, and she slept easily and without stirring on the cushions beside the pool where the faint play of the water lulled her.

Time had very little meaning in the oval room. She ate, slept, bathed, and looked at the tri-dees she asked Porpae to supply. Had she been as the others from the Hive, this existence would have been ideal. But instead, when there was no call to display her art, she grew restless. She was a prisoner here and none of the other inhabitants of the sky tower seemed aware of her.

There was one thing she could do, Tamisan decided upon her second waking. A dreamer was allowed, no, required, to study the personality of the master she must serve, if she were a private dreamer and not a lessee of the Hive. She had a right now to ask for tapes concerning Starrex. In fact, it might be considered odd if she did not, and accordingly she called for those. Thus she learned something of Starrex and his household.

Kas had had his personal fortune wiped out by some catastrophe when he was a child. He had been in a manner adopted by Starrex's father, the head of their clan, and, since Starrex's injuries, had acted in some fashion as his deputy.

The guard was Ulfilas, an off-world mercenary, Starrex had brought back from one of his star voyages.

But Starrex, save for a handful of bare facts, remained an enigma. That he had any human responses to others, Tamisan began to doubt. He had gone seeking change off world, but what he might have found there had not cured his eternal weariness of life. His personal recordings were meager. She now believed that to him anyone of his household was only a tool to be used, or swept from his path and ignored. He was unmarried and such feminine companionship as he had languidly attached to his household (and that more by the effort of the woman involved than through any direct action on his part) did not last long. In fact, he was so encased in a shell of indifference that Tamisan wondered if there was any longer a real man within that outer covering.

She began to speculate as to why he had allowed Kas to bring her as an addition to his belongings. To make the best use of a dreamer the owner must be ready to partake, and what she read in these tapes suggested that Starrex's indifference would raise a barrier to any real dreaming.

The more Tamisan learned in this negative fashion, the more it seemed a challenge. She lay beside the pool in deep thought, though that thought strayed even more than she herself guessed from the rigid mental exercises used by a pointten dreamer. To deliver a dream which would captivate Starrex was indeed a challenge. He wanted action, but her training, acute as it had been, was not enough to entice him. Therefore, *her* action must be able to take a novel turn.

This was an age of oversophistication, when star travel was a fact; and by the tapes, though they were not detailed as to what Starrex had done off world, the lord had experienced much of the reality of his time.

So he must be served the unknown. She had read nothing in the tapes to suggest that Starrex had sadistic or perverted tendencies, and she knew that if he were to be reached in such a fashion she was not the one to do it. Also, Kas would have stated such a requirement at the Hive.

There were many rolls of history on which one could draw, but those had also been mined and remined. The future had been overused, frayed. Tamisan's dark brows drew together above her closed eyes. It was trite; everything she thought of was trite! Why did she care anyway? She did not even know why it had become so strong a drive to build a dream that, when she was called upon to deliver it, would shake Starrex out of his shell, to prove to him that she was worth her rating. Maybe it was partly because he had made no move to send for her and try to prove her powers; his indifference suggesting that he thought she had nothing to offer.

She had the right to call upon the full library of tapes from the Hive, and it was the most complete in the star lanes. Why, ships were sent out for no other reason than to bring back new knowledge to feed the imaginations of the dreamers!

History ... her mind kept returning to the past. Though it was too threadbare for her purposes. History, what was history? It was a series of events, actions by individuals or nations. Actions had results. Tamisan sat up among her cushions. *Results of action!* Sometimes there were far-reaching results from a single action: the death of a ruler, the outcome of one battle, the landing of a star ship or its failure to land.

So . . .

Her flicker of an idea became solid. History could have had many roads to travel beside the one already known. Now, could she make use of that? Why, it had innumerable possibilities. Tamisan's hands clenched the robe lying across and then, who knows? Perhaps a solar system. She reined in more time ... She no longer resented his indifference. She would need every minute it was prolonged.

"Porpae!"

The android materialized from behind the web.

"I must have certain tapes from the Hive." Tamisan hesitated. In spite of the spur of impatience she must build smoothly and surely. "A message to the Foostmam: send to Tamisan 'n' Starrex the rolls of the history of Ty-Kry for the past five hundred years."

It was the history of the single city which based this sky tower. She would begin small, but she could test and retest her idea. Today it would be a single city, tomorrow a world, and then, who knows? Perhaps a solar system. She reined in her excitement. There was much to do; she needed a note recorder, and time. But by The Four Breasts of Vlasta ... *if* she could do it!

It would seem she would have time, though always at the back of Tamisan's mind was the small spark of fear that at any moment the summons to Starrex might come. But the tapes arrived from the Hive and the recorder, so that she swung from one to the other, taking notes from what she learned. After the tapes had been returned, she studied those notes feverishly. Now her idea meant more to her than just a device to amuse a difficult master, it absorbed her utterly, as if she were a low-grade dreamer caught in one of her own creations.

When Tamisan realized the danger of this, she broke with her studies and turned back to the household tapes to learn again what she could of Starrex.

But she was again running through her notes when at last the summons came. How long she had been in Starrex's tower she did not know, for the days and nights in the oval room were all alike. Only Porpae's watchfulness had kept her to a routine of eating and rest.

It was the Lord Kas who came for her, and she had just time to remember her role of bemused dreamer as he entered.

"You are well, happy?" he used the conventional greeting.

"I enjoy the good life."

"It is the Lord Starrex's wish that he enter a dream." Kas reached for her hand and she allowed his touch. "The Lord Starrex demands much; offer him your best, dreamer." He might have been warning her.

"A dreamer dreams," she answered him vaguely. "What is dreamed can be shared."

"True, but the Lord Starrex is hard to please. Do your best for him, dreamer."

She did not answer, and he drew her on, out of the room to a gray shaft and down that to a lower level. The room into which they finally went had the apparatus very familiar to her: a couch for the dreamer, the second for the sharer with the linkage machine between. But here there was a third couch; Tamisan looked at it in surprise.

"Two dream, not three."

Kas shook his head. "It is the Lord Starrex's will that another share also. The linkage is of a new model, very powerful. It has been well tested."

Who would be that third? Ulfilas? Was it that Lord Starrex thought he must take his personal guard into a dream with him?

The door swung open again and Lord Starrex entered. He walked stiffly, one leg swinging wide as if he could not bend the knee nor control the muscles, and he leaned heavily on

an android. As the servant lowered him onto the couch he
did not look at Tamisan but nodded curtly to Kas.

"Take your place also," he ordered.

Did Starrex fear the dream state and want his cousin as a
check because Kas had plainly dreamed before?

Then Starrex did turn to her as he reached for the dream
crown, copying the motion by which she settled her own circlet on her head.

"Let us see what you can offer." There was a shadow of
hostility in his voice, a challenge to produce something which
he did not believe she could.

II

She must not allow herself to think of Starrex now, but
only of her dream. She must create and have no doubt that
her creation would be as perfect as her hopes. Tamisan
closed her eyes, firmed her will, drew into her imagination all
the threads of the studies' spinning and began the weaving of
a dream.

For a moment, perhaps two fingers' count of moments, this
was like the beginning of any dream and then. . . .

She was not looking on, watching intently and critically, as
she spun with dexterity. No, it was rather as if that web suddenly became real and she was caught tightly in it, even as a
blue-winged drotail might be enmeshed in a fess-spider's
deadly curtain.

This was no dreaming such as Tamisan had ever known
before, and panic gripped so harshly in her throat and chest
that she might have screamed, save that she had no voice left.
She fell down and down from a point above, to strike among
bushes which took some of her weight, but with an impact
which left her bruised and half senseless. She lay unmoving,
gasping, her eyes closed, fearing to open them to see that she

was indeed caught in a wild nightmare and not properly dreaming.

As she lay there, she came slowly out of her dazed bewilderment and tried for control, not only over her fears, but also over her dreaming powers. Then she opened her eyes cautiously.

An arch of sky was overhead, pallidly green, with traces of thin, gray cloud like long, clutching fingers. It would have been as real as any sky might be, did she walk under it in her own time and world. *My own time and world!*

She thought of the idea she had built upon to astound Starrex; her wits quickened. Had the fact that she had worked with a new theory, trying to bring a twist to dreaming which might pierce the indifference of a bored man, precipitated *this?*

Tamisan sat up, wincing at the protest of her bruises, to look about her. Her vantage point was the crest of a small knob of earth. The land about her was no wilderness. The turf was smooth and cropped, and here and there were outcrops of rock cleverly carved and clothed with flowering vines. Other rocks were starkly bare, brooding. All faced downslope to a wall.

These forms varied from vaguely acceptable humanoid shapes to grotesque monsters. Tamisan decided that she liked the aspect of none when she studied them more closely. These were *not* of her imagining.

Beyond the wall began a cluster of buildings. Since she was used to seeing the sky towers and the lesser, if more substantial structures, beneath those, these looked unusually squat and heavy. The tallest she could see was no more than three stories high. Men did not build to the stars here; they hugged the earth closely.

But where was *here?* It was not her dream. Tamisan closed her eyes and concentrated on the beginnings of her planned dream. They had been about to go into another world, born of her imagining, but not this. Her basic idea had been simple enough, if not one which had been used, to her knowledge, by any dreamer before her. It all hinged on the idea that the past history of her world had been altered many times during its flow. She had taken three key points of alteration and studied what might have resulted had those been given the opposite decision by fate.

Now, keeping her eyes firmly closed against this seeming

reality into which she had fallen, Tamisan concentrated with fierce intentness upon her chosen points.

"The Welcome of the Over-queen Ahta." She recited the first.

What would have happened if the first starship on its landing had not been accepted as a supernatural event, and the small kingdom in which it had touched earth had not accepted its crew as godlings, but had greeted them instead with those poisoned darts the spacemen had later seen used? That was her first decision.

"The loss of the *Wanderer*." That was the second.

It had been a colony ship driven far from its assigned course by computer failure, so that it had to make a landing here or its passengers would die. If that failure had not occurred and the *Wanderer* landed to start an unplanned colony, what would have come to pass?

"The death of Sylt the Sweet-Tongued before he reached the Altar of Ictio."

That prophet might never have arisen to ruthless power, leading to a blood-crazed insurrection from temple to temple, setting darkness on three quarters of this world.

She had chosen those points, but she had not even been sure that one might not have canceled out another. Sylt had led the rebellion against the colonists from the *Wanderer*. If the welcome had not occurred . . . Tamisan could not be sure, she had only tried to find a pattern of events and then envision a modern world stemming from those changes.

She opened her eyes again. This was not her imagined world. Nor did one in a dream rub bruises, sit on damp sod, feel wind pull at them, and allow the first patter of rain to wet hair and robe. She put both hands to her head. *What of the dream crown?*

Her fingers found a weaving of metal, but there were no cords from it. For the first time she remembered that she had been linked with Starrex and Kas when this happened.

Tamisan got to her feet to look around, half expecting to see the other two somewhere near; but she was alone and the rain was falling heavier. There was a roofed space near the wall and Tamisan hurried for it.

Three twisted pillars supported a small dome of roof. There were no walls and she huddled in the very center, trying to escape the wind-borne moisture. She could not keep pushing away the feeling that this was no dream but true reality.

If . . . if one could dream *true*. Tamisan fought panic and tried to examine the possibilities. *Had* she somehow landed in a Ty-Kry which might have existed had her three checkpoints actually been the decisions she envisioned? If so, could one get back by simply visioning them in reverse?

She shut her eyes and concentrated.

There was a sensation of stomach-turning giddiness. She swung out, to be jerked back, swung out, to return once more. Shaking with nausea, Tamisan stopped trying. She shuddered, opening her eyes to the rain. Then again she strove to understand what had happened. That swing had in it some of the sensation of dream breaking, which meant that she was in a dream. But it was just as apparent that she had been held prisoner here. *How? And why?* Her eyes narrowed a little, though she was looking inward, not at the rain-misted garden before her. *By whom?*

Suppose . . . suppose one or both of those who had prepared to share my dream had also come into this place, though not right here . . . then I must find them. We must return together or the missing one will anchor the others. Find them, and now!

For the first time she looked down at the garment clinging damply to her slender body. It was not the gray slip of a dreamer, for it was long, brushing her ankles. And in color it was a dusky violet, a shade she found strangely pleasing and right.

From its hem to her knees there was a border of intricate embroidery so entwined and ornate that she found it hard to define in any detail. Though, oddly enough, it seemed the longer she studied it, the more it appeared to be not threads on cloth, but words on a page of manuscript, such as she had viewed in the ancient history video tapes. The threads were a metallic green and silver, with only a few minor touches of a lighter shade of violet.

Around her waist was a belt of silver links, clasped by a broad buckle of the same metal set with purple stones. This supported a pouch with a clasped top. The dress or robe was laced from the belt to her throat with silver cords run through metal eyelets in the material. Her sleeves were long and full, though from the elbow down they were slit into four parts, those fluttering away from her arms when she raised them to loosen the crown.

What she brought away from her head was not the familiar skullcap made to fit over her cropped hair, rather it was a circlet of silver with inner wires or strips rising to close in a conical point to add a foot or more on her height. On that point was a beautifully fashioned flying thing, its wings a little lifted as if to take off, the glitter of tiny jewels marking its eyes.

So was it made that, as she turned the crown around, its long neck changed position and the wings moved a fraction. Thus, at first, she was almost startled enough to drop the circlet, thinking it might be alive.

But the whole she recognized from one of the history tapes. The bird was the flacar of Olava. Wearing it so meant that she was a Mouth, a Mouth of Olava, part priestess, part sorceress and, oddly enough, part entertainer. But fortune had favored her in this; a Mouth of Olava might wander anywhere without question, search, and seem merely to be about her normal business.

Tamisan ran her hand over her head before she replaced the crown. Her fingers did not find the bristly stubble of a dreamer, but rather soft, mist-dampened strands which curled down long enough to brush her forehead and tuft at the nape of her neck.

She had imagined garments for herself in dreams, of course. But this time she had not provided herself with such, and so the fact that she stood as a Mouth of Olava was not of her willing. But Olava was part of the time of the Overqueen's rule. Had she somehow swept herself back in time? The sooner she found knowledge of where and when she was, the better.

The rain was slackening and Tamisan moved out from under the dome. She bunched up her robe in both hands to climb back up the slope. At its top she turned slowly, trying to find some proof that she had not been tossed alone into this strange world.

Save for the figures of stone and beds of rank-looking growth there was nothing to be seen. The wall and the dome lay below. But behind her when she faced the dome was a second slope leading to a still higher point, which was crowned by a roof to be seen only in bits and patches through a screen of oarn trees. The roof had a ridge which

terminated at either side in a sharp upcurve, giving the building the odd appearance of having an ear on either end. It
was green with a glittering surface, almost brilliantly so in
spite of the clouds overhead.

To her right and left Tamisan caught glimpses of the wall
curving and of more stone figures and flower or shrub plant-
ings. Gathering up her skirts more firmly, she began to walk
up the curve of the higher slope in search of some road or
path leading to the roof.

She came across what she sought as she detoured to avoid
a thicket of heavy brush in which were impaled huge scarlet
flowers. It was a wide roadway paved with small colored
pebbles embedded in a solid surface, and it led from an open
gateway up the swell of the slope to the front of the structure.

In shape the building was vaguely familiar, though Tamisan
could not identify it. Perhaps it resembled something she had
seen in the tri-dees. The door was of the same brilliant green
as the roof, but the walls were a pale yellow, cut sharply at
regular intervals by very narrow windows, so tall that they
ran from floor to roof level.

Even as she stood there wondering where she had seen
such a house before, a woman came out. As did Tamisan,
she wore a long-skirted robe with laced bodice and slit sleeves.
But hers was the same green as that of the door, so that,
standing against it, only her head and arms were clearly
visible. She gestured with vigor, and Tamisan suddenly realized that it must be she who was being summoned as if she
were expected.

Again she fought down unease. In dreams she was well
used to meetings and partings, but always those were of her
own devising and did not happen for a purpose which was
not of her wish. Her dream people were toys, game pieces,
to be moved hither and thither at her will, she being always
in command of them.

"Tamisan, they wait; come quickly!" the woman called.

Tamisan was minded in that instant to run in the other
direction, but the need to learn what had happened made
her take what might be the dangerous course of joining the
woman.

"Fha, you are wet! This is no hour for walking in the
garden. The First Standing asks for a reading from the
Mouth. If you would have lavishly from her purse, hurry,
lest she grows too impatient to wait!"

The door gave upon a narrow entry and the woman in green propelled Tamisan toward a second opening directly facing her. She came into the large room where a circle of couches was centered. By each stood a small table now burdened with dishes which serving maids were bearing away as if a meal had just been concluded. Tall candlesticks, matching Tamisan's own height, stood also between the divans; the candles in each, as thick as her forearm, were alight, to give forth not only radiance but also a sweet odor as they burned.

Midpoint in the divan circle was a tall-backed chair over which arched a canopy. In it sat a woman, a goblet in her hand. She had a fur cloak pulled about her shoulders hiding almost all of her robe, save that here and there a shimmer of gold caught fire from the candlelight. Only her face was visible in a hood of the same metal-like fabric, and it was that of a very old woman, seamed with deep wrinkles, sunken of eye.

The divans, Tamisan marked, were occupied by both men and women, the women flanking the chair and the men farthest away from the ancient noblewoman. Directly facing her was a second impressive chair, lacking only the canopy; before it was a table on which stood, at each of its four corners, small basins: one cream, one pale rose, one faintly blue, and the fourth sea-foam green.

Tamisan's store of knowledge gave her some preparation. This was the setting for the magic of a Mouth, and it was apparent that her services as a foreseer were about to be demanded. What had she done in allowing herself to be drawn here? Could she make pretense her savant well enough to deceive this company?

"I hunger, Mouth of Olava; I hunger not for that which will feed the body, but for that which satisfies the mind." The old woman leaned forward a little. Her voice might be the thin one of age, but it carried with it the force of authority, of one who has not had her word or desire questioned for a long time.

She must improvise, Tamisan knew. She was a dreamer and she had wrought in dreams many strange things, let her but remember that. Her damp skirts clung clammily to her legs and thighs as she came forward, saying nothing to the woman in return, but seating herself in a chair facing her client. She was drawing on faint stirrings of a memory which

seemed not truly her own for guidance, though she had not
yet realized that fully.

"What would you know, First Standing?" She raised her
hands to her forehead in an instinctive gesture, touching fore-
fingers to her temples, right and left.

"What comes to me ... and mine." The last two words
had come almost as an afterthought.

Tamisan's hands went out without her conscious ordering.
She stifled her amazement. It was as if she were repeating an
act as well learned as her dreamer's technique had been. With
her left hand she gathered up a palmful of the sand from the
cream bowl. It was a shade or two darker than the container.
She tossed this with a sharp movement of her wrist and it
settled smoothly as a film on the tabletop.

What she was doing was not of her conscious mind, as if
another had taken charge of her actions. By the way the
woman in the chair leaned forward, and by the hush which
had fallen on her companion, this was right and proper.

Without any order from her mind, Tamisan's right hand
went now to the blue bowl with its dark blue sand. But this
was not tossed. Instead, she held the fine grains in her upright
fist, passing it slowly over the tabletop so that a very tiny
trickle of grit fed down to make a pattern on the first film.

It was a pattern, not a random scattering. What she had so
drawn was a recognizable sword with a basket-shaped hilt
and a slightly curved blade tapering to a narrow point.

Now her hand moved to the pink bowl. The sand she
gathered up there was a dark red, more vivid than the other
colors, as if she dealt now with flecks of newly shed blood.
Once more she used her upheld fist, and the shifting stream
fed from her palm became a spaceship! It was slightly different in outline from those she had seen all her life, but it was
unmistakably a ship, and it was drawn on the tabletop as if it
threatened to descend upon the pointed sword. *Or is it that
the sword threatens it?*

She heard a gasp of surprise, or was it fear? But that sound
had not come from the woman who had bade her foretell. It
must have broken from some other member of the company
intent upon Tamisan's painting with the flowing sand.

It was to the fourth bowl now that her right hand moved.
But she did not take up a full fistful, rather a generous pinch
between thumb and forefinger. She held the sand high above

the picture and released it. The green specks floated down ...
to gather in a sign like a circle with one portion missing.

She stared at that and it seemed to alter a little under the
intensity of her gaze. What it had changed to was a symbol
she knew well, one which brought a small gasp from her. It
was the seal, simplified it was true, but still readable, of the
House of Starrex, and it overlaid both the edge of the ship
and the tip of the sword.

"Read you this!" the noblewoman demanded sharply.

From somewhere the words came readily to Tamisan. "The
sword is the sword of Ty-Kry raised in defense."

"Assured, assured." A murmur ran along the divans.

"The ship comes as a danger."

"That thing, a ship? But it is no ship."

"It is a ship from the stars."

"And woe, woe, and woe." That was no murmur, but a
full-throated cry of fright. "As in the days of our fathers
when we had to deal with the false ones. Ahta, let the spirit
of Ahta be a shield to our arms, a sword in our hands!"

The noblewoman made a silencing gesture with one hand.
"Enough! Crying to the revered spirits may bring sustenance,
but they are not noted for helping those not standing to arms
on their own behalf. There have been other sky ships since
Ahta's days, and with them we have dealt—to *our* purpose. If
another comes we are forewarned, which is also forearmed.
But what lies there in green, oh, Mouth of Olava, which surprised even you?"

Tamisan had had precious moments in which to think. If it
were true, as she had deduced, that she was tied to this world
by those she had brought with her, then she must find them;
and it was clear that they were not of this company. Therefore, this last must be made to work for her.

"The green sign is that of a champion, one meant to be
mighty in the coming battle. But he shall not be known save
when the sign points to him, and it may be that this can only
be seen by one with the gift."

She looked to the noblewoman, and, meeting those old
eyes, Tamisan felt a small chill rise in her, one which had not
been born from the still damp clothing she wore. There was
that in those two shadowed eyes which questioned coldly and
did not accept without proof.

"So should the one with the gift you speak of go sniffing

all through Ty-Kry and the land beyond the city, even to the boundaries of the world?"

"If need be." Tamisan stood firm.

"A long journey mayhap, and many strides into danger. And if the ship comes before this champion is found? A thin cord I think oh, Mouth, on which to hang the future of a city, a kingdom, or a people. Look if you will but I say we have more tested ways of dealing with these interlopers from the skies. But, Mouth, since you have given warning, let it so be remembered."

She put her hands on the arms of her chair and arose, using them to lever her. So did all her company come to their feet, two of the women hurrying to her so that she could lay her hands upon their shoulders for support. Without another look at Tamisan she went, nor did the dreamer rise to see her go. For suddenly she was spent, tired as she had been in the past when a dream broke and left her supine and drained. But this dream did not break; it kept her sitting before the table and its sand pictures, looking at that green symbol, still caught fast in the web of another world.

The woman in green returned, bearing a goblet in her two hands and offering it to Tamisan.

"The First Standing will go to the High Castle and the Over-queen. She turned into that road. Drink, Tamisan, and mayhap the Over-queen herself will ask you for a seeing."

Tamisan? That was her true name; twice this woman had called her by it. *How is it known in a dream?* Yet she dared not ask that question or any of the others she needed answers to. Instead she drank from the goblet, finding the hot, spicy liquid driving the chill from her body.

There was so much she must learn and must know; but she could not discover it, save indirectly, lest she reveal what she was and was not.

"I am tired."

"There is a resting place prepared," the woman returned. "You have only to come."

Tamisan had almost to lever herself up as the noblewoman had done. She was giddy and had to catch at the back of the chair. Then she moved after her hostess, hoping desperately to know.

III

Did one sleep in a dream, dream upon dream, perhaps?
Tamisan wondered as she stretched out upon the couch her
hostess showed her. Yet when she set aside her crown, laid
her head upon the roll which served as a pillow, she was once
more alert, her thoughts racing, or entangled in such wild
confusion that she felt as giddy as she had upon rising from
her seer's chair.

The Starrex symbol overlying both that of the sword and
the spaceship in the sand picture, could it mean that she
would only find what she sought when the might of this
world met that of the starmen? Had she indeed in some manner fallen into the past where she would relive the first
coming of the space voyagers to Ty-Kry? But the noblewoman had mentioned past encounters with them which had
ended in favor of Ty-Kry.

Tamisan had tried to envision a world of her own time,
but one in which history had taken a different road. Yet
much of that around her was of the past. Did that mean that,
without the decisions of her own time, the world of Ty-Kry
remained largely unchanged from century to century?

Real, unreal, old, new. She had lost all a dreamer's command of action. Tamisan did not play now with toys which
she could move about at will, but rather was caught up in a
series of events she could not foresee and over which she had
no control. Yet twice the woman had called her by her rightful name and, without willing it, she had used the devices of
a Mouth of Olava to foretell, as if she had done so many
times before.

Could it be? Tamisan closed her teeth upon her lower lip
and felt the pain of that, just as she felt the pain of the
bruises left by her abrupt entrance into the mysterious here.

Could it be that some dreams are so deep, so well woven, that they are to the dreamer real? Is this indeed the fate of those "closed" dreamers who were worthless for the Hive? Do they in their trances live a countless number of lives? But she was not a closed dreamer.

Awake! Once more, stretched as she was upon the couch, she used the proper technique to throw herself out of a dream, and once more she experienced that weird nothingness in which she spun sickeningly, as if held helplessly in some void, tied to an anchor which held her back from the full leap to sane safety. There was only one explanation, that somewhere in this strange Ty-Kry one or both of those who had prepared to share her dream was now to be found and must be sought out before she could return.

So, the sooner that is accomplished, the better! But where should I start seeking? Though a feeling of weakness clung to her limbs, making her move slowly as if she strove to walk against the pull of a strong current, Tamisan arose from the couch. She turned to pick up her Mouth's crown, and so looked into the oval of a mirror, startled thus into immobility. For the figure she looked upon as her own reflection was not one that she had seen before.

It was not the robe and the crown that had changed her; she was not the same person. For a long time, ever since she could remember, she had had the pallid skin, the close cropped hair of a dreamer very seldom in the sunlight. But the face of the woman in the mirror was a soft, even brown. The cheekbones were wide, the eyes large and the lips very red. Her brows ... she leaned closer to the mirror to see what gave them that odd upward slant and decided that they had been plucked or shaven to produce the effect. Her hair was perhaps three fingers long and not the well known fair coloring, but dark and curling. She was not the Tamisan she knew, nor was this stranger the product of her own will.

It would follow logically that if she did not look like her normal self, then perhaps the two she sought were no longer as she remembered either. Thus her search would be twice as difficult. Could she ever recognize them?

Frightened, she sat down on the couch facing the mirror. She dared not give way to fear, for if she once let it break her control she might be utterly lost. Logic, even in such a world of unlogic, must make her think lucidly.

Just how true was her soothsaying? At least she had not influenced that fall of the sand. Perhaps the Mouth of Olava did have supernatural powers. She had played with the idea of magic in the past to embroider dreams, but that had been her own creation. Could she use it by will now? It would seem this unknown self of hers did manage to draw upon some unknown source of power.

She must fasten her thoughts upon one of the men and hold him in her mind. Could the dream tie pull her to Kas or Starrex? All she knew of her master she had learned from tapes, and tapes gave one only superficial knowledge. One could not well study a person going through only half-understood actions behind a veil which concealed more than it displayed. Kas had spoken directly to her, his flesh had touched hers. If she must choose one to draw her, then it had better be Kas.

In her mind Tamisan built a memory picture of him as she would build a preliminary picture for a dream. Then suddenly the Kas in her mind flickered, changed; she saw another man. He was taller than the Kas she knew, and he wore a uniform tunic and space boots; his features were hard to distinguish. That vision lasted only a fraction of time.

The ship! The symbol had lain touching both ship and sword in the sand seeing. It would be easier to seek a man on a ship than wandering through the streets of a strange city with no better clue than that Starrex's counterpart might be there.

It was so little on which to pin a quest: a ship which might or might not be now approaching Ty-Kry, and which would meet a drastic reception when it landed. *Suppose Kas, or his double, is killed? Would that anchor me here for all time?* Resolutely Tamisan pushed such negative speculation to the back of her mind. *First things first; the ship has not yet planeted.* But when it came she must make sure that she was among those preparing for its welcome.

It seemed that having made that decision she at last able to sleep, for the fatigue which had struck at her in the hall returned a hundredfold and she fell back on the couch as one drugged, remembering nothing more until she awakened. She found the woman in green standing above her, one hand on her shoulder shaking her gently back to awareness.

"Awake, there is a summons."

A summons to dream, Tamisan thought dazedly, and then

the unfamiliar room and the immediate past came completely back to her.

"The First Standing Jassa has summoned." The woman sounded excited. "It is said by her messenger, he has brought a chair cart for you, that you are to go to the High Castle! Perhaps you will see for the Over-queen herself! But there is time, I have won it for you, to bathe, to eat, to change your robe. See, I have plundered my own bride chest." She pointed to a chair over which was spread a robe, not of the deep violet Tamisan now wore, but of a purple-wine. "It is the only one of the proper color, or near it." She ran her hand lovingly over the rich folds.

"But haste," she added briskly. "As a Mouth you can claim the need for making ready to appear before high company, but to linger too long will raise the anger of the First Standing."

There was a basin large enough to serve as a bath in the room beyond, and, as well as the robe, the woman had brought fresh body linen. When Tamisan stood once more before the mirror to clasp her silver belt and assume the Mouth crown, she felt renewed and refreshed and her thanks were warm.

But the woman made a gesture of brushing them aside. "Are we not of the same clan, cousin? Shall one say that Nahra is not open-handed with her own? That you are a Mouth is our clan pride, let us enjoy it through you!"

She brought a covered bowl and a goblet, and Tamisan ate a dish of meal into which had been baked dried fruit and bits of what she thought well-chopped meat. It was tasty and she finished it to the last crumb, just as she emptied the cup of a tart-sweet drink.

"Wellaway, Tamisan, this is a great day for the clan of Fremont, when you go to the High Castle and perhaps stand before the Over-queen. May it be that the seeing is not for ill, but for good. Though you are but the Mouth of Olava and not the One dealing fortune to us who live and die."

"For your aid and your good wishing, receive my thanks," Tamisan said. "I, too, hope that fortune comes before misfortune on this day." And that is stark truth, she thought, for I must gather fortune to me with both hands and hold it tight, lest the game I play be lost.

First Standing Jassa's messenger was an officer, his hair clubbed up under a ridged helm to give additional protection to his head in battle, his breastplate, enameled blue with the double crown of the Over-queen, and his sword very much to the fore. It was as if he already strode the street of a city at war. There was a small griffin between the shafts of the chair cart and two men-at-arms ready, one at the griffin's head, the other holding aside the curtains as their officer handed Tamisan into the chair. He briskly jerked the curtains shut without asking her pleasure, and she decided that perhaps her visit to the High Castle was to be a secret matter.

Between the curtain edges she caught sight of this Ty-Kry, and, though in parts it was very strange to her, there were enough similarities to provide her with an anchor to the real. The sky towers and other off-world forms of architecture which had been introduced by space travelers were missing. But the streets themselves and the many beds of foliage and flowers were those she had known all her life.

The High Castle, she drew a deep breath as they wound out of town and along the river, had been part of her world, too, though then as a ruined and very ancient landmark. Part of it had been consumed in the war of Sylt's rebellion, and it had been considered a place of misfortune, largely shunned, save for off-world tourists seeking the unusual.

Here it was in its pride, larger and more widely spread then in her Ty-Kry, as if the generations who had deserted it in her world had clung to it here, adding ever to its bulk. It was not a single structure, but a city in itself. However, it had no merchants or public buildings. It provided homes to shelter the nobles who must spend part of the year at court, all their servants and the many officials of the kingdom.

In its heart was the building which gave it its name, a collection of towers, rising far above the lesser structures at the foot. The buildings' walls were gray at their bases and changed subtly as they arose until their tops were a deep, rich blue. The other buildings in the great pile were wholly gray as to wall, a darker blue as to roof.

The chair creaked forward on its two wheels, the griffin being kept to a steady pace by the man at its head, and passed under the thick arch in the outer wall, then up a street between buildings which, though dwarfed by the towers, were in turn dwarfing to those who walked or rode by them.

There was a second gate, more buildings, a third gate and then the open space about the central towers. They passed people in plenty since they had entered the first gate. Many were soldiers of the guard, but some of the armed men had worn other colors and insignia, being, Tamisan guessed, the retainers of court lords. Now and then some lord came proudly, his retinue strung along behind him by threes to make a show which amused Tamisan. *As if the number of followers to tread on one's heels enhanced one's importance in the world.*

She was handed down with a little more ceremony than she had been ushered into the chair, and the officer offered her his wrist, his men falling in behind as a groom hurried forward to lead off the equipage, thus affording her a tail of honor, too.

But the towers of the High Castle were so awe-inspiring, so huge a pile, that she was glad she had an escort into their heart. The farther they advanced through the halls, the more uneasy she became. It was as if once she were within this maze there might be no retreat and she would be lost forever.

Twice they climbed staircases until her legs ached with the effort and they took on the aspect of mountains. Then her party passed into a long hall which was lighted not only by the candle trees, but some thin rays filtering through windows placed so high above their heads that nothing could be seen through them. Tamisan, in that part of her which seemed familiar with this world, knew this to be the Walk of the Nobles, and the company now gathered here were the Third Standing, nearest, then the Second, and, at the far end of that road of blue carpet onto which her guide led her, First Standing. They were sitting; there were two arcs of hooded and canopied chairs, with above them a throne on a three-step dais. The hood over that was upheld by a double crown which glittered with gems. On the steps were grouped men in the armor of the guard and others wearing bright tunics, their hair loose upon their shoulders.

It was toward that throne that the officer led her and they passed through the ranks of the Third Standing, hearing a low murmur of voices. Tamisan looked neither to right nor left; she wished to see the Over-queen, for it was plain she was being granted full audience. Something stirred deep within her as if a small pin pricked. The reason for this she did not know, save that ahead was something of vast importance to her.

Now they were equal with the first of the chairs and she saw that the greater number of those who so sat were women, but not all. Mainly they were at least in middle life. So Tamisan came to the foot of the dais, and in that moment she did not go to one knee as did the officer, but rather raised her fingertips to touch the rim of the crown on her head; for with another of those flashes of half recognition she knew that in this place that which she represented did not bow as did others, but acknowledged only that the Over-queen was one to whom human allegiance was granted after another and greater loyalty was paid elsewhere.

The Over-queen looked down with a deeply searching stare as Tamisan looked up. What Tamisan saw was a woman to whom she could not set an age; she might be either old or young, for the years had not seemed to mark her. The robe on her full figure was not ornate, but a soft pearl color without ornamentation, save that she wore a girdle of silvery chains braided and woven together, and a collarlike necklace of the same metal from which fringed milky gems cut into drops. Her hair was a flame of brightly glowing red, in which a diadem of the same creamy stones was almost hidden. Was she beautiful? Tamisan could not have said; but that she was vitally alive there was no doubt. Even though she sat quietly there was an aura of energy about her suggesting that this was only a pause between the doing of great and necessary deeds. She was the most assertive personality Tamisan had ever seen, and instantly the guards of a dreamer went into action. To serve such a mistress, Tamisan thought, would sap all the personality from one, so that the servant would become but a mirror to reflect from that moment of surrender onward.

"Welcome, Mouth of Olava who has been uttering strange things." The Over-queen's voice was mocking, challenging.

"A Mouth says naught, Great One, save what is given it to speak." Tamisan found her answer ready, though she had not consciously formed it in her mind.

"So we were told, though gods may grow old and tired. Or is that only the fate of men? But now, it is our will that Olava speak again if that is fortune for this hour. So be it!"

As if that last phrase were an order, there was a stir among those standing on the steps of the throne. Two of the guards brought out a table, a third a stool, the fourth a tray on which rested four bowls of sand. These they set up before the throne.

Tamisan took her place on the stool, again put her finger

to her temples. Would this work again, or must she try to force a picture in the sand? She felt a small shiver of nerves she fought to control.

"What desires the Great One?" She was glad to hear her voice steady, no hint of her uneasiness in it.

"What chances in, say, four passages of the sun?"

Tamisan waited. Would that other personality, or power, or whatever it might be, take over? Her hand did not move. Instead, that odd, disturbing prick grew the stronger; she was drawn, even as a noose might be laid about her forehead to pull her head around. So she turned to follow the dictates of that pull and looked where something willed her eyes to look. All she saw was the line of officers on the steps of the throne, and they stared at and through her, none with any sign of recognition. *Starrex!* She grasped at that hope, but none of them resembled the man she sought.

"Does Olava sleep? Or had his Mouth been forgotten for a space?"

The Over-queen's voice was sharper and Tamisan broke that hold on her attention, looking back to the throne and the woman on it.

"It is not meet for the Mouth to speak unless Olava wishes." Tamisan began, feeling increasingly nervous. That sensation gripped her left hand, as if it were not under her control but possessed by another will. She fell silent as it gathered up the brownish sand and tossed it to form a picture's background.

This time she did not seek next the blue grains; rather her fist dug into the red and moved to paint the outline of the spaceship, above it a single red circle.

Then, there was a moment of hesitation before her fingers strayed to the green, took up a generous pinch and again made Starrex's symbol below the ship.

"A single sun," the Over-queen read out. "One day until the enemy comes. But what is the remaining word of Olava, Mouth?"

"That there be one among you who is a key to victory. He shall stand against the enemy and under him fortune comes."

"So? Who is this hero?"

Tamisan looked again to the line of officers. Dared she trust to instinct? Something within her urged her on.

"Let each of these protectors of Ty-Kry," she raised a finger to indicate the officers, "come forward and take up the

sand of seeing. Let the Mouth touch that hand and may it
then strew the answer. Perhaps Olava will make it clear in
this manner."

To Tamisan's surprise the Over-queen laughed. "As good a
way as any perhaps for picking a champion. To abide by
Olava's choice, that is another matter." Her smile faded as
she glanced at the men, as if there was a thought in her mind
which disturbed her.

At her nod they came one by one. Under the shadows of
their helmets their faces, being of one race, were very similar
and Tamisan, studying each, could see no chance of telling
which Starrex might be.

Each took up a pinch of green sand, held out his hand,
palm down, and let the grains fall while she set fingertip to
his knuckles. The sand drifted but in no shape and to no purpose.

It was not until the last man came that there was a difference, for then the sand did not drift, but fell to form again
the symbol which was twin to the one already on the table.
Tamisan looked up. The officer was staring at the sand rather
than meeting her eyes, and there was a line of strain about
his mouth, a look about him as might shadow the face of a
man who stood with his back to a wall and a ring of sword
points at his throat.

"This is your man," Tamisan said. Starrex? She must be
sure; if she could only demand the truth in this instant!

But her preoccupation was swept aside.

"Olava deals falsely!" That cry came from the officer behind her, the one who had brought her here.

"Perhaps we must not think ill of Olava's advice." The
Over-queen's voice had a guttural, feline purr. "It may be his
Mouth is not wholly wedded to his service, but speaks for
others than Olava at times. Hawarel, so you are to be our
champion?"

The officer went to one knee, his hands clasped loosely before him as if he wished all to see he did not reach for any
weapon.

"I am no choice, save the Great One's." In spite of the
strain visible in his tense body he spoke levelly and without a
tremor.

"Great One, this traitor . . ." Two of the officers moved as
if to lay hands upon him and drag him away.

"No. Has not Olava spoken?" The mockery was very plain

in the Over-queen's tone now. "But to make sure that Olava's will be carried out, take good care of our champion-to-be. Since Hawarel is to fight our battle with the cursed starmen, he must be saved to do it. And," now she looked to Tamisan, startled by the quick turn of events and their hostility to Olava's choice, "let the Mouth of Olava share with Hawarel this waiting that she may, perhaps, instill in Olava's choice the vigor and strength such a battle will demand of our chosen champion." Each time the Over-queen spoke the word "champion" she made of it a thing of derision and subtle menace.

"The audience is finished." The Over-queen arose and stepped behind the throne as those about Tamisan fell to their knees; then she was gone. But the officer who had guided Tamisan was by her side. Hawarel, once more on his feet, was closely flanked by two of the other guards, one of whom pulled their prisoner's sword from his sheath before he could move. Then, with Hawarel before her, Tamisan was urged from the hall, though none laid a hand on her.

At the moment she was pleased enough to go, hoping for a chance to prove the rightness of her guess, that Hawarel and Starrex were the same and she had found the first of her fellow dreamers.

They transversed more halls until they came to a door which one of Hawarel's guards opened. The prisoner walked through and Tamisan's escort waved her after him. Then the door slammed shut, and at that sound Hawarel whirled around.

Under the beaking foreplate of his helmet his eyes were cold fire and he seemed a man about to leap for his enemy's throat.

His voice was only a harsh whisper. "Who ... who set you to my death wishing, witch?"

IV

His hands reached for her throat. Tamisan flung up her arm in an attempt to guard and stumbled back.

"Lord Starrex!" *If I have been wrong, if . . .*

Though his fingertips brushed her shoulders, he did not grasp her. Instead it was his turn to retreat a step or two, his mouth half-open in a gasp.

"Witch! Witch!" The very force of the words he hurled at her made them darts dispatched from one of the crossbows of the history tapes.

"Lord Starrex," Tamisan repeated, feeling on more secure ground at his stricken amazement and no longer fearing he would attack her out of hand. His reaction to that name was enough to assure her she was right, though he did not seem prepared to acknowledge it.

"I am Hawarel of the Vanora." He brought out those words as harsh croaking.

Tamisan glanced around. This was a bare-walled room, with no hiding place for a listener. In her own time and place she could have feared many scanning devices, but she thought those unknown to this Ty-Kry. To win Hawarel-Starrex into cooperation was very necessary.

"You are Lord Starrex," she returned with bold confidence, or at least what she hoped was a convincing show of it. "Just as I am Tamisan, the dreamer. And this, wherein we are caught, is the dream you ordered of me."

He raised his hand to his forehead, his fingers encountered his helmet and he swept it off unheedingly, so that it clanked and slid across the polished floor. His hair, netted into a kind of protecting cushion was piled about his head, giving him an odd appearance to Tamisan. It was black and thick, just as his skin was as brown-hued as that of her new body. Without the shadow of the helmet, she could see his face more clearly, finding in it no resemblance to the aloof master of the sky towers. In a way, it was that of a younger man, one less certain of himself.

"I am Hawarel," he repeated doggedly. "You try to trap me, or perhaps the trap has already closed and you seek now to make me condemn myself with my own mouth. I tell you, I am no traitor. I am Hawarel and my blood oath to the Great One has been faithfully kept."

Tamisan experienced a rise of impatience. She had not thought Lord Starrex to be a stupid man. But it would seem his counterpart here lacked more than just the face of his other self.

"You are Starrex, and this is a dream!" If it was not she did not care to raise that issue now. "Remember the sky tower? You bought me from Jabis for dreaming. Then you summoned me and Lord Kas and ordered me to prove my worth."

His brows drew together in a black frown as he stared at her.

"What have they given you, or promised, that you do this to me?" came his counterdemand. "I am no sworn enemy to you or yours, not that I know."

Tamisan sighed. "Do you deny you know the name Starrex?" she asked.

For a long moment he was silent. Then he turned from her, took a stride or two; his toe thumped against his helmet, sending it rolling ahead of him. She waited. He turned again to face her.

"You are a Mouth of Olava...."

She shook her head, interrupting him. "We have little time for such fencing, Lord Starrex. You do know that name, and it is in my mind that you also remember the rest, at least in some measure. I am Tamisan the dreamer."

It was his turn to sigh. "So you say."

"So I shall continue to say, and, mayhap as I do, others than you will listen."

"As I thought!" he flashed. "You would have me betray myself."

"If you are truly Hawarel as you state, then what have you to betray?"

"Very well. I am ... am two! I am Hawarel and I am someone else who has queer memories and who may well be a night demon come to dispute ownership of this body. There, you have it. Go and tell those who sent you and have me out to the arrow range for a quick ending there. Perhaps that will be better than to continue as a battlefield between two different selves."

Perhaps he was not just being obstinate, Tamisan thought. It might be that the dream had a greater hold on him than it did on her. After all, she was a trained dreamer, one used to venturing into illusions wrought from imagination.

"If you can remember a little, then listen." She drew closer to him and began to speak in a lower voice, not that she believed they could be overheard, but it was well to take no chance. Swiftly she gave her account of the whole tangle, or what had been her part in it.

When she was done she was surprised to see that a certain hardening had overtaken his features, so that now he looked more resolute, less like one trapped in a maze which had no guide.

"And this is the truth?"

"By what god or power do you wish me to swear to it?" She was exasperated now, frustrated by his lingering doubts.

"None, because it explains what was heretofore unexplainable, what has made my life a hell of doubt these past hours, and brought more suspicion upon me. I have been two persons. But if this is all a dream, why is that so?"

"I do not know." Tamisan chose frankness as best befitting her needs. "This is unlike any dream I have created before."

"In what manner?" he asked crisply.

"It is a part of a dreamer's duty to study her master's personality, to suit his desires, even if those be unexpressed and hidden. From what I had learned of you, of Lord Starrex, I thought that too much had been already seen, experienced and known to you, that it must be a new approach I tried, or else you would find that dreaming held no profit.

"Therefore, it came to me suddenly that I would not dream of the past, nor of the future, which are the common approaches for an action dreamer, but refine upon the subject. In the past there were times in history when the future rested upon a single decision. And it was in my mind to select certain of these decisions and then envision a world in which those decisions had gone in the opposite direction, trying to see what would be the present result of actions in the past."

"So this is what you tried? And what decisions did you select for your experiment at the rewriting of history?" He was giving her his full attention.

"I took three. First, the welcome of the Over-queen, Ahta, second, the drift of the colony ship *Wanderer,* third, the rebellion of Sylt. Should the welcome have been a rejection, should the colony ship never reach here, should Sylt have failed, these would produce a world I thought might be interesting to visit in a dream. So I read what history tapes I could call upon. Thus, when you summoned me to dream I had my ideas ready. But it did not work as it should have. Instead of spinning the proper dream, creating incidents in good order, I found myself fast caught in a world I did not know or build."

As she spoke she could watch the change in him. He had lost all the fervent antagonism of his first attack on her. More and more she could see what she had associated with the personality of Lord Starrex coming through the unfamiliar envelope of this man's body.

"So it did not work properly."

"No. As I have said, I found myself in the dream, with no control of action and no recognizable creation factors. I do not understand."

"No? There could be an explanation." The frown line was back between his brows, but it was not a scowl aimed at her. It was as if he were trying hard to remember something of importance which eluded his efforts. "There is a theory, a very old one. Yes, that of parallel worlds."

In her wide use of the tapes she had not come across that, and now she demanded the knowledge of him almost fiercely. "What are those?"

"You are not the first, how could you be, to be struck by the notion that sometimes history and the future hang upon a very thin cord which can be twisted this way and that by a small chance. A theory was once advanced that when that chanced it created a second world, one in which the decision was made to the right, when that of the world we know went to the left."

"But alternate worlds, where, how did they exist?"

"Thus, perhaps," he held out his two hands horizontally, one above the other, "in layers. There were even old tales created for amusement, of men traveling not back in time, nor forward, but across it from one such world to another."

"But here we are. I am a Mouth of Olava and I don't look like myself, just as to the eye you are not Lord Starrex."

"Perhaps we are the people we would be if our world had taken the other side of your three decisions. It is a clever device for a dreamer to create, Tamisan."

She told him now the last truth. "Only, I do not think I have created it. Certainly I cannot control it."

"You have tried to break this dream?"

"Of course, but I am tied here. Perhaps it is by you, and Lord Kas. Until we three try together maybe we cannot any of us return."

"Now you must go searching for him with that board and sand trick of yours?"

She shook her head. "Kas, I think, is one of the crew on the spacer about to set down. I believe I saw him, though not his face. She smiled a little shakily. "It seems that though I am mainly the Tamisan I have always been, yet also do I have some of the powers of a Mouth; likewise, you are Hawarel as well as Starrex."

"The longer I listen to you," he announced, "the more I become Starrex. So we must find Kas on the spacer before we wriggle free from this tangle? But that is going to be rather a problem. I am enough of Hawarel to know that the spacer is going to receive the usual welcome dealt off-world ships here: trickery and extinction. Your three points have been as you envisioned them. There was no welcome, but rather a massacre; no colony ship ever reached here, and Sylt was speared by a contemptuous man-at-arms the first time he lifted his voice to draw a crowd. Hawarel knows this as truth; as Starrex I am aware there is another truth which did radically change life on this planet. Now, did you seek me out on purpose, your champion tale intended to be our bridge to Kas?"

"No, at least I did not consciously arrange it so. I tell you, I have some of the powers of a Mouth; they take over."

He gave a sharp bark of sound which was not laughter but somewhat akin to it. "By the fist of Jimsam Taragon, we have it complicated by magic, too! And I suppose you cannot tell me just how much a Mouth can do in the way of foreseeing, forearming or freeing us from this trap?"

Tamisan shook her head. "The Mouths were mentioned in the history tapes; they were very important once. But after Sylt's rebellion they were either killed or disappeared. They were hunted by both sides, and most we know about them is only legend. I cannot tell you what I can do. Sometimes something, perhaps the memory and knowledge of this body, takes over and then I do strange things. I neither will nor understand them."

He crossed the room and pulled two stools from a far corner. "We might as well sit at ease and explore what we can of this world's memories. It just might be that united, we can learn more than when trying alone. The trouble is . . ." He reached out a hand and mechanically she touched fingertips to the back of it in an oddly formal ceremony which was not part of her own knowledge. He guided her to one of the stools and she was glad to sit down.

"The trouble is," he repeated as he dropped on the other stool, stretching out his long legs and tugging at his sword belt with that dangerously empty sheath, "that I was more than a little mixed up when I awoke, if you might call it that, in this body. My first reactions must have suggested mental imbalance to those I encountered. Luckily, the Hawarel part was in control soon enough to save me. But there is a second drawback to this identity: I am suspect as coming from a province where there has been a rebellion. In fact, I am here in Ty-Kry as a hostage, rather than a member of the guard in good standing. I have not been able to ask questions, and all I have learned is in bits and pieces. The real Hawarel is a quite uncomplicated, simple soldier who is hurt by the suspicion against him and quite fervently loyal to the crown. I wonder how Kas took his waking. If he preserves any remnant of his real self he ought to be well established by now."

Surprised, Tamisan asked a question to which she hoped he would give a true and open answer. "You do not like . . . you have reason to fear Lord Kas?"

"Like? Fear?" She could see that thin shadow of Starrex overlaying Hawarel become more distinct. "Those are emotions. I have had little to do with emotions for some time."

"But you wanted him to share the dream," she persisted.

"True. I may not be emotional about my esteemed cousin, but I am a prudent man. Since it was by his urging, in fact his arrangement, that you were added to my household, I thought it only fair he share in his plan for my entertainment. I know that Kas is very solicitous of his crippled cousin, ready handed to serve in any way, so generous of his time and his energy."

"You suspect him of something?" She thought she had sensed what lay behind his words.

"Suspect? Of what? He has been, as all would assure you freely, my good friend, as far as I would allow." There was a closed look about him warning her off any further exploration of that.

"His crippled cousin." This time Hawarel repeated those words as if he spoke to himself and not to her. "At least you have done me a small service on the credit side of the scale." Now he did look to Tamisan as he thumped his right leg with a satisfaction which was not of the Starrex she knew. "You have provided me with a body in good working order, which I may well need since, so far, bad has outweighed the good in this world."

"Hawarel, Lord Starrex . . ." She was beginning when he interrupted her.

"Give me always Hawarel, remember. There is no need to add to the already heavy load of suspicion surrounding me in these halls."

"Hawarel, then, I did not choose you for the champion; that was done by a power I do not understand, working through me. If they agree, you have a good chance to find Kas. You may even demand that he be the one you battle."

"Find him how?"

"They may allow me to select the proper one from the off-world force," she suggested. It was a very thin thread on which to hang any plan of escape, but she could not see a better one.

"And you think that this sand painting will pick him out, as it did me?"

"It did you, did it not?"

"That I cannot deny."

"And the first time I foresaw, for one of the First Standing, it made such an impression on her that she had me summoned here to foresee for the Over-queen."

"Magic!" Again he uttered that half laugh.

"To another world much that the space travelers can do might be termed magic."

"Well said. I have seen strange things; yes, I have seen things myself, and not while dreaming either. Very well, I am to volunteer to meet an enemy champion from the ship and then you sand paint out the proper one. If you are successful and do find Kas, then what?"

"It is simple; we wake."

"You take us with you, of course?"

"If we are so linked that we cannot leave here without one another, then a single waking will take us all."

"Are you sure you need Kas? After all, I was the one you were planning this dream for."

"We go, leave Lord Kas here?"

"A cowardly withdrawal you think, my dreamer. But one, I assure you, which would solve many things. However, can you send me through and return for Kas? It is in my mind I would like to know what is happening now for myself in our own world. Is it not by the dreamer's oath that he for whom the dream is wrought has first call upon the dreamer?"

He did have some lurking uneasiness tied to Kas, but in a manner he was right. She reached out before he was aware of what she would do and seized his hand, at the same time using the formula for waking. Once more that mist which was nowhere enveloped her. But it was no use, her first guess had been right, they were still tied. She blinked her eyes open upon the same room. Hawarel had slumped and was falling from his stool, so that she had to go to one knee to support his body with her shoulder or he would have slid full length to the floor. Then his muscles tightened and he jerked erect, his eyes opened and blazed into hers with the same cold anger with which he had first greeted her upon entering this room.

"Why?"

"You asked," she countered.

His lids drooped so she could no longer see that icy anger. "So I did. But I did not quite expect to be so quickly served. Now, you have effectively proven your point; three go or none. And it remains to be seen how soon we can find our missing third."

He asked her no more questions and she was glad, since that whirl into nowhere in the abortive attempt at waking had tired her greatly. She moved the stool a little so her back could rest against the wall and she was farther from him. In a little while he got to his feet and paced back and forth as if some driving desire for wider action worked in him to the point where he could not sit still.

Once the door opened, but they were not summoned forth.

Instead, food and drink were brought to them by one of the guards; the other stood ready with a crossbow at thigh, his eyes ever upon them.

"We are well served." Hawarel opened the lids of the bowls and inspected their contents. "It would seem we are of importance. Hail, Rugaard, when do we go forth from this room, of which I am growing very tired?"

"Be at peace; you shall have action enough, when the Great One desires it," the officer with the crossbow answered. "The ship from the stars has been sighted; the mountain beacons have blazed twice. They seem to be aiming for the plain beyond Ty-Kry. It is odd that they are so single-minded and come to the same pen to be taken each time. Perhaps Dalskol was right when he said that they do not think for themselves at all, but carry out the orders of an off-world power which does not allow them independent judgment. Your service time will come; and, Mouth of Olava," he took a step forward to see Tamisan the better, "the Great One says that it might be well to read the sand on your own behalf. False seers are given to those they have belittled in such seeing, to be done with as those they have so shamed may decide."

"As is well known," she answered him. "I have not dealt falsely, as shall be seen at the proper time and in the proper place."

When they were gone she was hungry, and so it seemed was Hawarel, for they divided the food fairly and left nothing in the bowls.

When they were done he said, "Since you are a reader of history and know old customs perhaps you remember one which it is not too pleasant to recall now, that among some races it was the proper thing to dine well as a prisoner about to die."

"You choose a heartening thing to think on."

"No, you chose it, for this is your world; remember that, my dreamer."

Tamisan closed her eyes and leaned her head and shoulders back against the wall. There was a clang of sudden noise, and she gasped out of a doze. The room had grown dark, but at the door was a blaze of light; in that stood the officer, with a guard of spearmen behind.

"The time has come."

"The wait has been long." Hawarel stood up, stretched

wide his arms as one who has been ready for too long. Then he turned to her and once more offered his wrist. She would have liked to have done without his aid, but she found herself stiff and cramped enough to be glad of it.

They went on a complicated way through halls, down stairs, until at last they issued out into the night. Waiting for them was a covered cart, much larger than the chair on wheels which had brought her to the castle, with two griffins between its shafts.

Into this their guard urged them, drawing the curtains and pegging those down tightly outside, so that even had they wished they could not have looked out. As the cart creaked out Tamisan tried to guess by sound where they might be going.

There was little noise to guide her. It was as if they now passed through a town deep in slumber. But in the gloom of the cart she felt rather than saw movement, and then a shoulder brushed hers and a whisper so faint she had to strain to hear it was at her ear.

"Out of the castle."

"Where?"

"My guess is the field, the forbidden place."

The memory of the this-world Tamisan supplied explanation. That was where two other spacers had planeted, not to rise again. In fact, the one which had come fifty years ago had never been dismantled; it stood, a corroded mass of metal, to be a double warning: to the stars not to invade and to Ty-Kry to be alert against such invasion.

It seemed to Tamisan that that ride would never come to an end. Then there was an abrupt halt which bumped her soundly against the side of the cart, and lights bedazzled her eyes as the curtains were pulled aside.

"Come, Champion and Champion-maker!"

Hawarel obeyed first and turned to give her assistance once more, but was elbowed aside as the officer pulled rather than led her into the open. Torches in the hands of spearmen ringed them. Beyond was a colorful mass of people, with a double rank of guards drawn up as a barrier between those and the dark of the land beyond.

"Up there." Hawarel was beside her again.

Tamisan raised eyes. She was almost blinded by the glare as a sudden pillar of fire burst across the night sky. A spacer was riding down on tail rockets to make a fin landing.

V

By the light of those flames, the whole plain was illumined. Beyond stood the hulk of the unfortunate spacer which had last planeted. There, drawn up in lines was a large force of spearmen, crossbowmen, officers with the basket-hilted weapons at their sides. However, as they waited they appeared a guard of honor for the Over-queen, who sat raised above the rest on a very tall chair cart, certainly not an army in battle array.

Those in the ship might well look contemptuously on such archaic weapons as useless. How *had* those of Ty-Kry taken the other ship and her crew? Was it by wiles and treachery, as the victims might declare, or by clever tricks, as suggested that part of Tamisan who was the Mouth of Olava.

The surface of the ground boiled away under the descent rockets. Then the bright fires vanished, leaving the plain in semidarkness until their eyes adjusted to the lesser light of the torches.

There was no expression of awe by the waiting crowd. Though they might be, by their trappings, dress and arms, accounted centuries behind the technical knowledge of the newcomers, they were braced by their history to know that they were not to face gods of unknown powers, but mortals with whom they had successfully fought before. *What gives them this attitude toward the star rovers,* Tamisan wondered, *and why are they so adverse to any contact with star civilization? Apparently they are content to stagnate at a level of civilization perhaps five hundred years behind my world. Do they not produce any inquiring minds, any who desire to do things differently?*

The ship was down; it gave no outward sign of life, though Tamisan knew its scanners must be busy feeding back what information they gathered to appear on video screens. If those had picked up the derelict ship, the newcomers would have so much of a warning. She glanced from the silent bulk of the newly landed spacer to the Over-queen just in time to see the ruler raise her hand in a gesture. Four men came forward from the ranks of nobles and guards. Unlike the latter they wore no body armor, or helmets, but only short tunics of an unrelieved black. In the hands of each was a bow, not the crossbow of the troops, but the yet older bow of expert archers.

That part of Tamisan which was of this world drew a catch of breath, for those bows were unlike any other in the land and those who held them unlike any other archers. It was no wonder ordinary men and women gave them wide room, for they were a monstrous lot. Over the head of each was fitted so skillfully fashioned a mask that it seemed no mask at all, but his natural features, save that the features were not human; the masks were copies of the great heads, one for each point of the compass, which surmounted the defensive walls of Ty-Kry. Neither human nor animal, they were something of both and something beyond both.

The bows they raised were fashioned of human bone and strung with cords woven of human hair. They were the bones and hair of ancient enemies and ancient heroes; the intermingled strength of both were ready to serve the living.

From closed quivers each took a single arrow, and in the torchlight those arrows glittered, seeming to draw and condense radiance until they were shafts of solid light. Fitted to the cords they had a hypnotic effect, holding one's attention to the exclusion of all else. Tamisan was suddenly aware of that and tried to break the attraction, but at that moment the arrows were fired. And her head turned with all the rest in that company to watch the flight of what seemed to be lines of fire across the dark sky, rising up and up until they were well above the dark ship, then following a curve, to plunge out of sight behind it.

Oddly enough, in their passing they had left great arcs of light behind, which did not fade at once, but cast faint gleams on the skin of the ship. It was ingathering one part of Tamisan's mind knew. A laying on of ancient power to influence those in the spacer. That of her which was a dreamer could not readily believe in the efficacy of any such ceremony.

There had been sound with those arrows' passing, a shrill,

high whistling which hurt the ears so that those in the throng put hands to the sides of their heads to shut out the screech. A wind arose out of nowhere, with it a loud crackling. Tamisan looked up to see above the Over-queen's head a large bird flapping wings of gold and blue. A closer look revealed it was no giant bird, but rather a banner so fashioned that the wind set it flying to counterfeit live action.

The black-clad archers still stood in a line a little out from the ranks of the guards. Now, though the Over-queen made no visible sign, those about Hawarel and Tamisan urged them forward until they came to front both the archers and the Over-queen's tall throne-cart.

"Well, Champion, is it in your mind to carry out the duties this busy Mouth has assigned you?" There was jeering in the Over-queen's question, as if she did not honestly believe in Tamisan's prophecy but was willing to allow a dupe to march to destruction in his own way.

Hawarel went to one knee, but as he did so he swung his empty sword sheath across his knee, making very visible the fact that he lacked a weapon.

"At your desire, Great One, I stand ready. But is it your will that my battle be without even steel between me and the enemy?"

Tamisan saw a smile on the lips of the Over-queen and at that moment glimpsed a little into this ruler, that it might just please her to will such a fate on Hawarel. But if the Over-queen played with that thought for an instant or two, she put it aside. Now she gestured.

"Give him steel, and let him use it. The Mouth has said he is the answer to our defense this time. Is that not so, Mouth?"

The look she gave to Tamisan had a cruel core.

"He has been chosen in the farseeing, and twice has it read so." Tamisan found the words to answer in a firm voice, as if what she said was a decree.

The Over-queen laughed. "Be firm, Mouth; put your will behind this choice of yours. In fact, do you go with him, to give him the support of Olava!"

Hawarel had accepted a sword from the officer on his left. He rose to his feet and, swinging the blade, he saluted with a flourish which suggested that, if he knew he were going to extinction, he intended to march there as one who moved to trumpet and drums.

"The right be strength to your arm, a shield to your body,"

intoned the Over-queen. There was that in her voice which one might detect to mean that the words she spoke were only ritual, not intended to encourage this champion.

Hawarel turned to face the silent ship. From the burned and blasted ground about its landing fins arose trails of steam and smoke. The faint arcs left in the air from the arrow flights were gone.

As Hawarel moved forward, Tamisan followed a pace or two behind. If the ship remained closed to them, if no hatch opened, no ramp ran forth, she did not see how they could carry out their plans. If that were so, would the Over-queen expect them to wait hour after hour for some decision from the spacer's commander as to whether or not he would contact them?

Fortunately, the space crew were more enterprising. Perhaps the sight of that hulk on the edge of the field had given them the need to learn more. The hatch which opened was not the large entrance hatch, but a smaller door above one of the fins. From it shot a stunner beam.

Luckily it caught its prey, both Hawarel and Tamisan, before they had reached the edge of the sullenly burning turf, so that their suddenly helpless bodies did not fall into the fire. They did not lose consciousness, but only the ability to control slack muscles.

Tamisan had crumpled face down, and only the fact that one cheek pressed the earth gave her room to breathe. Her sight was sharply curtailed at the edge of burning grass which crept inexorably toward her. Seeing that she forgot all else.

These moments were the worse she had ever spent. She had conjured up narrow escapes in dreams, but always there had been the knowledge that at the last moment escape was possible. Now there was no escape, only her helpless body and the line of advancing fire.

With the suddenness of a blow, delivering shock through her still painful bruises, she was caught, right side and left, in what felt like giant pincers. As those closed about her body, she was drawn aloft, still face down, the fumes and heat of the burning vegetation choking her. She coughed until the spasms made her sick, spinning in that brutal clutch, being drawn to the spacer.

She came into a burst of dazzling light. Then hands seized her, pulling her down, but holding her upright. The force of the stunner was wearing off; they must have set the beam on lowest power. There was a prickle of feeling returning in her legs and her heavy arms. She was able to lift her head a fraction to see men in space uniforms about her. They wore helmets as if expecting to issue out on a hostile world, and some of them had the visors closed. Two picked her up easily and carried her along, down a corridor, before dropping her without any gentleness in a small cabin with a suspicious likeness to a cell.

Tamisan lay on the floor recovering command of her own body and trying to think ahead. Had they taken Hawarel, too? There was no reason to believe they had not, but he had not been put in this cell. She was able to sit up now, her back supported by the wall, and she smiled shakily at her thought that their brave boast of a championship battle had certainly been brought quickly to naught. It was not that what the Over-queen desired might have run far counter to what happened, but she and Starrex had gained this much of their own objective: they were in the ship she believed also held Kas. Only let the three of them make contact, and they could leave the dream. *And, would our leaving shatter this dream world? How real is it?* She was sure of nothing, and there was no reason to worry over side issues. The time had come to concentrate upon one thing only: Kas.

What should I do? Pound on the door of this cell to demand attention, to speak with the commander of this ship? Would she ask to see all the crew so she could pick out Kas in his this-world masquerade? She had a suspicion that while Hawarel-Starrex had accepted her story, no one else might.

The important thing was some kind of action to get her free and let her search.

The door was opening. Tamisan was startled by what seemed a quick answer to her need.

There was no helmet on the man who stood there, though he wore a tunic bearing the insignia of a higher officer, slightly different from that Tamisan knew from her own Ty-Kry. He also had a stunner aimed at her; at his throat was the box of a vocal interpreter.

"I come in peace."

"With a weapon in hand?" she countered.

He looked surprised; he must have expected a foreign tongue in answer, but she had replied in the Basic which was the second language of all Confederacy planets.

"We have reason to believe that weapons are necessary with your people. I am Glandon Tork of Survey."

"I am Tamisan and a Mouth of Olava." Her hand went to her head and discovered that somehow, in spite of her passage through the air and her entrance into the ship, her crown was still there. Then she pressed the important question:

"Where is the champion?"

"Your companion?" The stunner was no longer centered on her, and his tone had lost some of its belligerency. "He is in safe keeping. But why do you name him champion?"

"Because that is what he is—come to engage *your* selected champion in right battle."

"I see. And we select a champion in return, is that it? What is right battle?"

She answered his last question first. "If you claim land, you meet the champion of the lordship of that land in right battle."

"But we claim no land," he protested.

"You made claim when you set your fiery ship down on the fields of Ty-Kry."

"Your people then consider our landing a form of invasion? But this can be decided by a single combat between champions? And we pick our man . . ."

Tamisan interrupted him. "Not so. The Mouth of Olava selects; or rather the sand selects, the seeing selects. That is why I have come, though you did not greet me in honor."

"You select the champion how?"

"As I have said, by the seeing."

"*I* do not see, but doubtless it will be made plain in the proper time. And where then is this combat fought?"

She waved to what she thought were the ship walls. "Out there on the land being claimed."

"Logical," he conceded. Then he spoke as if to the air around them. "All that recorded?" Since the air did not answer him, he was apparently satisfied by silence.

"This is your custom, Lady, Mouth of Olava. But since it is not ours, we must discuss it. By your leave, we shall do so."

"As you wish." She had this much on her side, he had introduced himself as a member of Survey, which meant that he had been trained in the necessity of understanding alien folkways. The simple underlying principle of such training was, wherever possible, to follow planet customs. If the crew did accept this idea of championship, then they might also be willing to follow it completely. She could demand to see every member of the crew and thus find Kas. Once that was done she could break dream.

But, Tamisan told herself, *do not count on too easy an end to this venture.* There was a nagging little doubt lurking in the back of her mind, and it had something to do with those death arrows, and the hulk of the derelict. The people of Ty-Kry, seemingly so weakly defended, had managed through centuries to keep their world free of spacers. When she tried to plumb the Tamisan-of-this-world's memories as to how that was accomplished she had no answer but what corresponded to magic forces only partly understood. That the shooting of the arrows was the first step in bringing such forces into being she was aware. Beyond that seemed only to lie a belief akin to her Mouth power, and that she did not understand even when she employed it.

She was accepting all of this, Tamisan realized suddenly, as if this world did exist, as if it was not a dream out of her control. Could Starrex's suggestion be the truth, that they had by some means traveled into an alternate world?

Her patience was growing short; she wanted action. Waiting was very difficult. She was sure that scanners of more than one kind were trained on her and she must play the part of a Mouth of Olava, displaying no impatience, only calm confidence in herself and her mission. That she held to as best she could.

Perhaps the time she waited seemed longer than it really was, but Tork returned, to usher her out of the cell and escort her up a ladder from level to level. She found the long skirts of her robe difficult to manage. The cabin they came into was large and well furnished, and there were several men seated there. Tamisan looked from one to another searchingly. She could not tell; she felt none of the uneasiness she had known in the throne room when Hawarel had been there. Of course, that could mean Kas was not one of this group, though a Survey ship did not carry a large crew, mainly specialists of several different callings. There were probably ten, perhaps twenty more than the six before her.

Tork led her to a chair which had some of the attributes of an easirest, molding to her comfort as she settled into it.

"This is Captain Lowald, Medico Thrum, Psycho-Tech Sims and Hist-Techneer El Hamdi." Tork named names and each man acknowledged with a half bow. "I have outlined your proposal to them and they have discussed the matter. By what means will you select a champion from among us?"

She had no sand; for the first time Tamisan realized the handicap. She would have to depend upon touch alone, but somehow she was sure that would reveal Kas to her.

"Let your men come to me, touching hand to mine." She raised hers to lay it, palm up, on the table. "When I clasp that of he whom Olava selects, I shall know it."

"It seems simple enough," the Captain returned. "Let us do as the lady suggests." And he leaned forward to rest his own for a minute on hers. There was no response, nor was there any in the others. The Captain called an order on the intercom and one by one the other members of the crew came to her, touching palm to palm. Tamisan, with mounting uneasiness, began to believe she had erred; perhaps only by the sand could she detect Kas. Though she searched the face of each as he took his seat opposite her and laid his hand on hers, she could see no resemblance to Starrex's cousin, nor was there any inner warning her man was here.

"That was the last," the Captain said as the final man arose. "Which is our champion?"

"He is not here." She blurted out the truth, her distress breaking through her caution.

"But you have touched hands with every man on board this ship," the Captain answered her. "Or is this some trick?"

He was interrupted by a sound sharp enough to startle. The numbers which spilled from the com by his elbow meant nothing to Tamisan, but brought the rest in that cabin into instant action. A stunner in Tork's hand caught her before she could rise, and once more she was conscious but unable to move. As the other officers pushed through the door on the run, Tork put out his hand, holding her limp body erect in the chair, while with the other he thumped some alarm button set into the table.

His summons was speedily answered by two crewmen who carried her along, to thrust her once more into a cabin. *This is getting to be far too regular a procedure*, Tamisan thought ruefully, as they tossed her negligently on a bunk, hardly pausing to see if she landed safely on its surface or not. Whatever that alert had meant it had certainly once more brought her to the status of prisoner.

Apparently sure of the stunner beam her guard went out,

leaving the door open a crack so that she could hear the pad of running feet and the clangs of what could be secondary alarms.

What possible attack could the forces of the Over-queen have launched against a well-armed and already alert spacer? Yet it was plain that those men believed themselves in danger and were on the defensive. *Starrex and Kas. Where is Kas?* The Captain said she had met all on board. Did that mean that the vision she had earlier seen was false, that the faceless man in spacer dress was a creature of her too-active imagination?

I must not lose confidence. Kas is here, he has to be! She lay now trying vainly to guess by the sounds what was happening. But the first flurry of noise and movement were stilled, there was only silence. *Hawarel, where is Hawarel?*

The stunner's power was wearing off. She had pulled herself up somewhat groggily when the door of the cabin shot into its wall crack and Tork and the Captain stood there.

"Mouth of Olava, or whatever you truly are," the Captain said, with a chill in his voice which reminded Tamisan of Hawarel's earlier rage, "the winning of time may not have been of your devising, this nonsense of champions and right battle, or perhaps it was. Your superiors perhaps deceived you, too. At any rate now it does not matter. They have done their best to make us prisoners and will not reply now to our signals for a parley; so we must use you for our messenger. Tell your ruler that we hold her champion and we can readily use him as a key to open gates shut in our faces. We have weapons beyond swords and spears, even beyond those which might not have saved those in that other ship. She can tie us here for a measure of time, but we can sever such bonds. We have not come as invaders, no matter what you believe, nor are we alone. If our signal does not reach our sister ship in orbit above, there will be such an accounting as your race has not seen, nor can conceive of. We shall release you now and you shall tell your Queen this. If she does not send those to talk with us before the dawn, then it will be the worse for her. Do you understand?"

"And Hawarel?" Tamisan asked.

"Hawarel?"

"The champion. You will keep him here?"

"As I have said, we have the means to make him a key for your fortress doors. Tell her that, Mouth. From what we have read in your champion's mind, you have certain authority here which ought to impress your Queen."

Read from Starrex's mind? What do they mean? Tamisan was suddenly fearful. *Some kind of mind probe? But if they did that, then they must know the rest.* She was utterly confused now, and found it very hard to center her attention on the matter at hand, that she must relay this defiant message to the Over-queen. Since there seemed to be nothing she could do to protest that action, she would do so. *What reception might I have in Ty-Kry?* Tamisan shuddered as Tork pulled her from the bunk and half carried, half led her along.

VI

For the third time Tamisan sat in prison, but this time she looked not at the smooth walls of a spaceship cabin, but at the ancient stones of the High Castle ringing her in. Captain Lowald's estimation of her influence with the Over-queen had fallen far short, and her plea in favor of a parley with the spacemen had been overruled at once. The threat concerning their strange weapons and their mysterious use of Hawarel as a "key" was laughed at. The fact that those of Ty-Kry had successfully dealt with this menace in the past made them confident that their same devices would serve as well now. What those devices were Tamisan had no idea, save that something had happened to the ship before she had been unceremoniously bundled out of it.

Hawarel they had kept on board, Kas had disappeared, and until she had both to hand she was indeed a captive. Kas . . . her thoughts kept turning back to the fact that he had not been among those who had faced her. Lowald had assured her that she had seen all his crew.

Wait! She set herself to recall his every word. *What had he said?* "*You have touched hand with every man aboard this ship.*" But he had not said all the crew. *Had there been one outside the ship?* All she knew of space travel she had learned from tapes, but those had been very detailed as they needed to be to supply the dreamers with factual background and inspiration from which to build fantasy worlds. This spacer claimed to be a Survey vessel and not operating alone. *Therefore, it might have a companion in orbit and there Kas could be.* But, if that were so, she had no chance of reaching him.

Now if this were only a true dream ... Tamisan sighed, leaned her head back against the dank stone of the wall, and then jerked away from that support as its chill struck into her shoulders. *Dreams ...*

She sat upright, alert and a little excited. *Suppose I could dream within a dream and find Kas that way? Is it possible? You cannot tell until you proved it one way or another.* She had no stabilizer, no booster, but those were only needed when a dream was shared. She might venture as well on her own. *But, if I dreamed within a dream, can I do aught to set matters right? Why ask questions I cannot answer until it is put to proof!*

She stretched out on the stones of the cell floor resolutely blocking off those portions of her mind which were aware of the present discomfort of her body. Instead, she began the deep, even breathing of a dreamer, fastened her thoughts on the pattern of self-hypnosis, which was the door to her dreams. All she had as a goal was Kas and he as he was in his real person. *So poor a guide ...*

She was going under; she could still dream.

Walls built up around her, but these were of a translucent material through which flowed soft and pleasing colors. It could not be a spaceship. Then the scene wavered, and swiftly Tamisan thrust aside that doubt which might puncture the dream fabric. The walls sharpened and fixed into a solid state; this was a corridor; facing her was a door.

She willed to see beyond, and was straightway, after the manner of a proper dream, in that chamber. Here the walls were hung with the same sparkling web of stuff which had lined her chamber in the sky tower. Seeking Kas, she had returned to her own world. But she held the dream, curious as to why her aim had brought her here. Had she been wrong and Kas had never come with her? If that were so, why had she and Starrex been marooned in the other dream?

There was no one in the chamber, but she felt a faint pull drawing her on. She sought Kas; there was that which promised he was here. There was a second room; entering, she was startled. This she knew well: it was the room of a dreamer. Kas stood by an empty couch, while the other was occupied.

The dreamer wore a sharing crown, but what rested on the other couch was not a second sleeper but a squat box of metal, to which her dream cords were attached, and Tamisan was not the dreamer. She had expected to see herself. Instead, the entranced was one of the locked minds, the blankness of her countenance unmistakable. Dream force was being created here by an indreamer, and seemingly it was harnessed to the box.

Given such clues, Tamisan projected the rest. This was not the same dreaming chamber where she had fallen asleep; it was a smaller room. Kas was very much awake, intent upon some dials on the top of the box. The indreamer and the box, locked so together, could be holding them in the other world. *But what of that faint vision of Kas in uniform? To mislead me? Or is this a misleading dream, dictated by the suspicions I detected in Starrex concerning his cousin?* This was the logical reasoning from such suspicions, that she had been sent with Starrex into a dream world and therein locked by an indreamer and machine. *Real, or dream . . . which?*

Am I now visible to Kas? If this were a dream she should be; if she had come back to reality . . . Her head reeled under the listing of things which might be true, untrue, half true. To prove at least one small fraction, she moved forward and laid her hand on Kas's as he leaned over to make some small adjustment to the box.

He gave a startled exclamation, jerked his hand from under hers and glanced around. But, though he stared straight at her, it was plain he saw nothing; she was as disembodied as a spirit in one of the old tales. *Yet if he has not seen me still he has felt something . . .*

Again he leaned over the box, eyeing it intently as if he thought he must have felt some shock or emanation from it. The dreamer never moved. Save for the slow rise and fall of her breathing, which told Tamisan she was indeed deep in her self-created world, she might have been dead. Her face was very wan and colorless. Seeing that, Tamisan was uneasy. This tool of Kas's had been far too long in an uninterrupted dream. She would have to be awakened if she made no move to break it for herself. One of the dangers of indreaming was this possible loss of the power to break a dream. That occurring, the guardian must break it. Most of the dreamers' caps provided the necessary stimuli to do so. But the cap on this dreamer's head had certain modifications Tamisan had never seen before, and these might prevent breaking.

What would happen if Tamisan could evoke waking? Would that also release her and Starrex, wherever he might be, from *their* dream and return them to the proper world? She was well drilled in the technique of dream breaking. Those she had used when she stood in reality beside a victim who had overstayed the proper dream time.

She reached out a hand, touched the pulse on the sleeper's throat and applied slight massage. But, though her hands seemed corporeal and solid to her, there was no response in the other. To prove a point Tamisan aimed a finger, thrusting it deeply as she could into the pillow on which the dreamer's head rested. Her finger did not dent that soft roundness, but went into it as if her flesh and bone had no substance.

There was yet another way; it was harsh and used only in cases of extremity. But to Tamisan this could be no else. She put those unsubstantial fingers on the temples of the sleeper, just below the rim of the dream cap, and concentrated on a single command.

The sleeper stirred, her features convulsed and a low moan came from her. Kas uttered an exclamation and hung over his box, his fingers busy pushing buttons with a care which suggested he was about a very delicate task.

"Awake!" Tamisan commanded with such force as she could summon.

The sleeper's hands arose very slowly and unsteadily from her sides and they wavered toward the cap, though her eyelids did not rise. Her expression was now one of pain. Kas, breathing hard and fast, kept to his adjustments on the box.

So they fought their silent battle for possession of the dreamer. Slowly Tamisan was forced to concede that whatever force lay in that box overrode all the techniques she knew. But the longer Kas kept this poor wretch under, the weaker she would grow. Death would be the answer, though perhaps that did not trouble him.

If she could not wake the dreamer and break the bonds which she was certain now were what tied her and Starrex to that other world, then she must somehow get at Kas himself. He had responded to her touch before.

Tamisan slipped away from the head of the couch and came to stand behind Kas. He straightened up, a faint relief mirrored on his face as apparently his box reported that there was no longer any disturbance.

Now Tamisan raised her hands to either side of his head, spreading wide her fingers so they might resemble the covering of a dreamer's cap, and then brought them swiftly down to cover his head, putting firm touch on his temples though she could not exert real pressure there.

He gave a muffled cry, tossed his head from side to side as if to free himself from a cloud. But Tamisan, with all the determination of which she was capable, held fast. She had seen this done once in the Hive; however, then it had been used on a docile subject and both the controlled and the dreamer had been on the same plane of existence. Now she could only hope that she could disrupt Kas's train of thought long enough to make him release the dreamer himself. So she brought to bear all her will to that purpose. He was not only shaking his head from side to side now, making it very hard to keep her hands in the proper position, but he was swaying back and forth, his hands up, clawing as if to tear her hold away. It appeared he could not touch her any more than she could lay firm grip on him.

That fund of energy which had enabled her to create strange worlds and hold them for a fellow dreamer was bent to the task of influencing Kas. But, to her dismay, though he ceased his frenzied movements, his clawing for the hands he could not clutch growing feebler, his eyes closed and his face screwed into an expression of horror and rejection of a frightened child. He did not move to the box.

Instead he slumped forward so suddenly that Tamisan was taken wholly unaware, falling half across the divan. In that fall he flailed out with an arm to send the box smashing to the floor, its weight dragging the cap from the dreamer.

She drew several deep breaths, her haggard face now displaying a small trace of returning color. Tamisan, still startled at the results of her efforts to influence Kas, began to wonder if she might have made matters worse. She did not know how much the box had to do with their transportation to the alternate world and whether, if it was broken, they could ever return.

There was one precaution, if she could take it. *If I return to that prison cell in the High Castle, I must, or leave Star-rex-Hawarel lost forever, then to leave Kas here, perhaps able again to use his machine, no! But how, since I cannot? . . .*

Tamisan looked to the stirring dreamer. The girl was struggling out of the depths of so deep a state of unconsciousness that she was not aware of what lay about her. In this state she might be pliable. Tamisan could only try.

Leaving Kas she went back to the dreamer. Once more touching the girl's forehead, she sought to influence her.

The dreamer sat up with such slow movements of body as one might use were almost unbearable weights fastened to every muscle. In a painfully slow gesture she raised her hands to her head, groping for the cap no longer there. Then she sat, her eyes still shut, while Tamisan drew heavily on her own strength to deliver a final set of orders.

Blindly, for she never opened her eyes, the dreamer felt along the edge of the couch on which she had lain, until her hand swept against the cords which fastened the cap to the box. Her lax fingers fumbled and tightened as she gave a feeble jerk, then another until both cords pulled free. Holding those still in one hand, she slipped from the couch in a forward movement which brought her to her knees, the upper part of her body on the other couch, one cheek touching that of the unconscious Kas.

The strain on Tamisan was very great. She was wavering in her control now, several times those weak hands fell limply as her hold on the dreamer ebbed. But each time she found some small surge of energy which brought them back into action again, so that at last the cap was on Kas, the cords which had connected it to the box in a half coil on which the dreamer's head rested.

So big a chance and with such poor equipment! Tamisan could not be sure of any results, she could only hope. Tamisan released her command of the dreamer who lay against the couch on one side as Kas half lay on the other. She summoned all that she had, all that she sensed she had always possessed, that small difference in dream power she had secretly cherished. Once more she touched the forehead of the sleeping girl and broke her dream within a dream.

It was like climbing a steep hill with an intolerably heavy burden lashed to one's aching back, like being forced to pull the dead weight of another body through a swamp which sucked one down. It was such an effort as she could not endure . . .

Then that weight was gone and the relief of its vanishing was such that Tamisan savored the fact that it did not drag at her. She opened her eyes at last and even that small movement required such an effort that it left her spent.

She was not in the sky tower. These walls were stone, and the light was dusky, coming from a slit high in the opposite wall. She was in the High Castle from which she had dreamed her way back to her own Ty-Kry in a dream within a dream. But how well had she wrought there?

For the present she was too tired to even think connectedly. Bits and pieces of all she had seen and done since she had awakened first in this Ty-Kry floated through her mind, not making any concrete pattern.

It was the mind picture of Hawarel's face as she had seen it last while they marched toward the spacer which roused her from that uncaring drift. She remembered Hawarel and the threat the ship's Captain had made, which the Over-queen had pushed aside. If Tamisan had truly broken the lock Kas had set up to keep them here, then it would be escape. There was no strength in her. She tried to remember the formula for breaking, and knew a stroke of chilling fear when her memory proved faulty. She could not do it now; she must have more time to rest both mind and body. Now she was hungry and thirsty, with such a need for both food and drink that it was a torment. *Do they mean to leave me here without any sustenance?*

Tamisan lay still, listening. Then she inched her head around slowly to view the deeper dusk of her surroundings at floor level. She was not alone.

Kas!

Had she successfully pulled Kas with her? If so, was it that he had no counterpart in this world and so was still his old self?

However, she did not have time to explore that possibility, for there was a loud grating and a line of light marking an opening door. In the beam of a torch stood that same officer who had earlier been her escort. Using her hands to brace her body, Tamisan raised herself. At the same time there was a cry from the far corner.

Someone moved there, raised a head and showed features she had last seen in the sky tower. It was Kas in his rightful body. He was scrambling to his feet and the officer and the guardsman behind him in the doorway stared as if they could not believe their eyes. Kas shook his head as if to clear away some mist.

His lips pulled back from his teeth in a terrible rictus which was no smile. There was a small laser in his hand. She could not move; he was going to burn her. In that moment she was so sure of that she did not even fear, but only waited for the crisping of her flesh.

But the aim of the weapon raised beyond her and fastened on the doorway. Under it both officer and guard went down. With one hand on the wall to steady himself, Kas pulled along until he came to her. He stood away from the stone, transferred his laser to the other hand and reached down to hook fingers in the robe where it covered her shoulder.

"On . . . your . . . feet." He mouthed the words with difficulty, as if his exhaustion nearly equaled hers. "I do not know how, or why, or who. . . ."

The torch, dropped from the charred hand which had carried it, gave them dim light. Kas swung her around, thrusting his face very close to hers. He stared at her intently, as if by the very force of his glare he could strip aside the mask her body made for her and force the old Tamisan into sight.

"You are Tamisan—it cannot be otherwise! I do not know how you did this, demon-born." He shook her with a viciousness which struck her painfully against the wall. "Where is he?"

All that came from her parched throat were harsh sounds without meaning.

"Never mind." Kas stood straighter now; there was more vigor in his voice. "Where he is, there shall I find him. Nor shall I lose you, demon-born, since you are my way back. And for Lord Starrex, here there will be no guards, no safe shields. Perhaps this is the better way after all. What is this place; answer me!" He slapped her face, his palm bruising her, once more thumping her head back against the wall so that the rim of the Mouth crown bit into her scalp and she cried out in pain.

"Speak! Where is this?"

"The High Castle of Ty-Kry," she croaked.

"And what do you in this hole?"

"I am prisoner to the Over-queen."

"Prisoner? What do you mean? You are a dreamer; this is your dream. Why are you a prisoner?"

Tamisan was so shaken she could not marshal words easily, as she had to explain to Starrex. She thought, a little dazedly, that Kas might not accept her explanation anyway.

"Not ... wholly ... a dream," she got out.

He did not seem surprised. "So the control has that property, has it; to impose a sense of reality." His eyes blazed into hers. "You cannot control this dream, is that it? Again fortune favors me it seems. Where is Starrex now?"

She could give him a truthful answer she was glad, as it seemed to her she could not speak falsely with any hope of belief. It was as if he could see straight into her mind with those demanding eyes of his. "I do not know."

"But he is in this dream somewhere?"

"Yes."

"Then you shall find him for me, Tamisan, and speedily. Do we have to search this High Castle?"

"He was, when I saw him last, outside."

She kept her eyes turned from the door, from what lay there. But he hauled her toward that, and she was afraid she was going to be sick. Where they might be in the interior of the small city which was the High Castle she did not know. Those who had brought her here had not taken her to the core towers, but had turned aside along the first of the gateways and gone down a long flight of stairs. She doubted if they would be able to walk out again as easily as Kas thought to do.

"Come." He pulled at her, dragging her on, kicked aside what lay in the door. She closed her eyes tightly as he brought her past. But the stench of death was so strong that she staggered, retching, with his hand dragging at her, keeping her on her feet and reeling ahead.

Twice she watched glassily as he burned down opposition. His luck at keeping surprise on his side held. They came to the foot of the stairs and climbed. Tamisan held to one hope. Now that she was on her feet and moving, she found a measure of strength returning, so that she no longer feared falling if Kas released his hold upon her. When they were out at last in the night, the damp smell of the underways wafted away by a rising wind, she felt clean and renewed and was able to think more clearly.

Kas had gotten her this far because of her weakness, so to

his eyes she must continue to counterfeit that, until she had a chance to act. It might be that his weapon, so alien to this world and thus so effective, might well cut their way to Starrex. That did not mean that once they had reached him she need obey Kas. She felt that, face to face with his lord, Kas would be less confident of success.

It was not a guard that halted them now but a massive gate. Kas examined the bar and laughed before he raised the laser and sent a needle-thin beam to cut as he needed. There was a shout from above and Kas, almost languidly, swung the beam to a narrow stair leading from the ramparts, laughing again as there came a choked scream, the sound of a falling body.

"Now." Kas put his shoulder to the gate and it swung more easily than Tamisan would have thought possible for its weight. "Where is Starrex? And if you lie . . ." His smile was threatening.

"There." Tamisan was sure of her direction, and she pointed to where there was a distant blaze of torches about the bulk of the grounded spacer.

VII

"A spacer!" Kas paused.

"Besieged by these people," Tamisan informed him. "And Starrex is a hostage on board, if he still lives. They have threatened to use him in some manner as a weapon and the Over-queen, as far as I know, does not care."

Kas turned on her, his merriment had vanished; his laugh was now a snarl; and he shook her back and forth. "It is your dream; control it!"

For a moment Tamisan hesitated. Should she try to tell him what she believed the truth? Kas and his weapon might be her only hope of reaching Starrex. Could he be persuaded to a frontal attack if he thought that was their only chance of reaching their goal? On the other hand, if she admitted she could not break this dream, he might well burn her down out of hand and take his chances. She thought she had a solution.

"Your meddling has warped the pattern, Lord Kas. I cannot control some elements, nor can I break the dream until I have Lord Starrex with me, since we are pattern-linked in this sequence."

Her steady reply seemed to have some effect on him. Though he gave her one more punishing shake and uttered an obscenity, he looked ahead to the torches and the half-seen bulk of the ship with calculation in his eyes.

They made a lengthy detour away from most of the torches, coming up across the open land to the south of the ship. There was a graying in the sky and a hint that dawn might perhaps be not far away. Now that they could see better, it was apparent that the ship was sealed. No hatch opened on its surface, no ramp ran out. The laser in Kas's hand could not burn their way in, by the method he had opened the gate of the High Castle.

Apparently the same difficulty presented itself to Kas, for he halted her with a jerk while they were still in the shadows, well away from the line of torches forming a square around the ship. Surveying the scene, they sheltered in a small dip in the ground.

The torches were no longer held by men, but had been planted in the ground at regular intervals, and they were as large as outsize candles. The colorful mass which had marked the Over-queen and her courtiers on Tamisan's first visit to the landing field were gone, leaving only a line of guardsmen in a wide encirclement of the sealed ship.

Why did the spacemen not lift and planet elsewhere, Tamisan wondered. Perhaps the confusion in the last moments she had been on board meant that they could not do so. They had spoken then of a sister ship in orbit above. It would seem that had made no move to aid them, though she had no idea how much time had elapsed since last she had been here.

Kas turned on her again. "Can you get a message to Starrex?" he demanded.

"I can try. For what reason?"

"Have him ask for us to come to him." Kas had been silent for a moment before replying. *Is he so stupid as to be-*

lieve that I would not give a warning with whatever message I could deliver, or has he precautions against that?

But can I reach Starrex? She had gone into the secondary dream to make contact with Kas. There was no time for such a move now. She could only use the mental technique for inducing a dream and see what happened thereby. She said as much to Kas now, promising no success.

"Be about what you can do now!" he told her roughly.

Tamisan closed her eyes to think of Hawarel as she had seen him last, standing beside her on this very field. She heard a gasp from Kas. Opening her eyes she saw Hawarel, even as he had been then, or rather a pallid copy of him, wavering and indistinct, already beginning to fade, so she spoke in a swift gabble.

"Say we come from the Queen with a message, that we must see the Captain."

The shimmering outline of Hawarel faded into the night. She heard Kas mutter angrily. "What good will that ghost do?"

"I cannot tell. If he returns to that of which he is a part, he can carry the message. For the rest ..." Tamisan shrugged. "I have told you this is no dream I can control. Do you think if it were, we two would stand here in this fashion?"

His thin lips parted in one of his mirthless grins.

"You would not, I know, dreamer!"

His head went from left to right as he slowly surveyed the line of planted torches and the men standing on guard between them. "Do we move closer to this ship, expect them to open to us?"

"They used a stunner to take us before," Tamisan warned him. "They might do so again."

"Stunner." He gestured with the laser. Tamisan hoped his answer would not be a headlong attack on the ship with that.

He used it as a pointer to motion her on toward the torch line. "If they do open up," he commented, "I shall be warned."

Tamisan gathered up the long skirt of her robe. It was torn by rough handling, frayed in strips at the hem where she could trip if she caught those rags between her feet. The rough brush growing knee high about them caught at it so that she stumbled now and again, urged on continually by

Kas's pulling, when he dug his fingers painfully into her already bruised shoulder.

They reached the torch line. The guards there faced inward to the ship and in this crease of light Tamisan could see that they were all armed with crossbows, not with those of bone which the black-dressed men had earlier worn. Bolts against the might of the ship. The answer seemed laughable, a jesting to delight the simple. Yet the ship lay there and Tamisan could well remember the consternation of those men who had been questioning her within it.

There was a dark spot on the hull of the ship and a hatch suddenly swung open. She recognized it as a battle hatch, though she had only seen those via tapes.

"Kas, they are going to fire." With a laser beam from there they could crisp everything on this field, perhaps clear back to the walls of the High Castle!

She tried to turn in his grasp, to race back and away, knowing already that such a race was lost before she took the first lunging stride. He held her fast.

"No muzzle," he said.

Tamisan strained to see through the flickering light. Perhaps it was a lightening of the sky which made it clear that there was no muzzle projecting to spew a fiery death across them all. But that was a gunport.

As quickly as it had appeared, the opening was closed. The ship was again sealed tightly.

"What?"

Kas answered her half question, "Either they cannot use it, or else they have thought better of doing so, which means, by either count, we have a chance. Now, stay you here! Or else I shall come looking for you in a manner you shall not relish; never fear that I can find you!" Nothing in Tamisan disputed that.

She stood; for after all, apart from Kas's threats, where did she have to go? If she were sighted by any of the guards she might either be returned to prison or dealt with summarily in another fashion. She had to reach Starrex if she were to escape.

She watched Kas make good use of the interest which riveted the eyes of the guards on the ship. He crept, with more ease than she thought possible for one used to the luxury of the sky towers, behind the nearest man.

What weapon he used she could not see; it was not the

laser. Instead he straightened to his full height behind the un-
suspecting guard, reached out an arm and seemed only to
touch the stranger on the neck. Immediately the fellow
collapsed without a sound, though Kas caught him before he
had fallen to the ground and dragged him backward to the
slight depression in the field where Tamisan waited.

"Quick," Kas ordered, "give me his cloak and helmet."

He ripped off his own tunic with its extravagantly padded
shoulders, while Tamisan knelt to fumble with a great brooch
and free the cloak from the guard. Kas snatched it out of her
hands, dragged the rest of it loose from under the limp body,
and pulled it around him, taking up the helmet and settling it
on his head with a tap. Then he picked up the crossbow.

"Walk before me," he told Tamisan. "If they have a field
scanner on in the ship I want them to see a prisoner under
guard. That may bring them to a parley. It is a thin chance,
but our best."

He could not guess that it might be a better chance than he
hoped, Tamisan knew, since he did not know that she had
been once within the ship and the crew might be expecting
some such return with a message from the Over-queen. But to
walk out boldly past the line of torches, surely Kas's luck
would not hold so well; they would be seen by the other
guards before they were a quarter of the way to the ship. But
she had no other proposal to offer in exchange.

This was no adventure such as she had lived through in
dreams. She believed that if she died now she died indeed
and would not wake unharmed in her own world. Her flesh
crawled with a fear which made her mouth go dry and her
hands quiver as they held wet upon the folds of her robe.
*Any second now I will feel the impact of a bolt, hear a shout
of discovery, be . . .*

But still Tamisan tottered forward and heard, with alerted
ears, the faint crunch of boots which was Kas behind her.
His contempt for a danger which was only too real for her,
made her wonder, fleetingly, if he did indeed still believe this
a dream she could control, and need not then watch for anyone but her. She could not summon words to tell him of his
woeful mistake.

So intent was she upon some attack from behind that she
was not really conscious of the ship toward which they went,
until suddenly she saw another of the ports open and steeled
herself to feel the numbing charge of a stunner.

However, again the attack she feared did not come. The sky was growing lighter, although there was no sign of sunrise. Instead, the first drops of a storm began to fall. Under the onslaught of moisture from lowering clouds, the torches hissed and sputtered, finally flickering out. The gloom was hardly better than twilight.

They came close enough to the ship to board, when one of the ramps lowered to them, they stood waiting. Tamisan felt the rise of hysterical laughter inside her. *What an anticlimax if the ship refuses to acknowledge us!* They could not stand here forever and there was no way they could battle a way inside. Kas's faith in her communication with the ghost of Hawarel seemed too high.

But even as she was sure that they faced failure, there was a sigh of sound from above them. The port hatch wheeled back into the envelope of the ship's wall, and a small ramp, hardly more than a steep ladder, swung creaking out, dropped to hit the charred ground not far from them.

"Go!" Kas prodded her forward.

With a shrug, Tamisan went. She found it hard to climb with the heavy, frayed skirts dragging her back. But by using her hands to pull along the single rail of the ramp, she made progress. Why had not the rest of the guards along that watching line of torches moved? Had it been that Kas's disguise had indeed deceived them, and they thought that Tamisan had been sent under orders to parley a second time with the ship's people?

She was nearly at the hatch now, could see the suited men waiting in the shadows above. They had tanglers ready to fire, prepared to spin the webs to enmesh them both as easily handled prisoners. But before those slimy strands writhed forth to touch (patterned as they were to seek flesh to anchor) both the waiting spacemen jerked right and left, clutched with already dead hands at the breasts of charred tunics from which arose small, deadly spirals of smoke.

They had expected a guard armed with a bow; they had met Kas's laser, to the same undoing as the guardsmen at the castle. Kas's shoulder in the middle of her back sent her sprawling, to land half over the bodies of the two who had awaited them.

She heard a scuffle, was kicked and rolled aside, fighting the folds of her own long skirt, trying to get out of the confines of the hatch pocket. Somehow, on her hands and knees, she made it forward, since she could not retreat. Now she fetched up against the wall of a corridor and managed to pull around to face the end of the fight.

The two guards lay dead. But Kas held the laser on a third man. Now, without glancing around, he gave an order which she mechanically obeyed.

"The tangler, here!"

Still on her hands and knees, Tamisan crawled far enough back into the hatch compartment to grip one of those weapons. The second she eyed with awakening need for some protection herself, but Kas did not give her time to reach it.

"Give it to me."

Still holding the laser pointed steadily at the middle of the third spaceman, he groped back with his other hand. *I have no choice, no choice, but I do!*

If Kas thinks he has me thoroughly cowed . . . Swinging the tangler around without taking time to aim, Tamisan pressed the firing button.

The lash of the sticky weaving spun through the air, striking the wall, from which it dropped away. Then it struck one arm of the motionless captive, who was still under Kas's threat, and there it clung, across his middle, and on through the air until it caught Kas's gun hand, his middle, his other arm and adhered instantly, tightening with its usual efficiency and tying captor to captive.

Kas struggled against those ever-tightening bands to bring the laser round to bear on Tamisan. Whether he would have used it even in his white-hot rage, she did not know. It was enough that the tangler made sure she could keep from his line of fire. Having ensnared them enough to render them both harmless for a time, Tamisan drew a deep breath and relaxed somewhat.

She had to be sure of Kas. She had loosed the firing button of the tangler as soon as she saw that he could not use his arms. Now she raised the weapon, and with more of a plan, tied his legs firmly together. He kept on his feet, but he was as helpless as if they had used a stunner on him.

Warily she approached him. Guessing her intent, he went into wild wrigglings, trying to bring the adhesive tangler strands in contact with her flesh also. But she stooped and tore at the frayed hem of her robe, ripping up a strip as high as her waist and winding it about her arm and wrist to make sure she could not be entrapped.

In spite of his struggles she managed to get the laser out of his hold, and for the second time knew a surge of great relief. He made no sound, but his eyes were wild and his lips so tightly drawn against his teeth, that a small trickle of spittle oozed from one corner to wet his chin. Looking at him dispassionately, Tamisan thought him nearly insane at that moment.

The crewman was moving. He hitched along as she swung around with the laser as a warning, his shoulders against the wall keeping him firmly on his feet, his unbound legs giving him more mobility, though the cord of the tangler anchored him to Kas. Tamisan glanced around searching for what he appeared desperate to reach. There was a com box.

"Stand where you are!" she ordered.

The threat of the laser kept him frozen. With that still trained on him she darted small glances over her shoulder to the hatch. Sliding along the wall in turn, she managed, the tangler thrust loosely into the front of her belt, to slam the hatch door and give a turn to its locking wheel.

Using the laser as a pointer she motioned him to the com, but the immobile Kas was too much of an anchor. Dared she face the crewman? There was no other way. She motioned with one hand.

"Stand well away."

He had said nothing during their encounter; but he obeyed with an agility which suggested he liked the sight of that weapon in her hand even less than he had liked it when Kas had held it. He stretched to the limit the cord would allow so she was able to burn it through.

Kas spit out a series of obscenities which were only a meaningless noise as far as Tamisan was concerned. Until he was released he was no more now than a well-anchored bundle. But the crewman had importance.

Reaching the com before him, she gestured him on to it. She played the best piece she had in this desperate game.

"Where is Hawarel, the native who was brought on board?"

He could lie, of course, and she would not know it. But it seemed he was willing to answer, probably because he thought that the truth would strike her worse than any lie.

"They have him in the lab, conditioning him." He grinned at her with some of the malignancy she had seen in Kas.

She remembered the Captain's earlier threat to make of

Hawarel a tool to use against the Over-queen and her forces. Was she too late? There was only one road to take and that was the one she had chosen in those few moments when she had taken up the tangler and used it.

She spoke as she might to one finding it difficult to understand her. "You will call, and you will say that Hawarel will be released and brought here."

"Why?" the crewman returned with visible insolence. "What will you do? Kill me? Perhaps, but that will not defeat the Captain's plans; he will be willing to see half the crew burned."

"That may be true," she nodded. Not knowing the Captain she could not tell whether or not that was a bluff. "But will his sacrifice save his ship?"

"What can you do?" began the crewman, and then he paused. His grin was gone, now he looked at her speculatively. In her present guise she perhaps did not look formidable enough to threaten the ship, but he could not be sure. One thing she knew from her own time and place: a spaceman learned early to take nothing for granted on a new planet. It might be that she did have command over some unknown force.

"What can I do? There is much." She took quick advantage of that hesitation. "Have you been able to raise the ship?" She plunged on, hoping very desperately that her guess was right. "Have you been able to communicate with your other ship or ships in orbit?"

His expression was her answer, one which fanned her hope into a bright blaze of excitement. The ship *was* grounded, and there was some sort of a hold on it which they had not been able to break.

"The Captain won't listen." He was sullen.

"I think he will. Tell him that we get Hawarel here, and himself, or else we shall truly show you what happened to that derelict across the field."

Kas had fallen silent. He was watching her, not with quite the same wariness of the crewman, but with an emotion she was not able to read. Surprise? Did it mask some sly thought of taking over her bluff, captive though he was?

"Talk!" The need for hurry rode Tamisan now. By this time those above would wonder why their captives had not been brought before them. Also, outside, the Over-queen's men would certainly have reported that Tamisan and a guard had entered the ship; from both sides enemies might be closing in.

"I cannot set the com," her prisoner answered.

"Tell me then."

"The red button."

But she thought she had seen a slight shift in his eyes. Tamisan raised her hand, to press the green button instead. Without accusing him of the treachery she was sure he had tried, she said again more fiercely,

"Talk!"

"Sannard here." He put his lips close to the com. "They, they have me; Rooso and Cambre are dead. They want the native . . ."

"In good condition," hissed Tamisan, "and now!"

"They want him now, in good condition," Sannard repeated. "They threaten the ship."

There came no acknowledgment from the com in return. Had she indeed pressed the wrong button because she was overly suspicious? What was going to happen? She could not wait.

"Sannard." The voice from the com was metallic, without human inflection or tone.

"Sir?"

But Tamisan give the crewman a push which sent him sliding back along the wall until he bumped into Kas and the bonds of both men immediately united to make them one struggling package. Tamisan spoke into the com.

"Captain, I do not play any game. Send me your prisoner or look upon that derelict you see and say to yourself, 'that will be my ship.' For this is so, as true as I stand here now, with your man as my captive. Send Hawarel alone, and pray to whatever immortal powers you recognize that he can so come! Time grows very short and there is that which will act if you do not, to a purpose you shall not relish!"

The crewman, whose legs were still free, was trying to kick away from Kas. But his struggles instead sent them both to the floor in a heaving tangle. Tamisan's hand dropped to her side as she leaned against the wall, breathing heavily. With all her will she wanted to control action as she did in a dream, but only fate did that now.

VIII

Though she sagged against the wall Tamisan felt rigid, as if she were in a great encasement of su-steel. As time moved at so slow a pace as not to be measured normally, that prisoning hold on her body and spirit grew. The crewman and Kas had ceased their struggles. She could not see the crewman's face, but that which Kas turned to her had a queer, distorted look. It was as if before her eyes, though not through any skill of hers, he was indeed changing and taking on the aspect of another man. Since her return to the sky tower in the second dream, she had known he was to be feared. In spite of the fact that his body was securely imprisoned, she found herself edging away, as if by the very intentness of that hostile stare he could aim a weapon to bring her down. But he said nothing and lay as broodingly quiet and impassive as though he had foreknowledge of utter failure for her.

She knew so little, Tamisan thought, she who had always taken pride in her learning, in the wealth of lore she had drawn upon to furnish her memory for action dreaming. The space crew might have some way of flooding this short corridor with a noxious gas, or using a hidden ray linked with a scanner to finish them. Tamisan found herself running her hands along the walls and studying the unbroken surface a little wildly, striving to find where death might enter quietly and unseen.

There was another bulkhead door at the end of the short corridor; at a few paces away from the outer hatch a ladder ascended to a closed trap. Her head turned constantly from one of those entrances to the other, until she regained a firmer control of herself. *They have only to wait to call my bluff . . . only to wait . . .*

Yes! They have waited and they are . . .

The air about her was changing; there was a growing scent in it. It was not unpleasant, but even a fine perfume would have seemed a stench when it reached her nostrils under present conditions. The light which radiated from the juncture of the corridor roof and ceiling was altering. It had been that of a moderately sunlit day; now it was bluish. Under it her own brown skin took on an eerie look. *I have lost my throw! Maybe, if I could open the hatch again, let in the outer air . . .*

Tamisan tottered to the hatch, gripped the locking wheel and brought her strength to bear. Kas was writhing again, trying to break loose from his unwilling partner. Oddly enough, the crewman lay limp, his head rolling when Kas's heaving disturbed his body, but his eyes were closed. At the same time Tamisan, braced against the wall, her full strength turned on the need for opening the door, knew a flash of surprise. Was it her overvivid imagination alone which made her believe that she was in danger? When she rested for a moment and drew a deep breath . . .

In her startlement she could have cried out aloud; she did utter a small sound. She was gaining strength, not losing it. She breathed in every lungful of that scented air, and she was breathing deeper and more slowly, as if her body desired such nourishment. It was a restorative.

Kas, too? She turned to glance at him again. Where she breathed deeply, with lessening apprehension, he was gasping, his face ghastly in the change of light. Then, even as she watched, his struggles ended and his head fell back so that he lay as inert as the crewman he sprawled across.

Whatever change was in progress here affected Kas and the crewman, the latter faster than the former, but not her. Now her trained imagination took another leap. Perhaps she had not been so far wrong in threatening those on this ship with danger. Though she had no guess as to how it was done, this could be another strange weapon in the armament of the Over-queen.

Hawarel? The spacemen had probably never intended to send him. *Dare I go to seek him?* Tamisan wavered, one hand on the hatch wheel, looking to the ladder and the other door. If all within this ship had reacted to the strange air, there would be none to stop her. If she fled the ship she would face the loss of the keys to her own world and might be met by some evil fate at the hands of the Over-queen. She had broken prison, and she had left dead men behind her. As the Mouth of Olava she shuddered from the judgment which would be rendered one deemed to have practiced wrongful supernatural acts.

Resolutely Tamisan went to the door at the end of the corridor. It was true that she had no choice at all. She must find Starrex and somehow bring him here, so that they three could be together. They must win a small space of time in which to arrange a dream breaking, or she was totally defeated.

She loosened her belt a little so she could draw up her robe through it, shortening its length and leaving her legs freer. There was the tangler and Kas's laser. In addition, there was the mounting feeling of strength and well being, though an inner warning suggested she beware of overconfidence.

The door gave under her push and she looked out upon a scene which first startled and then reassured her. There were crewmen in the corridor. But they lay prone as if they had been caught while on their way to the hatch. Lasers (a slightly different pattern than that Kas had brought) had fallen from their hands, and three of the four wore tanglers.

Tamisan picked her way carefully around them, gathering up all the weapons in a fold of her robe, as if she were some maiden in a field plucking an armful of spring flowers. The men were alive, she saw as she stooped closer, but they breathed evenly as if peacefully asleep.

She took one of the tanglers, discarding the one she had used, fearing its charge might be near exhaustion. As for the rest of the collection, she dropped them at the far end of the passageway and turned the beam of Kas's weapon on them, so she left behind a metal mass of no use to anyone.

Her idea of the geography of the ship was scanty. She would simply have to explore and keep exploring until she found Starrex. She would start at the top and work down. She found a level ladder and three times came upon sleeping crewmen. Each time she made sure they were disarmed before she left them.

The blue shade of light was growing deeper, giving a very weird cast to the faces of the sleepers. Making sure her robe was tightly kilted up, Tamisan began to climb. She had reached the third level when she heard a sound, the first she had noted in this too silent ship since she had left the hatchway.

She stopped to listen, deciding it came from somewhere in
the level into which she had just climbed. With laser in hand
she tried to use it as a guide, though it was misleading and
might have come from any one of the cabins. Each door she
passed Tamisan pushed upon. There were more sleepers:
some stretched in bunks, others on the floors, seated at tables
with their heads lying on them. But she did not halt now to
collect weapons; the need to be about her task, free of this
ship, built in her as sharp as might a slaver's lash laid across
her shrinking shoulders.

Suddenly the sound grew louder as she came to a last door
and pushed it. Now she looked into a cabin not meant for
living but perhaps for a kind of death. Two men in plain
tunics were crumpled by the threshold as if they had had
some limited warning of danger to come and had tried to flee
and fell before they could reach the corridor. Behind them
was a table and on that a body, very much alive, struggled
with dogged determination against confining straps.

Though his long hair had been clipped and the stubble of it
shaven to expose the full nakedness of his entire scalp, there
was no mistaking Hawarel. He not only fought against the
clamps and straps which held him to the table, but in addition he jerked his head with sharp, short pulls, to dislodge
disks fastened to his forehead, which were connected to a
vast box of a machine that filled one quarter of the cabin.

Tamisan stepped over the inert men, reached the side of
the table, and jerked the disks away from the prisoner's head;
perhaps his determined struggles had already loosened them
somewhat. His mouth had opened and shut as she came to
him as if he were forming words she could not hear, or could
not voice. But as the apparatus came away in her hands he
gave a cry of triumph.

"Get me loose!" he commanded. She was already examining the underpart of the table for the locking mechanism of
the straps and clamps. It was only seconds before she was
able to obey his order.

Bare to the waist, he sat upright, and she saw beneath,
where his shoulders and the upper part of his spine had
rested on the table, a complicated series of disks.

"Ah." Before she could move, he scooped up the laser she
had laid on the edge of the table when she had freed him.
The gesture he made with it might not have been only to indicate the door and the need for hurry, but perhaps also was

a warning that with a weapon in his hands he now thought he was in command of the situation.

"They sleep everywhere," she told him. "And Kas, he is a prisoner."

"I thought you could not find him; he was not one of the crew."

"He was not. But I have him now, and, with him, we can return."

"How long will it take?" Starrex was down on one knee, searching the two men on the floor. "What preparation will you need?"

"I cannot tell." She gave him the truth. "But how long will these sleep? Their unconsciousness is, I think, some trick of the Over-queen's."

"It came unexpectedly for them," Starrex agreed. "And you may be right that this is only preliminary to taking over the ship. I have learned this much: their instruments and much of their equipment has been affected so they cannot trust them." Hawarel's face was grim under its bluish, dead man's coloring. "Otherwise, I would not have survived this long as myself."

"Let us go!" Now that she had miraculously (or so it seemed to her) succeeded, Tamisan was even more uneasy, wanting nothing to spoil their escape.

They found their way back to the corridor before the hatch while the ship still slept. Starrex knelt by Kas and then looked with astonishment at Tamisan. "But this is the real Kas!"

"It is Kas, real enough," she agreed. "And there is a reason for that. But need we discuss it now? If the Over-queen's men come to take this ship, I tell you her greeting to us may be worse than any you have met here. I remember enough of the Tamisan who is the Mouth of Olava to know that."

He nodded. "Can you break dream now?"

She looked around her a little wildly. *Concentration ... no, somehow I cannot think so clearly.* It was as if the exultation the fumes of that scented air had awakened in her was draining. With that sapping went what she needed most.

"I . . . I fear not."

"It is simple then." He stopped again to examine the tangle cords. "We shall have to go to where you can." She saw him set the laser on its lowest beam and burn through the cords which united Kas to the crewman, though he did not free his cousin from the rest of his bonds.

*But what if we march out of the hatch into a waiting party
of the Over-queen's guards?* They had the tangler, the laser,
and perhaps the half-smile of fortune on their side. They
would have to risk it.

Tamisan opened the inner door of the pressure chamber.
The dead men lay there as they had fallen, and fighting
nausea, she dragged one aside to make room for Starrex, who
carried Kas over his shoulder, moving slowly under that burden. There was a fold of cloak wrapped about the prisoner to
prevent any contact between the cords and Starrex's own
flesh. The outer hatch was open.

A blast of icy rain, with the added bite of the wind which
drove it, struck violently at them. It had been dawn when Tamisan had entered the ship, but outside now the day was no
lighter; the torches had been extinguished. Tamisan could see
no lights, as, shielding her eyes against the wind and rain, she
tried to make out the line of guards.

Perhaps the severe weather had driven them all away. She
was sure no one waited at the foot of the ramp, unless they
were under the fins of the ship, sheltering there. That chance
they would have to take. She said as much and Starrex
nodded.

"Where do we go?"

"Anywhere away from the city. Give me but a little shelter
and time . . ."

"Vermer's Hand over us and we can do it," he returned.
"Here, take this!"

He kicked an object across the metal plates of the deck
and she saw it was one of the lasers used by the crewmen.
She picked it up in one hand, the tangler in the other. Burdened as he was by Kas, Starrex could not lead the way. She
must now play in real life such an action role as she had
many times dreamed. But this held no amusement, only a
wish to scuttle quickly into any form of safety wind and rain
would allow her.

The ramp being at a steep angle, she feared slipping on it,
and had to belt the tangler, hold on grimly with one hand
and moving much more slowly than her fast-beating heart demanded. She was anxious that Starrex in turn might lose
footing and slam into her, carrying them both to disaster.

The strength of the storm was such that it was a battle to
gain step after step even though she reached the ground without mishap. Tamisan was not sure in which direction she

must go to avoid the castle and the city. Her memory seemed befuddled by the storm and she could only guess. Also, she was afraid of losing contact with Starrex, for, as slowly as she went, he dragged even more behind.

Then she stumbled against an upright stake, and putting out her hand, fumbled along it enough to know that this was one of the rain-quenched torches. It heartened her a little to learn that they had reached the barrier and that no guards stood there. Perhaps the storm was a lifesaver for the three of them.

Tamisan lingered, waiting for Starrex to catch up. Now he caught at the torch, steadying himself as if he needed that support.

His voice came in wind-deadened gusts; it was labored. "I may have in this Hawarel a good body, but I am not a heavy-duty android. We must find your shelter before I prove that."

There was a dark shadow to her left, it could be a coppice. Even trees or tall brush could give them some measure of relief.

"Over there." She pointed, but did not know if, in this gloom, he could see.

"Yes." He straightened a little under the burden of Kas and staggered in the direction of the shadow.

They had to beat their way into the vegetation. Tamisan, having two arms free, broke the path for Starrex. She might have used the laser to cut, but the ever-present fear that they might need the charges for future protection kept her from a waste of their slender resources.

At last, at the cost of branch-whipped and thorn-ripped weals in their flesh, they came into a space which was a little more open. Starrex allowed his burden to fall to the ground.

"Can you break dream now?" He squatted down beside Kas, as she dropped to sit panting near him.

"I can . . ."

But she got no further. There was a sound which cut through even the tumult of the storm, and that part of them which was allied to this world knew it for what it was, the warning of a hunt. Since they *were* able to hear it, they must be the hunted.

"The Itter hounds!" He put their peril into words.

"And they run for us!" Mouth of Olava or not, when the

Itter hounds coursed on one's track there was no defense, for they could not be controlled once they were loosed to chase.

"We can fight them."

"Do not be too sure of that," he answered. "We have the lasers, weapons not of this world. The weapon which put the ship's crew to sleep did not vanquish us; so might an off-world weapon react the other way here."

"But Kas . . ." she thought she had found a weak point in his reasoning, much as she wanted to believe he had guessed rightly.

"Kas is in his own form, which is perhaps more akin to the crewmen now than to us. And, by the way, how is it that he is?"

She kept her tale terse, but told him of her dream within a dream and how she had found Kas. She heard him laugh.

"I was right then in thinking my dear cousin might well be at the center of this web. However, now he is as completely enmeshed as the rest of us. As a fellow victim, he may be more cooperative."

"Entirely so, my noble lord." The voice out of the dark between them was composed.

"You are awake then, cousin. Well, we would be even more awake. There is a struggle here in progress between two sets of enemies who are both willing to make us a third. We had better travel swiftly elsewhere if we would save our skins. What of it, Tamisan?"

"I must have time."

"What I can do to buy it for you, I will." That carried the force of a sworn oath. "If the lasers act outside the laws of this world, it may be that they can even stop the Itter hounds. But get to it!"

She had no proper conductor, nothing but her will and the need. Putting out her hands she touched the bare, wet flesh of Starrex's shoulder, but was more cautious in seeking a hold on Kas, lest she encounter one of the tangle cords. Then she exerted her full will and looked far in, not out.

It was no use; her craft failed her. There was a momentary sensation of suspension between two worlds. Then she was back in the dark brush where the growing walls did not hold off the rain.

"I cannot break the dream. There is no energy machine to step up the power." But she did not add that perhaps she might have done it for herself alone.

Kas laughed then. "It would seem my sealer still works in spite of all your meddling, Tamisan. I fear, my noble lord, you will have to prove the effectiveness of your weapons after all. Though you might set me free and give me arms, necessity making allies of us after all."

"Tamisan!" Starrex's voice was one to bring her out of the dull anguish of her failure. "This dream, remember, it may not be a usual dream after all. Could another world door be opened?"

"Which world?" At that moment her memories of reading and viewing tapes were a whirl in her head. The voiceless call of the Itter hounds to which *this* Tamisan was attuned made her whole body cringe and shiver and addled her thinking even more.

"Which world? Any one ... think, girl, think! Take a single change, if you must, but think!"

"I cannot. The hounds, aheeee; they come, they come! We are meat for the fangs of those who course the dark runnels under moonless skies. We are lost." The Tamisan who dreamed slipped into the Mouth of Olava, and the Mouth of Olava vanished in turn, and she was only a naked, defenseless thing crouching under the shadow of a death against which she could raise no shield. She was ...

Her head rocked, the flesh of her cheeks stung as she swayed from the slaps dealt her by Starrex.

"You are a dreamer!" His voice was imperative. "Dream now then as you have never dreamed before, for there is that in you which can do this, if you will it."

It was like the action of that strange-scented air in the ship; her will was reborn, her mind steadied. Tamisan the dreamer pushed out that other, weak Tamisan. *But what world? A point, give me but a decision point in history!*

"Yaaaah!" The cry from Starrex's throat was not now meant to arouse her. Perhaps it was the battle challenge of Hawarel.

There was a pallid snout about which hung a dreadful sickening phosphorescence, thrust through the screen of brush. She sensed rather than saw Starrex fire the laser at it.

A decision, water beating in on me. Wind rising as if to claw us out of the poor refuge to be easy meat for the hunter. Drowning, sea, sea, the Sea Kings of Nath!

Feverishly she seized upon that. She knew little of the Sea

Kings who had once held the lace of islands east of Ty-Kry. They had threatened Ty-Kry itself so long ago that that war was legend, not true history. And they had been tricked, their king and his war chiefs taken by treachery.

The Ill Cup of Nath. Tamisan forced herself to remember, to hold on that. And, with her choice made, again her mind steadied. She threw out her hands, once more touching Starrex and Kas, though she did not choose the latter, her hand went without her conscious bidding as if he must be included or all would fail.

The Ill Cup of Nath—this time it would not be drunk!

Tamisan opened her eyes. *Tamisan, no, I am Tam-sin!* She sat up and looked about her. Soft coverings of pale green fell away from her bare body. And, inspecting that same body, she saw that her skin was no longer warmly brown; instead it was a pearl white. What she sat within was a bed fashioned in the form of a great shell, the other half of it arching overhead to form a canopy.

Also, she was not alone. Cautiously she turned somewhat to survey her sleeping companion. His head was a little hidden from her so that she could see only a curve of shoulder as pale as her own and hair curled in a tight-fitting cap, the red-brown shade of storm-tossed seaweed.

Very warily, she put out a fingertip, touched it to his hunched shoulder, and knew! He sighed and began to roll over toward her. Tamisan smiled and clasped her arms under her small, high breasts.

She was Tam-sin, and this was Kilwar, who had been Starrex and Hawarel, but was now Lord of LockNar of the Nearer Sea. But there had been a third! Her smile faded as memory sharpened. *Kas!* Anxiously she looked about the room, its nacre-coated walls, its pale green hangings, all familiar to Tam-sin.

There was no Kas, which did not mean that he might not be lurking somewhere about, a disruptive factor if his nature held true.

A warm arm swung up about her waist. Startled, she looked down into sea-green eyes, eyes which knew her and which also knew that other Tamisan. Below those very knowledgeable eyes, lips smiled.

His voice was familiar and yet strange, "I think that this is going to be a very interesting dream, my Tam-sin."

She allowed herself to be drawn down beside him. Perhaps, no, surely he was right.

PART TWO

SHIP
OF
MIST

Ship of Mist

I

Tam-sin, she who had been born Tamisan, the dreamer, stood in the narrow slit of the craig tower. Below the sea washed, tossing a lace of foam up so near that she might lean forward to gather the salt spinning into one hand. This was going to be a wild storm-troubled night. Yet, for all the rage growing in the lash of water below, she felt no fear, rather excitement, as heady as thorson wine, warmed her scantily clothed, pearl-fair body.

Behind her lay the room of her awakening, its nacre-coated walls, its shell bed, its hanging draperies and carpet of green-blue as much a part of the sea world as the people of the Nearer Sea were akin to the element guarding and encompassing their islands. Their sea was life, and what one feared the breath of life?

"My lady . . ." The voice came drowsily, lazy from that same shell bed, "it would seem that you seek . . ."

She turned slowly to face the man who still lounged at ease, the silk coverlet half drifting from his body.

"My lord," she raised her voice to a pitch above the cease-less song of the waves, "I am remembering Kas."

His green eyes narrowed and that satisfied content which had been a part of his smile was gone. In his face, this new face, she saw the elements which perhaps only she could see:

the stoical repression of Starrex, the bewilderment of Hawarel, those he had been in past and now must still carry in his mind.

"Yes, there is Kas." Now his voice had lost its first warmth, sounded tired as if he had been awakened from a pleasant half dream to take up once more some burden.

Half dream? Now what held them now was more than any dream. Tam-sin knew dreams; she had been able to summon and dismiss them at her own will, they and the people in them had been but toys with which she could play at desire. Until she had dreamed for Lord Starrex and plunged them both into such a venture as she could not control. Fleeing that she had somehow brought them here: to new identities, new adventures, and doubtless, new dangers. But where was Kas, her Lord's cousin and his enemy, who had striven to put an end to them both in two times, two worlds, and who must also have been wrenched with them into this, though not in their company?

The man sat up in the bed. His skin was as palely fair as her own. Where the cover lay against him that soft fabric seemed to impart a green reflection to his body. His hair was the red-brown of living seaweed, even as she could see her own in a polished mirror of silver metal on the wall.

"I am Kilwar, Lord of LockNar," he said slowly, as if to assure himself of the truth of that identification. "What dream have you wrought this time, my Tam-sin?"

"That of the world in which the Ill Cup of Nath came not to the lips of these, our people, Lord."

"The Ill Cup of Nath, the betrayal of the Sea Kings." He frowned a little as if it were an effort to remember, not with Kilwar's memories but those of Starrex. "So that piece of black doing did not engulf Nath?"

"So I desired, Lord."

He smiled. "Tam-sin, if you can alter the writing of history then you are indeed a mighty dreamer. But I think that I shall find LockNar closer to my taste than was the world of Hawarel. Still, as you have said, there is the matter of Kas. And we shall have no easy dealings with that one. You did pull him with us?"

"We were tight-linked, Lord. We could not have come here was he not drawn with us."

"But it would seem not so closely," Kilwar stood up. His body was not as sturdy as that of Hawarel, and the gill pockets on his throat formed a half collar of loose skin. Yet there was about him, bare bodied as he now stood, the same aura of command which had been Starrex's. "And," he added, "I do not altogether relish the thought that Kas is *not* here where I can keep an eye on him. Could he have gone back to the beginning?"

"Not so," Tam-sin was sure of that. "His dreamer awoke there, before I drew him through. No, he is linked too closely with us."

"My lady of power!" He crossed to her in two strides and her body melted against his, joyfully, in a way as if they were designed to do so by the very power which had given them birth. "You are very lovely," his breath was warm against her cheek. "And you are Tam-sin who has chosen life united with me."

She surrendered to his caresses, aware that Tamisan, the dreamer, now faded, that she was indeed Tam-sin and he desired her. Within her was a warm content.

His lips touched her closed eyes gently, right and then left. Then the spell of their closeness was broken by a mournful, hooting call.

"The signal shell . . ." He loosed his hold upon her.

He was no longer lover, but Lord of the hold as he reached for shell-set belt and kilt of scaled skin. She held ready his sword, wrought from one of the huge, murderous saw snouts of a spallen, its toothed edges hidden in a sheath of the spallen's own tough hide.

As he belted it on, she herself tidied her short, sleeveless robe pulled thread loops about the pearls of its breast fastening, took up her dagger of curved taskan tooth. While they dressed thus, hastily the boom of the shell horn sounded twice more, echoing through rooms carved from the very stuff of the sea cliff.

The part of her which was Tam-sin told her that the summons was such as might be a forewarning of danger. And with that thought came again a wondering concerning Kas and what mischief he might be about.

He had striven with such power as she had hardly been able to meet to kill his cousin during the first dream she had been required to set. With Starrex gone the fortune and power he held would fall to Kas. But in the Ty-Kry Tamisan had first dreamed Kas had failed. Would he find here some more potent threat?

She followed Kilwar from the chamber. The walls beyond lacked the smooth casing of the living quarters, were rather rock, rough and natural, with narrow, twisting inner ways between the larger rooms. They descended steps worn into hollows by centuries of use. And the rock carried through to them the vibration of the waves beating beyond the wall to their left.

Tam-sin knew they were now close to sea level and she was close on Kilwar's heels as he passed through a tool-smoothed portal into a vast space which was rock roofed overhead, but into which the sea washed, forming a long ribbon between two level areas above the highest reach of the tides. A small ship rode the water there. Though the Sea People were at home in the waters, yet they also needed ships for the transport of their trade, and such a one was this. Men dropped from its deck, leaping expertly to the natural docks between which it now was anchored.

And other men, armed, yet with their swords and water guns still sheathed, saluted Kilwar as he passed through their lines to meet the seamen from the ship. They were all of the *Nath,* for though Land traders came, those did not use in the inner harbors. Their leader held up his hand in a greeting which Kilwar acknowledged in turn.

Only four of them, that was not a full crew. Yet no more showed from beneath the deck. And there was about them a strain which Tam-sin picked up as easily as if they had come shouting alarm.

She knew that captain, Pihuys. Not a man easily shaken. A hunter of spallen in their own waters was not one to know fear as a side-by-side comrade. Yet that uneasiness she had sensed, it held the substance of fear.

"Lord . . ." Pihuys spoke that one word and then hesitated, as if what he had to say was such that he could not find the proper words with which to tell it.

"You have come," Kilwar moved to drop clan-chief's grip on the other's shoulder, "with some news which is dire. Speak, Captain. Do the Land people show their teeth? But that would not rouse one who commanded at the Battle of the Narrows."

"Land scum?" Pihuys shook his head. "Not in whole truth, Lord. Though there may be some witchery of theirs behind this thing. It is thus . . ." He drew a deep breath and then spoke, with one word tumbling over the next in his haste to explain.

"We were examining the reefs off Lochack, for there were reports that spallen have come inward to those shallows for some reason. There was the mist as comes then before the true day and in the mist we found a deserted ship. It was one of the Land traders, and its cargo hold was full, sealed. I think that it had drifted from the eastern lands. Salvage it was, for there was nothing living on board. Yet the small boats were all in place. Since the land scum cannot live long in the water they would have taken those.

"Within there was even food from which men had risen hastily yet there were no signs of any battle, nor other trouble, no battering as if a storm had hit them. We thought that Vlasta had smiled on us, the ship being sound in every way and heavy laden with goods. So I left on board four men and we looped a tow to the *Talquin*.

"The mist continued very thick and, even though we held the ship in tow, we could not see her as we went, only the rope which held her. I had told Riker, he who I left in command on board, to sound the shell at each turn of the sand glass. Three times he sounded; then, Lord, there was silence.

"We hailed and got no answer. Thus we swam back and boarded once again. Lord, my men were gone as if they had never been! Yet if they had taken to the sea there was no reason they would not have come to the *Talquin*. We found only the shell horn lying on the deck as if dropped."

"And the ship?"

"Lord, for the second time, I made an evil choice. Wund, who was brother to Riker, and Vitkor, his sword-companion, demanded that I let them take up vigil and discover what manner of strange thing this boat was. And to that I agreed. Once more we were mist-hidden and the horn stopped. Once more the men were gone." Pihuys opened his hands in a small gesture of helplessness. "So I swore that I would bring in this ship that those of LockNar could examine it. But when we went once more into the *Talquin* and the mist closed . . . Lord, it sounds beyond a man's belief, but the rope went slack and when we pulled it aboard it was cut!"

II

"A Landsman's ship," Kilwar repeated thoughtfully. "I know you must have searched her well each time."

Pihuys nodded. "Lord, any place a man could go within, that we sought. And the cargo hatch was sealed with an unbroken seal."

"Yet somehow, Captain, there is an answer to your mystery!"

The voice was high pitched and so unpleasant was its tone that Tam-sin looked over her shoulder to where another man had come out upon the cave dock. He walked clumsily, with a sidewise lurch, and his face had a petulant twist. Under that there lay a resemblance to Kilwar. And Tam-sin, with the part memories of this time, knew him, Rhuys, Kilwar's brother, whose injuries during the winter hunting of two seasons ago left him sour and sharp of tongue.

There was another stir of knowledge within her mind. In the craig castle Rhuys was her enemy. Not openly, but with such an ill will as any sensitive (and above all a dreamer had to cultivate such sensitivity) could read. He did not even glance in her direction now, rather limped on to stand with Kilwar facing the Captain.

"Lord Rhuys," Pihuys's voice was far more formal in tone, "I can only tell of what I saw. We searched the vessel from bow to stern; the small boats hung in their lashings, there was naught living aboard."

"Naught living?" Kilwar echoed those words. "That is said, Pihuys, as if you have some explanation which is not of the living world."

The Captain shrugged. "Lord, we have lived in, by, and of the sea for all our generations. Yet do we not still come upon mysteries none of us, nor our records, can explain? There are great depths into which our species cannot venture. What may lurk there: who knows?"

"But this," persisted Rhuys, "is not a tale of the Great Depths, but rather of the surface, and of a Landsman's ship. They do not deal in any of our mysteries; they fear us." Tam-sin thought there was a thread of pride in that statement. Perhaps, because he had lost so much in his life, Rhuys clung to the thought that their race was feared by others.

"I tell only what I saw, what I heard, what happened," Pihuys repeated stolidly. And he did not look in Rhuys's direction at all, rather made a point of speaking directly to Kilwar. Rhuys was not greatly cherished within the hold of LockNar; his peevish temper too often flashed to life.

"I would have your chart, Pihuys," Kilwar said. "Perhaps the ship still floats free. You say the rope was cut, could it have been the work of a spallen?"

Pihuys half turned, gestured to one of his seamen. The man leaped back to the deck of the anchored vessel, returned with a coil of heavy rope slung over his shoulder. The Captain caught at the dangling end and held it out for their inspection. Even Tam-sin, knowing little of the ship's equipment, could see that end was cleanly cut, and it must have taken a sharp knife or hatchet to accomplish that so easily.

Kilwar ran his finger over the severed end. "This took strength," he commented, "as well as a sharp edge. Was it cut on board the ship, or when the rope lay between you and it?"

"Close on the ship, Lord, by the measurement," Pihuys answered at once. "There is no roughage as one would find at a saw-through. No, it was done by a single blow."

Rhuys laughed spitefully. "It could have been cut by a man who determined that the cargo was worth the risk of losing his comrades. If the Landsmen's ship was as intact as you say, it could easily be sailed to Insigal which, as all men know, is inhabited by those who are not too honest."

Pihuys, for the first time, faced Rhuys squarely. "Lord, if there had been any man hidden on board, him we would have flushed out. We know ships and on that one we even sniffed into the bilges. And if it is suggested that *my* men thought of playing such a trick ..." The glare he turned now on Kilwar's brother was one verging on the murderous.

"Not so, Pihuys." Kilwar broke in. "No one would suggest that you or your men might be responsible for a ship taken to

Insigal so that the salvage came not into our hands." He was frowning, but he did not glance at his brother.

Tam-sin sighed inwardly. Some time Kilwar would have to see Rhuys for what he was: a soured man, a troublemaker who stirred up many fires and depended upon Kilwar to see that he was not scorched when those burst into open flame. She could urge nothing on her Lord, that she knew. Rhuys was persuasive with Kilwar when he wished, and he hated her. She must allow no wedge to be driven between them.

"Bring me your chart," Kilwar was continuing. "Also I shall ask of the Lord of Lockriss and he of Lochack, what they might have seen or had reported. For if you came across this derelict off the Reefs, that territory is well patrolled by their forces."

The chart of the reef territory was spread out on the table in the council chamber and Kilwar made a point of assembling there those Elders whose knowledge of the strange tales of the sea outrivaled the many accounts in their archives. He had Pihuys relate his version of the mist-concealed ship and then looked to the Elders.

"Has there been a like happening known?" the Lord of LockNar asked, when the silence fell after Pihuys' detailed report.

For a long moment no one answered. Then Follan, who all men knew, had made the eastern voyage near a dozen times, arose and went to the màp, using his forefinger to trace the line Pihuys had indicated.

"Lord, this has happened before, but not in these waters."

"Where and when?" Kilwar's question was brief.

"There is a place off Quinquare in the east in which ships have been sighted, yes, even boarded, to be found deserted. Nor has any Captain been able to bring in those ships. At one time this was so great a danger that men would no longer sail for Quinquare and that city's trade died, its people fled inland or overseas, and it became a shadowed ruin. But years passed and the ghost ships were not seen. So Quinquare arose again, yet never was it the great city it had once been."

"Quinquare," Kilwar mused. "That is a full sea away. But such ships have not been seen on *this* coast?"

"That is so," Follan replied. "Lord, I do not like it. Just so acting were the ghost ships of Quinquare. If some power holds them that now lies on our lee, then it is trouble indeed."

"Lord, the message hawks ..." He who had charge of

those swift flying birds moved to the table, one on either wrist. The birds looked about them with bright and fierce eyes, moving their feet uneasily on the heavy gauntlets covering the Hawkmaster's wrists. They were sea eagles, able to wing tirelessly over the waves, bred for intelligence, and trained to carry the messages from one craig-island castle to the next for the Sea Kings.

Kilwar drew a small piece of cured sea snake skin and inked on it coded words. When he had done he took each bird in turn to fasten his message in the tube bound to one leg.

"Release them now," he ordered. "And be alert for any quick return."

"Lord, it is done."

"Meanwhile," Kilwar said, "let our battleship be made ready. We shall seek out this ghost vessel for ourselves, if it still floats and seeks men as a bait lies within a trap. Pihuys, what manner of seal lay upon the cargo hatch? Did you know it?"

"Lord, it was of this design," the Captain had picked up another square of snakeskin and the writing stick Kilwar had dropped. He sketched in some lines. "I have not seen it before," he added as he put aside the pen and pushed the sketch over to his Lord.

Tam-sin moved forward a pace or so, in spite of Rhuys's glare, to peer down over Kilwar's shoulder. She drew a gasping breath when the significance of those lines became clear. Tam-sin of LockNar would not have recognized it, but Tamisan of Ty-Kry knew . . . And she saw, almost felt, the sudden tensing of Kilwar's body as he made the same identification.

"It would seem, brother," Rhuys said, "even if the brave Captain knows not this symbol, she who shares your bed does."

The six-point star with a jaggered bolt of lightning through it, Starrex's own badge out of Ty-Kry, the real Ty-Kry from which they had come, no, there was no mistaking that!

III

Tam-sin did not answer the words Rhuys had made into an accusation. She was sure that Kilwar himself had recognized instantly that sign of his own House in the other time before they had been caught, by Kas's planning, in these dreams. She would leave it to him to say yes or no. But it was Follan who spoke first, with a gravity which seemed a part of his personality.

"Lady Tam-sin, is this sign truly known to you?" She studied him, not sensing any of the hatred which her sensitive's power could pick up from Rhuys. And that part of her which was Tam-sin knew that Follan had been her friend from the beginning in this place, for she was not born of LochNar but had come from a small, less important craig keep which was nearer to the land.

"It is known to both of us," Kilwar replied before she could summon words. "It is the sign of a land house, one in its time of no little power. And now it can be the sign of an enemy." He was thinking of Kas she was certain. Could it be in *this* dream world Kas was Lord of Starrex's clan, should that clan exist at all? "I do not like it being a part of this ghost-ship matter."

Kilwar's answer drew their eyes from her. She caught only a malicious glance from Rhuys and her chin lifted determinedly as she allowed herself a return stare. Rhuys could not make trouble between this Kilwar and her, no matter how he had been able to deal in the past with that other Tam-sin who had given her form and body here. There was such a tie between this Sea Lord and herself that none standing here could understand nor trouble.

"Landsman!" the Captain exploded. "They are ever a threat to us and whyfor? We do not want their territories ashore, and we do not forbid them the sea when they gather courage enough to venture out on it! Then why should they set themselves against us as they are ever minded to do?"

"They have a greed born in them," Follan answered. "What they have is never enough, always they want more. The High Queen likes it not that our Lords do not bow knee in her court nor send her gifts. Also they say that because we can live where they dare not, for the sake of their lives, venture ..." his hand arose to finger the edge of his now closed gills, "we are not of their species. And what they do not understand, that they hate and fear. Nor can we say that we do not do the same upon occasion. This was a Landsman's ship, therefore it is natural that it bears a House seal."

"Bait for a trap." Rhuys lurched forward another step so that he stood to Kilwar's other hand, flanking him on the left as did Tam-sin on the right. "This ship could be the bait of a trap, brother. Have not already six of our men gone into it and not come out again? What they may want is for us to try it farther, losing more men each time. It would be better to use sea fire and destroy it utterly ..."

"Thus making sure," Pihuys commented dryly, "that we destroy also any means of learning where are our men and whether we can find them once again."

"Do you think they still live?" Rhuys flung at him. "Do not be a complete fool, Captain!"

Pihuys's hand went to the hilt of the knife at his belt and Rhuys smiled. That he had deliberately provoked the Captain for some purpose of his own Tam-sin had no doubts.

"Be quiet, Rhuys." Kilwar's voice was calm but the tone of it was such as to raise a flush on his brother's bitter face. "We shall," he gave the final word, "await word from Lochack and Lochriss; if they have further news of this ship it would be well to have it. Then, at sunrise we shall take out the battleship and see what we can discover. Meanwhile, have you aught in the way to offer as advice, Elders, Captain, do you think upon it so that when we gather for further council that we may listen."

They went, silently, as men who had much upon their minds. Kilwar watched them through the doorway, his hand still resting on the chart. Only Rhuys did not move.

"I still say it is a trap."

"Perhaps you are right, brother. But we must make sure of what kind of a trap before we attempt to render it useless.

And who set such a trap off Quinquare in years past? We have no touch with the northeastern lands now, not since they were overrun by the Kamocks, who care nothing for the sea, and will not let traders into the borders of the lands they have seized. It might well be that whoever devised a way of leveling Quinquare has, because of those very Kamocks, changed his arena of action hither. Yet I cannot see the profit in this thing. They do not loot ships, it would seem, unless that bark was emptied and the hatch resealed, which I do not believe. Pihuys is too experienced a seaman not to tell between the riding of a ship in ballast and one which is well laden. Therefore, it seems a very elaborate trap indeed for the catching of a handful of venturesome seamen who lay aboard what they believe to be a derelict."

"Six men from a crew of ten, brother, is no small catch," Rhuys returned.

"Not by our counting. But if this game is played long . . ." Kilwar frowned. "Let me but hear from Lochack and Lochriss and we may know a little more. If the messages come I shall be in our chamber." He held out his hand and Tam-sin laid her fingers lightly on his wrist, as they both turned away from the table, leaving Rhuys alone.

Nor did they exchange any words until they were once more in the chamber where they had awakened together. Once there Kilwar walked to the window slit and looked out.

"There is a storm coming fast," he observed. "It may well be that no ship can sail no matter how pressing the need."

"Kilwar."

At the sound of his name he swung about to face her. Tam-sin looked quickly right and left. She had a queer feeling that even here they were overlooked, perhaps spied upon. Yet the part of her who knew this keep well recognized no such form of spying was possible.

"The seal . . ." she continued.

"Yes, the seal." He came closer as if he, too, had that sense of being under observation. "You told me before that these dreams made us the people we would have been had history taken a different turn in the past."

"That is what I believed."

"You say now 'believed,' have you then changed your mind?"

"I don't know. I have no sea people in my ancestry. Have you, Lord?"

"Not that I know of. Yet it would seem that there is my House here, yet I am no longer a member of it."

"There is Kas."

"Yes, Kas. Could he be Clan Lord then by some quirk of fate? Is there any way you would know, Tam-sin?"

She shook her head. "Lord, as I told you, in our first venture, these are not ordinary dreams wherein I can influence the flow of action. I myself am enmeshed in them, which is not natural. I can break the dream, or so I hope, but as you know there must be the three of us together to do this thing. And we have not Kas."

"Unless he is a part of this ghost-ship mystery and in searching out its secret we can fasten on him," commented Kilwar. "Meanwhile, I am not a man of uncontrolled fancy, but I sense trouble here, even as it awaited us at the court of the High Queen."

"Watch for Rhuys," she gave the warning which seemed most important to her. "He is a bitter man, and, like Kas, he resents that you have what he lacks. Kas wants your clan leadership, your wealth. Rhuys wants the same, but with it burns resentment that you are a whole man, and he is maimed and cut off from a full life."

"Part of me, that which is native here," Kilwar said slowly, "resents that saying. But you are right. Ties of blood hold him fast so far; after all we are brothers. But brother-hate can be worse than many other rages. And you he hates even more. To him our mating is a shameful thing because you are a Tide-Singer and of a lesser House. Also he would have kept me if he could from any heir."

"Tide-Singer . . ." Tam-sin repeated slowly and searched the memories of this personality. Yes, she was indeed a Tide-singer, once she released the memories of Tam-sin, knowledge awoke in her. It was strange knowledge, alien to any she knew. She must search those other memories, find more about this power which was of a different race and time.

There was a fierce blast of wind fingering at them through the window slit and Kilwar quickly drew the shield across the opening.

"A storm indeed," he observed.

But Tam-sin thought that one hardly less fierce might even now be gathering strength within this very pile.

IV

The storm battered and worried at the craig keep throughout the night. Tam-sin slept only in snatches, awakening at intervals to hear the drums of fury without. Twice as she did so, lying tense and shivering, Kilwar's hands sought her and she found comfort in his nearness and touch.

She tried to search the memories of Tam-sin and discover what powers that other whose form she now wore had. Once she had been a dreamer, then a Voice of Olava in a different world wherein she had fronted the anger of the High Queen; now she was a Tide-Singer, one who "sang" the fish into the nets, could "see" from a distance any ship of the Sea Kings. In each life she had talents which were not those of the common sort.

A Tide-Singer might follow a ship with her mind, if she were linked with any on board it. But she could not pick out such a ship unless those ties existed. And she herself must be given time to absorb from the Tam-sin personality what she could now put to use.

"Lord," she whispered, "what think you lies at the heart of this matter?"

"Any guess could equal mine," he returned in a murmur no louder than that she had used. "But I am uneasy that the cargo seal was the one I know."

He fell silent then and she lay as quiet, with her head upon his shoulder, knowing that, even as she, he sniffed danger for them ahead.

But they spoke no more and when the first gray light appeared around the edge of the shutter he had pulled across their outer window, he slipped from the bed, arousing her in an instant.

"Lord, let me go also when you hunt this derelict."

"You know I cannot. By the Law of these folk I am constrained not to take any female into what might be battle."

That lay within the Tam-sin memory, too. Yet to have him vanish now was more than she thought she could bear. To be alone . . .

As Tam-sin arose to face him she read in his face that he could or would not go against the customs of the Sea People.

"You know," she said, her lips feeling stiff even as she shaped those words, "that if aught happens to you and I am not near, then this dream will never be broke."

Kilwar nodded. "I know. But there lies no other answer. I must, being who I am, follow this course. You are a Singer, you can link with me."

"Well enough, but I will have no power to aid, even if my thoughts ride with yours and I learn that dire fate befalls you."

She turned away, not wishing him to read what might be written on her face. There was no appeal from his decision, from the customs of the Sea Kings. Kilwar would ride the waves when the storm had blown itself out. And she would be left alone . . . here.

Yet later she was able to master herself and stand outwardly unmoved to watch him aboard the battleship, his liegemen in their scaled armor and their sea given weapons raising a salute as he swung to the deck. And Tam-sin watched the ship loose off its mooring ropes, to slide under the direction of the helmsman into the passage leading to the sea.

The storm had indeed blown itself out. Also the birds had returned at an hour after first light, each bringing a message. The ghost ship had been sighted by those of Lockriss, who had lost four men to its mystery. But Lochack reported no such haunted vessel. However, each keep lord would now join with Kilwar at the Reefs.

Tam-sin watched the ship bearing her lord slip into the open beyond the anchor cave. There a weak sunlight made brighter scale armor, and the banner of LockNar was the scarlet of new-shed blood as the wind played with its flods.

She still watched, until that vanished. Only then was she aware of Rhuys, who was not looking toward the going of the battle vessel, but rather regarding her through narrowed eyes. His stare was boldly measuring, as if she were some spell book whose hidden secrets he would make his own.

Tam-sin returned that study with a level gaze.

Rhuys's lips parted, for a moment she expected him to speak. But he did not, merely hunched his shoulders as if to face into a stiff sea wind, and limped away, his back turned insolently upon her, leaving her without any form of courtesy, to return to the inner ways alone.

She held her head high; no one lingering here among the women who had watched their men sally forth on such a dubious mission must think that she felt aught of embarrassment at this open flaunting of her rank within LochNar.

Instead, returning to the inner passages, she sought one with a narrow, steep stair hacked out to rise and rise, past all the levels of the keep, until she came out on the crown of the craig. There, though the wind whipped her, she cupped her hands about her eyes and searched for last sighting of Kilwar's ship. But it must now have drawn farther out, enough to be hidden behind the rising craig of Lochack which stood between this keep and the norther reefs.

Seabirds called and shrieked about her, swooping to search among the storm wrack piled below for the debris of the storm, fish or other food things, entrapped by high waves washing among the sharp lacework of the rocks. As she looked down she could see many of the women and children of LochNar were already busied there, seeking the sea's lavish bounty even as did the birds. But Tam-sin had no mind to join them.

Instead she settled down with a rise of rock to her back, her arms about her knees, crouched small under the freshness of the wind, her eyes still on the sea. Again she searched diligently the memory of Tam-sin, putting into order all she might learn from this other self of hers.

There was much to astonish her therein. Even as the occult learning of the Voice of Olava had come to her in the last dream, so now did seep or rush into her mind those talents which were Tam-sin's. Some she pushed aside, working ever to find what might serve them best now. But for the moment she did not try linkage with Kilwar, rather she wished to learn what she might against that time when such linkage became vital.

"My Lady."

The voice startled her so quickly out of that study that she gave a gasp as she turned her head. It was the Elder Follan who had followed her here. And he was watching her with an intentness which matched that Rhuys had earlier turned upon her, yet this study had no twinge of malice such as she knew moved Rhuys whenever he thought or looked at her.

"Follan," she asked, "what else do you know of these ships of Quinquare?"

"No more than I told our Lord, Lady. It was a puzzle which had no ending that I have ever heard."

"But how can men vanish from the deck of a ship, one in tow, and no way known?"

"I do not know. With Landsmen . . . yes, a sudden panic, a quick squall which might threaten a ship with upturning . . . even a madness of mind to grip one and all, sending them plunging to their deaths. There is such a madness which comes with the eating of spoiled grain. Men can list such explanations. But those would not account for what happened to Pihuys's men. And the Captain is a wary and careful ship master. There might be some hidden place on board which searchers could not find . . ."

"With what menace in that?" Tam-sin urged when Follan hesitated.

"Lady, there are a many things in this world, or in the sea of which there has never been any report. But . . ." again he paused and then added somberly, "Lady, you are faithful to my Lord in all things and his chosen. Now I must warn you: walk carefully."

"Well have I guessed that, Elder. I am not loved elsewhere in LochNar."

There was a shadow of relief on his face as if he were glad that she accepted his warning so promptly.

"There is always talk," he said. "And for thoughtless hearers talk holds a shadow of truth, or so they believe. You are an out-craig, and there are those who believe, and now say, that our Lord could have done better. Nor does one who is a Tide-Singer seem close to others."

"Follan, my thanks for your plain speaking. I had already known there were those who wished me away from this place. But I had not thought they were becoming so open."

Her hand clenched tightly. Rhuys had supporters, but had she ever believed that he did not? What sort of tale could he spin for her undoing? What if Kilwar did not return?

"You are our Lord's chosen," Follan returned. "As such, Lady, you have only to command, you will find the most of us ready to harken to those commands."

She smiled a little thinly. "Elder, such words are as a shield and a blade to me. I only hope that I shall not have to take up such weapons."

But his expression remained troubled. "Lady, walk carefully. After our custom the Lord Rhuys commands while our Lord is gone. He is maimed and we would not choose him Sea King, but that fact adds to his desire to give orders while he can."

V

Tam-sin lay within the shell bed. Her eyes were wide open but she did not see the intricate mosaic of shells set in the ceiling over her. Rather she drew upon that other sight of hers so that Kilwar was before her, standing brace-legged on a ship's deck which was never still. Around him wreathed tendrils of fog, gray as the bones of men long dead.

So clearly was he in her mind that it seemed she need only reach out her hand, which arose a little from the bed cover at her thought, and lay it upon the well-muscled arm of the Sea King, to make him turn and look eye to eye with her. Yet there were distances separating them in body, if not in mind.

"Kilwar," her lips shaped his name, though she did not speak it aloud. And she was sure that somehow he heard her summons, soundless, as it was, for his head turned a little as if to glance over his shoulder.

But at that very moment he started and his body tensed. So Tam-sin was aware he must have heard something which she did not. For it was the nature of this mind-linkage that it could not carry any sound, only sight with it. Sight, and a kind of nonverbal communication which she was still hesitant to use, lest she distract him from what must be his primary concern.

Another man loomed out of the wreathing mist, and Tam-

sin could see it was Pihuys, even though his image wavered
and did not show as plainly as that of Kilwar, perhaps because there was no true linkage.

The Captain waved an arm toward the left, as if calling his
Lord's full attention to something there. And, when Kilwar
strode to the rail to peer into the ever-thickening fog, Tam-
sin could see it, too . . . the narrow prow of a vessel piercing
the folds of the mist as a needle might prick cloth.

Yet the strange vessel did not keep its course, but shifted
with every wave. And she could believe there was no helms-
men in control. She saw Kilwar's head turn again, the movement of his lips. Men appeared on the deck behind him, a
small boat was loosed, lowered over the side. So her Lord
had indeed come upon the ghost ship of the mists!

At that moment a stab of terror struck into her so deeply
that she lost control. Kilwar, the mist-hung ships—all were
gone and Tam-sin lay panting, her palms damp, her mouth
feeling dry. This fear . . . she assessed it as well as she could.
It was not the normal fear of one who faces an unknown
danger. No, it was a panic which she had not felt before. As
if there was some charnel house emanation from the strange
vessel which had struck directly at the seat of her own sensitive talent.

No, she must go back, see Kilwar, even though her flesh
crawled and her body shook as if she lay bare under the ice-
rimmed wind of full winter.

Kilwar! Once more she strove to steady herself, to push
away the fear and renew the linkage. There was . . . death?
No, something else, but as devastating for her kind, which
crouched waiting on the half-visible ship. Tam-sin knew that
as well as she had seen a monster rise up behind the rail,
reach forth claws to capture its prey.

Kilwar! Tam-sin summoned her nearly demoralized forces,
built his image in her mind. There was a queasy shaking of
the world, and she was back, but in a different place. For
with the Sea Lord she stood on what could only be the deck
of the derelict.

It was a vessel, she judged from what the fog would allow
her to see, of a size between that of Pilhuys's ship and the
battle one her Lord commanded. Nor did it have the clean
lines of a sea-folks' design, but was rounder, fashioned to
carry more cargo than any Sea King's possession. There was
a hatch before Kilwar, the rope fastenings of which were

stoutly tied and impressed with a seal as big as her palm. When Kilwar went down on one knee to inspect the pattern on that, she was not in the least surprised to see the impression Pilhuys had drawn for them.

Kilwar gestured, gave orders, she could not hear. Men climbed from the boat below, spread out, going in pairs and with drawn weapons, to the search. As Kilwar himself ventured into the officers' quarters drawing far sight with him.

There was the table, bolted to the floor for safety in times of storm. A single-backed chair, a bench, and against the far wall a bunk covered with salt-stained crimson cloth. On the deck rolled a jar which had dribbled its contents long since in a meaningless, sticky swirl across the planks. And there was a rack in which hung swords, none missing; set upright below those a stand of double-headed boarding axes. But there was no trace of any living thing save Kilwar and the men who had come with him. And, as the Sea King sat in the chair and men reported to him, coming in pairs, Tam-sin could tell from his expression that he was learning nothing save that which Pilhuys had already reported: the ship was empty.

Yet that menace which she had felt with the thrust of panic, still lurked here, and she held linkage only by all the willpower she could summon. It seemed to her that it was unbelievable that she did not sight some lurking thing which was more substance than shadow. Yet, for all the determined use of her powers, she could fasten on nothing concrete, save the knowledge that it was indeed present.

The last pair of searchers had reported. Now Kilwar sat, elbow planted on the table, his firm jaw supported by his fist, a considering look about him. When he spoke Pilhuys made a gesture of dissent. It was apparent he launched into some vehement argument. But Kilwar cut him off with a word or two. And, looking beyond the Captain, he pointed to two of the waiting warriors, both of whom the Tam-sin part of her recognized as being men long battle-bound to their Lord. At his gesture they raised naked blades to salute him.

Once more Pilhuys made protest but at Kilwar's manifest order he tramped from the cabin. With him went all but the two the Sea King had selected. Tam-sin could guess what Kilwar's orders were. He, himself, chose to remain on board the haunted ship, seeking to solve its mystery. Again that panic overwhelmed her, so that her talent failed, returning her to the keep and to another battle with that strong fear.

This time her struggle was more protracted. Perhaps her will had been a little weakened in the first encounter. Yet she fought valiantly, with all the strength she could summon. When she at last won to Kilwar it was to see a shadowed cabin. Two ship's lanterns were set on the table, the light flaring low within them, giving radiance only to the section immediately about them. She could see Kilwar who was still, or again, seated in the chair.

On the board before him lay not only a bared sword, but two of the double-headed axes, also placed close to his hand. The rack wherein those and the swords had been was now empty. Tam-sin guessed that he had taken the armament, determined that no one, or nothing, could secretly equip itself from that collection.

His attitude was one of listening, though she believed he had not yet heard anything suspicious but waited for such to manifest itself. Now and then his mouth opened and she believed that he called to his men, doubtless checking them at sentry posts without.

It seemed as if time dragged on thus forever. The lantern light flickered. Sometimes Kilwar arose to his feet and tramped back and forth. When he did so he went sword in hand, as if he did not intend to be caught unawares by the unknown enemy.

Suddenly he shouted again, whirled to the table and snatched up one of the waiting axes with his left hand. Then he leaped into the shadows beyond the reach of the lantern light. The deck, was he bound for the deck?

That must be so, for now Tam-sin saw a curtain of mist, silvery light. This was no normal mist, that she knew, for within it were small motes of glitter which were like insects flying back and forth. Through this blundered a dark form, staggering. The shadow man fell just as Kilwar broke into the thickness of the mist. He made a second leap, until he stood one foot on either side of that supine body, his sword ready to slash, and his head a little bent as if he had difficulty in seeing.

At that moment the terror which had exiled her twice struck full. Tam-sin was swept into a darkness of sheer horror, racing ahead of that which she dared not see, could never hope to imagine. Until, at last, she knew nothing at all, taking a last refuge in mindlessness.

VI

"Lady!"

It was a calling from far off; she would not listen. Here was safety . . . there . . .

"Lady!"

Tam-sin became aware of her body, though not yet would she open her eyes. Memory had returned to her bringing the last mind picture of her Lord wrapped round by that mist sparkling with unholy light. But there was a hand on her shoulder and for the third time the voice came urgently:

"Lady!"

Reluctantly she opened her eyes. Althama, who was her own waiting woman, leaned over her, her face showing distress. Behind her shoulder Tam-sin saw Follan. That the Elder would come thus into her inner chamber argued some dire happening.

Tam-sin sat up. "Our Lord . . ." she croaked the words as if for too long she had been without speech. "He faces the danger."

"Lady," Follan replied somberly, "word has come by hawk that when he of Lochriss and he of Lochack came to the meeting place, our Lord was gone to gather with two of his men, and the derelict drifted, empty of life."

"He is not dead!"

"Lady, they have searched the ghost ship once again. They found no life, no sign of any on board her."

"He is not dead," she repeated sharply. "For that I would know, Elder. When one is mind-linked and death comes, then there is such a shock of loss as no one can mistake. I stood mind-linked when our Lord went to battle . . ."

"To battle what?" Follan demanded eagerly. "What saw you then, Lady?"

"Naught but a mist filled with whirling specks of light. But it was not of any energy that I know. And I was cut off—"

Follan shook his head. "Lady, the news has been too clear. Our Lord is gone from us, dead or no, yet he has gone. Now it is Rhuys's day, for when the message came he proclaimed a regency. A man of twisted body may not rule the keep, but he can hold the power until time passes and men at last agree our Lord is truly dead."

"But I shall say that our Lord lives."

"Lady, which one of the men now pledged to Rhuys will harken to an assurance they believe you make only to hold sway here? Rhuys has spoken much during the past hours. It is his tale that you have laid a bewitchment upon our Lord since your first meeting, and that it is because of this bewitchment, Kilwar went to his death. He tells a logical story and one those without your talents can well believe."

Tam-sin ran her tongue across her lips, lips which suddenly felt dry. She could, indeed, see the logic in Rhuys's argument and what had she to stand against it? She was a Tide-Singer right enough, but those who had not such gifts were wary of the ones who had, resenting often their own lack.

"What would he do with me?" she asked directly of Follan.

"Lady, there are already two guards without your door. What lies in his mind I cannot say, save that it means no good to you."

"Yet you came hither to warn me."

"Lady, I have known you since the first day my Lord went wooing. You are his chosen and to my mind you have never worked any mischief. Now you say my Lord lives, but where is he?"

He leaned forward, his eyes holding her. There was something fierce and demanding in his gaze. Just so did the sea eagles look upon one.

"I do not know, only am I sure he is not dead. And now there is that I must do . . . go in search of him. We have been mind-linked; there must lie some trace on board that evil ship which I can trace. But I cannot do it from here. And you say there are guards without the door . . ." Now she looked swiftly to her maid.

"Althama, how much will you serve me?" Tam-sin demanded bluntly.

"Lady, I am your woman," the maid replied simply. "What is your wish is my desire."

"Will they let you go forth?"

"I think so, Lady. After they make sure that I am no messenger."

"What do you plan?" the Elder wanted to know.

"That which is my only hope. Follan, you have ever shown yourself a true liegeman to my Lord, how stand you for me?"

"You say our Lord is not dead, and yours is said to be the talent which can separate life from death in such matters. Lady, I am with you. What *is* your plan?"

"There is this," she looked again to Althama, "I can use my talent to set upon me the look of Althama. Such a disguise cannot be long held, but perhaps it would get me out of here. And that she may not be held by Rhuys for my escapement, I shall leave her bound upon this bed. How say you?"

The maid nodded vigorously. "Lady, if you can do this thing, then do it speedily. There are many whispers among the women and some of them are ill to hear. Lord Rhuys holds power now and you he fears and hates. But where will you go? There cannot any ship set forth from here without the knowledge of those who will speedily tell him of it, or prevent its sailing."

"I will not go by ship. And, Althama, neither shall I say how I go, thus they cannot press you for such an answer. Put on the pretense of hatred for me, saying that I am wild of thought because of my Lord's loss and that you believe I have taken the Dark Road of self-destruction because of my love for him and my fear of Rhuys. To think that I fear him so much will be pleasant hearing for that one."

She arose from the bed and it was Follan who made tight the bonds about Althama's wrists and ankles, also putting a gag of cloth within her mouth, but in such a way that she could work that out and then call to the guards for deliverment.

Tam-sin set on the maid's kilt and then she stood with closed eyes for a long moment, willing upon herself the dream talent to be what she was not. She heard a gasp from Follan as she opened her eyes once again.

"Lady, had I not seen this, I would have said it could not be so."

"I cannot hold the illusion long," she told him. "Let me get to the beach where they glean among the storm wrack."

"That I can insure you will do," he replied readily.

So, wearing the illusion of Althama, she went along the corridors a respectful two paces behind the Elder who brushed past the guards as if they were unseen. Down they traveled by a narrow stair, and then by a wider one. She could hear now the calls of the women who were busy with the storm gift upon the shore as they came out into the open. There Tam-sin hurried before the Elder, as if, having been somehow kept from this treasure hunt she was now the more eager to reach the debris. But since all that nearer the keep entrance was already well swept she needs must hunt farther toward the point.

Once there she clambered up over a tumble of rocks which were water washed, to find beyond a pocket of cover wherein but two women tugged and pulled apart the water-sodden strands of weed to see what might lie within its broken folds.

Follan caught up with her. "Lady, there is no ship to be launched from here."

She nodded. "Well do I know that, Elder. But I have my own talents and such can bring me to where my Lord disappeared." She went again toward farther rocks about which spray tossed, wetting their surfaces and streaming from their sides.

As Tam-sin climbed up on the outermost of those she looked down and back at Follan.

"Elder, what will Rhuys do if he finds you have given me such countenance."

Follan smiled wryly. "Nothing. I shall be witness to your giving yourself to the sea, Our Mother, in your frenzy of mind. But be sure of this, my Lady, Rhuys will not find it easy to rule in LochNar, regnant or no. And I shall not give *him* any countenance at all."

"Good friend," Tam-sin smiled a little unsteadily. Follan was not a man easy to fathom but that he had done this for her, that was enough to give near kin-kindness. "Say what you will, but perhaps not the truth."

She unfastened the kilt, to stand bare of body save for a belt which held the long-bladed knife Kilwar had given her at their choosing. Then she swung to the sea and, cupping her hands about her mouth, she sent forth a high ringing call. Three times did she so call, and at the third she saw the dis-

tant form leap above the waves for an instant and knew that
she had been heard and answered.

Content for so much, Tam-sin slid into the embrace of the
sea, choosing well her moment that she might not be crushed
between wave and rock, and began to swim. She was not far
beyond the rocks when those she had summoned flanked her
on either side, their round, bluish bodies only half seen. She
flung out a hand to each, felt that hand seized in a gentle but
firm grip by mouths which were armed with wicked teeth, but
whose weapons would never be turned on one who had the
secret of their calling. Now she was drawn forward at a
speed no swimmer, not even the sea-born of the keeps could
equal. She needed no ship to reach the Reefs with these at
her service.

VII

At intervals Tam-sin swam by herself but the loxsas still
flanked her, ready to offer help when she tired. That weak
sunlight was gone and the sky, whenever she arose to the surface for a sighting, bore the deep purplish red of the after-
glow. The water world through which she now headed was as
known to the Tam-sin part of her as her own room in the
Hive of the dreamers from which the other person in her had
come. Though there were dark bulks which plowed these
ways, yet none would turn toward her with the loxsas on
watch.

Those were of high intelligence, but of a thinking pattern
so alien to her own that it was a difficult effort to contact
them. So the messages of such communication were necessar-
ily very limited. They knew where she would go, the why was
not needed for they would ask no explanation of her.

The moon arose and once more she was towed by her
finned companions. Then, out of the waters, whirled two

more of their kind swiftly and efficiently taking their places to offer her the same aid.

She was hungry and thirsty, but the needs of her body could be set aside for now. Let her but reach the Reefs and she could relax the inflexible will which kept rein on the loxsas and carried her along.

Time ceased to have any real meaning. Tam-sin felt as if she had so traveled for hours without number. Then she sighted, during a surfacing, the dark bulk of a ship. For a single wild moment she thought perhaps this was the ghost vessel, until she heard the sound of a gong ring across the water and knew that it must be one of those set on guard by the Sea People.

At this moment she had no desire to seek out any ship save the ominous one which drifted in the billows of the fog. Should she chance to be picked up by Kilwar's own vessel there was good chance of being taken into custody by those among the crew who might be Rhuys's men. For she never doubted that he had his spies on board. And, were she to hail the battleships of either Lochack and Lochriss, the result might well be the same in the end. Therefore, she must head for the Reef itself and there await a chance to find the ghostly sea trap which had taken Kilwar's party.

The loxsas angled left now, drawing her away from proximity with the ship. And they swam underwater, where at night they could not be detected. There arose rocks high before them, and the girl knew she had reached the roots of that wall whose jaggered crest formed the surface Reefs. Getting the loxsas to loose their hold she swam slowly toward that and, sought hand- and footholds to raise her out of the waves and into the night air which was so frosty cold on her bare skin that she gave a gasp as she crept up the jaggered surface. Huddling below the crest line where the movement of her body might well reveal her to some keen-eyed watcher, she breathed deeply to loose the action of her gills and return once again to that of her lungs.

From this point she could see lights on three ships. They were apparently riding at anchor well off the danger of the Reef. There was no mist and she began to wonder if the ghost vessel itself had something to do with that as a cloak for the evil which undoubtedly inhabited it.

Her eyes could not serve her now, she must seek with that other talent, search out through the cloak of the night for the

mind to which she could link. There was a faint in-and-out
pattern which she caught first, but did not attempt to clarify.
That was loxsas' thoughts and of no value to her. Farther,
wider, she must spread her net, hoping to catch in it the faintest flicker of Kilwar to guide her. But it would seem that
she could not find . . .

She had pushed near to the limit such a seeking could go if
it were unfed by linkage. Then she tightened her hands into
fists, her head whipped left, to the north. Again she summoned the full of her power and sent it probing in that
direction.

Not true linkage, no. It was like finding only an end of a
raveling thread when one sought the whole piece of weaving.
But there was enough to assure her that in that direction lay
her field of search. So heartened, Tam-sin slipped once more
into the water, her sea guard closing in about her without her
call.

Her escort had grown to six now. The loxsas had a vast
curiosity, especially about men. It was well known that they
often accompanied Sea People at a distance, merely, it would
seem, to watch their actions. That they came so close to her
was because she had used the old summoning. Now they sped
along beside her, and her sea ears caught the faintest traces
of their shrill cries which, as their thoughts, sped in and out
of her own range of consciousness. Their sleek bodies, twice
as long as her own, made a formidable ring of defense, but
that they would serve her so once her goal was found, that
she knew could not happen.

Since they swam now below the surface and towed her at
the speed they could easily maintain, Tam-sin left her
transport to her companions and centered all her mind upon
picking up and holding that trace which had lured her in this
direction.

It was not a true linkage, that she already knew. Rather it
was closer to seeing a thin shadow in place of the substance
of a man. But she knew that she was not mistaken, some
form of contact with Kilwar endured.

Only that grew no stronger as they went, though she had
expected it would. And in that she was disappointed. Finally
she loosed her ties with the loxsas and swam to the surface.
About her . . .

Her heart raced with mingled triumph and apprehension.
The mist lay heavy, a rolling fog. It hid the surface of the sea

so that she could not tell now east, west, north, or south. The loxsas who had last borne her company raised their snouts free from the waves and faced ahead. She strove once more for communication and got a faint reassurance. The fog did not baffle the sea creatures—here was a man-made thing there.

That could only be the ghost ship! With all her will Tamsin sent forth her desire—to come beside the thing hidden in the mist. But, to her astonishment, for the first time the creatures refused their help.

She could sense their protest even though she could not hear their supersonic voices, nor meet them squarely thought to thought. Whatever swung with the roll of wave within the fog frightened them.

Just as it frightened her. Yet she would not yield to that fear and she swam resolutely ahead, aware that the loxsas, upset, flashed around her at a distance, striving to herd her back to what they considered less dangerous territory.

It was only the strength of her will which made them reluctantly give way. Now they no longer flanked her, rather drifted back, following her at a distance which grew the greater as she kept determinedly on. Their breed feared nothing in the sea as she well knew. So that this present uneasiness of theirs was a warning of what she deliberately took the wild chance to face.

Here the fog was so thick that it seemed a wall to ward her off. She dropped below the surface where she could not see it. Ahead, ahead was a trail of phosphorescence outlining what could only be the keel of a ship. That phosphorescence was a warning in itself, for it was born from the shells of those creatures who lived best on wood long washed by salt waves. And for so many to gather in one place meant that this ship had been far too long at sea ... no attention given to the cleaning of its hull.

Tam-sin headed directly for the source of the wan light. She knew that the loxsas had dropped completely behind and her all thought was for how she might win aboard. Unless there remained some line dropped along the side she might not be able to win to the deck.

Surfacing one more she raised her head, treading water, one hand against the weed-grown side of the derelict. As far as she could see there was no rope or trailing line here. The anchor chain?

She paddled toward the stern and there she saw it, heard it,
too, rasping along the wood it had already polished bare of
weed and shell. The anchor was gone, but the chain still hung
as if weighted, near enough so that Tam-sin managed a push
upward to hook a hand in a half-open link.

It was a difficult climb and one which left her breathless.
However, she reached the opening where the chain fed in.
That was too small for even her slight-boned figure to use, so
she sought for a hold above and, gasping with effort, at least
swung over a splintered rail onto the deck. The mist hid all
from view except for perhaps an arm's-length away. She
crouched to listen, with her ears, not her mind.

VIII

There was life here, she could sense it. But it was as alien
as that of the loxsas, overlying and near smothering the traces
of Kilwar which she sought. Of one thing was Tam-sin sure,
she would not find anything in the common cabins and passages of the wallowing vessel. The searches which had been
made there had not been slighted. There was naught left for
any seeker to find.

Yet something brooded here . . .

The girl's bare feet were silent on the deck as she crept
forward, her knife ready in her hand. To draw that was only
instinct for she was sure that what lurked in hiding was nothing one could overcome by any blade, no matter how skillfully wielded.

Not in the ship, then where?

The curdling of the fog cloaked near all the deck save that
which was immediately about her. Though she listened, all
she could hear was the slap of waves against the vessel's side,
the scrape of the anchor chain rubbing ever back and forth
like a pendulum.

There was something in the mist, close to the desk. Very slowly Tam-sin edged toward that shadow. This could only be the edge of that hatch so battened down and sealed. With her left hand resting on it, slipping over the web of ropings that kept it secure, she made the circuit of the wide square. This was the only place they had not searched, those who had been drawn into the trap of the ghost ship.

Because the lashings were taut and looked undisturbed, because of the seal, none boarding the derelict had given it a second thought. But it was the only place left to hide whatever made the derelict a menace.

Tam-sin had reached the seal. It was near as wide as her palm, and, through the wan light which seemed a part of the fog itself, she could indeed see that impression of the House which Starrex ruled in the real world.

Tam-sin sank to her knees. The deck was runneled with damp, perhaps condensed from the fog. And there was a cold which made her shiver. But she raised the seal where it crossed the final knotting of the ropes and gave it a hard tug.

It seemed to her that something in the crisscross of ropes had yielded to her grasp. She pulled again, harder. The seal slipped free and rope ends fell away, far too easily. This had not been truly sealed after all, merely the appearance of being so had been craftily given.

She worked hurriedly, throwing off the latchings of the hatch. Whether she would have the strength to raise the cover was another problem. It was divided into two leaves, which split down the middle. Putting her knife between her teeth for safekeeping, the girl hooked fingers in that center crack and heaved with all her might.

She nearly lost her balance as the half she worried at arose swiftly as if it were far lighter than she had thought it, or as if she had activated some spring to aid in the opening. From the void below burst a light: pale, greenish, and wholly unpleasant. And with the light there arose a stench, the foul like of which she had never been forced to inhale before.

Choking with nausea Tam-sin fell back, waiting for whatever horror might then dare to show. But there was nothing save the light and the smell. With one hand over her nose to ward off all she could of the latter, Tam-sin once more approached the half-open hatch.

She made herself look down, though all her sensitive's warnings, every fiber of her body, opposed that act.

What she saw she could not first understand, the horror of it was too great. But she forced herself to study the contents of the hold below, catalogue them with her mind.

Immediately below the center break of the hatch was a long box or coffer. And in that lay a man. At his head rested a globe of light from which spread the greenish illuminance. But . . .

On either side of the open coffer were tumbled . . . bodies! Tam-Sin pressed her hand, knuckles hard against her lips, so stifling a scream. Some sprawling there must have been old, the skin was only parchment stretched over bone, husks of what had once been men. But slumped against that open coffer, close by the head was Kilwar! And with him his liege-men, beyond those three others which must be some of those Pihuys had sent on board, though they had a curious sunken and wasted look and she was sure they were dead.

Kilwar! Her seeking thought probbed into mind of the limp body. No, not dead!

But how could she get him free of that pestilent prison?

The ropes which had lashed down the hatch! She caught at the fog-wet lengths, striving to knot the longer together. The meaning of what she had uncovered she did not know, but that there might be very little time left for Kilwar, of that she was sure.

Tam-sin made fast her rope to the nearest deck rail, testing each knot as she came back along her improvised ladder to the edge of the hatch.

She had to face now what was the greatest test of all: she must descend herself into that charnel house and seek to rouse Kilwar, and his men, if those still lived. And it took all her resolution to climb over and work her way down the ropes.

It was when she stood over the Sea Lord that she realized whatever power this terrifying trap was rousing. For that was the sensation she caught, something horribly sated stirred from a gluttoned sleep. She would be caught in turn . . . only the fact that it had feasted well had so far served her.

Reaching down she caught at Kilwar's sword. It was far heavier than her knife and she drew it awkwardly, not being schooled in the use of such a weapon. The light, that was growing stronger. She glanced to the globe, saw a swirling deep inside.

There was . . . life!

The globe . . .

Something closed upon her, wrapped her around as if to smother, driving air from her lungs, leaving only the nauseating stench which made her retch. It would . . . take . . . her!

She dug fingers into Kilwar's shoulder, shook him. There was still a spark of life flickering in him, of that she was sure. He must awaken, help himself. For she now faced a power which far outreached any she had fronted, in dreams or out.

"Kilwar!" Tam-sin shrieked his name, felt him stir feebly. She could not pull him nearer to the rope; he was too heavy for her as a dead weight. Instead he toppled a little toward her, driving her back against the side of the coffer. For the first time she saw directly the face of the man within it. Saw and knew . . .

Kas! Was he dead, drained of life force as the others here, or did he sleep?

The globe pulsated with light. A vast, arrogant confidence spread from it to her. This thing had never known defeat, it had gathered its victims as *It* chose and none could stand against it.

Tam-sin drew upon that part of her which was dreamer, Tide-Singer. The thing was not man as she knew it, but something far beyond any classification her knowledge could offer her. Only to find Kas lying here . . . in a queer way that steadied and strengthened that part of her which had never been defeated either.

It was the globe which fed, fed the man it guarded or itself? There was no sign of corruption about Kas's body. She thought she even saw his breast rise and fall in a very shallow breathing.

The globe . . .

That which abode within it was growing stronger—ready to overpower her. Tam-sin reversed the sword she still held. Though the sharp-toothed edges cut painfully into her flesh, she raised it high, and brought the pommel down on the globe.

That did not shatter as she had hoped, though under her blow the light whirled malignantly and she swayed under return blow of willed force. A second time she struck at the bubble, blood from her scored hands making the blade slippery in her grip.

It would not break. And in another breath, perhaps two, she would be overtaken by its power. What . . .

Once more Tam-sin reversed the weapon, the blood flowing down her wrists. She had only a second left, and a wild
guess which was only that. Holding the sword as best she
could, she aimed the point straight down, into the breast of
the man in the coffer, realizing that she had no other choice.

IX

There was a howling screech which did not burst from
Tam-sin's throat, mainly because she could not at that moment make a sound. All sense failed her under a vicious
blow. She reeled and fell among the tangle of bodies, clinging
desperately to the spark of life within her.

The howling was a torture to her ears. And there was surge
of light as blinding. She moaned feebly. No longer could she
muster any strength, she could only endure as best she might.

There was movement beside her.

The thing in the coffer, she had not known in that back
lash of power whether she had struck true or not. No, *no*,
and no!

Somehow Tam-sin drew on her last dregs of strength. She
struggled up, loathing what lay beneath, about her. The light,
it no longer seared her tearing eyes. It was flickering in the
globe, as if it, too, now fought extinction.

That terrible hate which had struck at her ... she was free
of it. Tam-sin set one hand to the side of the coffer, her
fingers clamping on the edge. And by that hold she fought to
draw herself upright again.

That within the globe coiled back and forth as might a ser-
pent sore wounded. She longed for an ax and the power to
strike without mercy or hindrance.

"Tam-sin!"

Though the howling had lessened she could barely hear her
name. Rather she was staring down into the coffer. There

Kilwar's sword stood hilt upright, caught between the ribs of the sleeper. But this was no sleeper . . . the flesh fast shriveled, dropped away, to pull skin tightly over bones.

"Tam-sin," there was an arm around her shoulders as she fought the heaving nausea which gripped her.

"Kas," she pointed a shaking hand into what lay there, now with the seeming of a man many months dead.

Anger, incredulous anger, impotent anger. Though she felt an arm about her she could not look away from the globe. That was no longer a perfect sphere of light, it bulged as if that which lay within were fighting to be free.

"Out," she mouthed the word twice before she could say it aloud, "out."

The arm about her was drawing her back toward the rope, away from the coffer, the globe. The greenish glow in that still writhed, but its struggles were weakening. Another's hands swung her around to face the rude ladder, lifted her body from the noisome mass on the floor. Only half conscious of what she did, Tam-sin gripped the rope.

But there was no strength left in her. To climb . . . she could not make it.

"Tam-sin, climb!"

The sharpness of that order broke through the daze, long enough for her to weakly strive to obey. There was someone still behind her urging her up. Somehow she gathered a last spurt of both courage and energy and fell out upon the mist-clouded deck.

There was not even strength enough left in her now to raise herself from where she lay.

"Stay!" Again that sharp order. "I go for Trusend and Lother."

Her eyelids dropped, never had she been so tired. That which now fought in the globe had seemed to suck from her all energy and purpose. She no longer cared, it was enough to be out of that pestilent hold, into the sea wind.

But at length she edged around so she might see the hatch. The rope was drawn very taut, and it moved in little jerks.

A head arose over the hatch edge and a man stood on deck.

Kilwar. She did not even feel relief at seeing him. Too much had gone from her. He turned and began to pull on the rope, until a second head drooped limply into sight. Then he drew that still body to fall beside her own, and once more disappeared into the depths. Only to bring out a second man as unconscious as the first had been.

Hard upon their rescue there came a flare of eye blinding light. Flames spurted up from the hatch, clawing spitefully at the rescuer as he drew the second man to safety.

"Fire!" Kilwar shouted. "By the Face of Vlasta there is no fighting this!"

He stooped and caught at her, dragging her to her unsteady feet. "Get you down," he had pulled her as far as the rail.

As she clung to that she watched him jerk at the open cover of the hatch, hacking at part of it with a sword. Then he drew the length of seasoned wood to the rail, heaved it over. Having seen it hit the waves, Kilwar turned and shook Tam-sin.

"Get down! I will lower them to you. Hold them on that raft."

Somehow she was able to leap out and down, cleaving the water not too cleanly, but welcoming the wash of the cleansing sea about her body. She swam for the raft and worked her way up on it. Then Kilwar lowered the bodies of his liegemen to that half-awash surface, leaped to swim and join her where she lay flat, one hand locked upon each of the unconscious men's belts.

Behind the mist glowed as if it, also, had caught fire. Tam-sin watched dully a line of flames creep along the rail she had left behind only moments earlier. And something, perhaps the heat of the burning ship, was conquering the mist, drying it away as they bobbed off from the side of ghost vessel.

Kilwar unhooked her fingers from the belts, rolled the bodies together in the center of his improvised raft.

"That," he gestured toward the burning ship, "should bring them to investigate. We can hold here until that happens."

"The fire ..." Tam-sin watched the destruction of the ghost ship with no emotion. Feeling seemed to have been wrung out of her by the experiences of this night.

"The thing, that which rested in the globe," he told her, "it broke its dwelling place, and this is the result."

There was something else she must tell him, but her mind seemed unable to think logically. Something important, but she was too spent to care.

"*Rrrruuuul!*"

Out beyond the derelict someone had sounded a shell horn. Kilwar rose to his knees, balancing carefully on the bobbing raft. He sent back a call as ringing as the blast of the horn. A second later a shout answered him.

"Tam-sin," his hand was warm and gentle on her shoulder, "they are coming for us."

She could not answer, even when he raised her head to rest upon his knee. Through the haze of fatigue she saw one of those others Kilwar had saved, turn his head, look to his Lord.

The mist was fast going. She could see the wink of a star overhead. While the fierce burning of the ship sent a full light over the water. The nose of a ship cut into that light, heading toward them.

She was hardly conscious of being hoisted aboard, carried to a bunk where Kilwar left her, a soft quilt pulled over her. He was back before she was aware fully that he was gone, holding a goblet. Bracing her against his shoulder he put the container to her lips, and, because she was too tired to protest, though she smelled the strongness of the wine it held, she swallowed what was liquid fire.

"The . . . the thing," she half whispered. "If it got out . . ."

A nightmare shadow built in her mind. What if the thing, now freed from its container, could follow to haunt them?

"It is dead, or at least it is gone," he reassured her quickly. "Now sleep my lady, and know that naught can harm us here."

She allowed him to lay her back on the bunk. Sometime she must sort out what had happened. Now she no longer cared, and sleep waited.

X

There was an edge of gray light spreading from one of the cabin windows, touching upon Kilwar as he sprawled in a chair, his head thrown back, his eyes closed. Tam-sin watched him sleep as she marshaled a host of broken memories from the immediate past: the ghost ship, and what lay in its hold. Once more she looked down upon one who seemed to sleep under the baneful light of that globe.

Kas!

Then only did she understand what might have come from her attack upon that sleeper. The three of them were bound together in this dream which existed seemingly beyond her control. And if Kas was dead . . .

But the evidence of her eyes, the body which, when she had used the sword, certainly it had withered, shrunk into the corpse of one who had been dead, not for moments, but for days, or longer. Could this have been the same ship which had haunted the coast off Quinquare? If that was so, then Kas on this plane had been dead for a long time, or in a half-life secured by the globe.

What matter of strange and frightening sorcery lay behind what had existed in the hold of that ship?

Kilwar stirred, his eyes opened, and he straightened in the chair. Then he looked quickly to her and from somewhere Tam-sin drew the strength to smile.

"My Lady!"

He was quickly at her side.

"My Lord!" She warmed to his concern, felt his need of her as an anchor in the midst of so much she could not understand.

"You dared to go . . . *there*." He caught her hands, held

them in a grip too tight for comfort, but she would not have it otherwise.

"When there was such a need, how else could it be?" she asked. "But it was your strength that got us forth in the end, Kilwar. What was that thing?"

He shook his head slowly. "That I cannot name. It ... it *fed* ... upon the life force of those it took. And it had many victims."

Tam-sin shivered, remembering what had lain about that coffer. Now she slid her tongue over her lips. If he did not know she must tell him at once. And it was a thing which laid heavy on her.

"Kilwar, did you see what lay within the coffer?"

"Another of the dead ..."

"Not wholly ... I think. Not until I slew it with your sword. Kilwar, it was Kas who lay there."

"Kas!" He stared at her. "You saw him so?"

"I saw him, knew him. He was not changed as are you and I, but wore the face I first knew. And ... do you understand, Kilwar ... I killed him!"

The astonishment had not left his face.

"Kas?" he repeated wonderingly. "But that ship, it must have voyaged so for a long time."

She knew a sudden sickness rising in her as the full meaning of what she had witnessed flashed into her mind. Kas transported to this dream world, imprisoned in his counterpart here, part of a dead-alive body ruled by the globe thing! Had he been conscious of what had happened to him? No, she could not, dared not believe that!

Kilwar's arms were about her, drawing her close to the warmth of his body, as if he would keep her safe even from her thoughts ... those thoughts now spinning out sheer horror.

"If that was the Kas in this world, then you had no part of it."

"But, Lord, it was my power and will which brought us here."

"Out of very certain death," he reminded her. "I do not know what was the reason for the death ship. Since the globe strove to keep alive the counterpart of my cousin, perhaps he was the one who fashioned such a trap in the beginning. It must have been that the two were close linked for as you slew him, then the globe went wild. It was a murderous being whatever its nature. And the blame for none of this can you take upon yourself, Tam-sin."

"But I brought him here ... to *that* ..." her voice was near a whisper.

"You brought us all to what meant safety as you could see it. Kas on this plane must have dealt with devilment, or he would not have been linked to that eater of men's life force."

"We cannot be sure," she wanted to be comforted, to believe that Kilwar had guessed rightly, but how could they ever know?

"I was there, remember," he brushed her hair from her forehead with a tender hand. "I was the prey that thing sought. If it meant slaying half a hundred men and them all blood kin to me, then I would have given the order, for that unclean thing was not fit to endure in this world. It had slain and slain again, ruthlessly and for a greed which sickens a man to think on. Kas, dead or alive, was what tied it to that trap. Do you think that any will say that his death under those circumstances was not merited?"

"You do not yet understand," Tam-sin tried to pull out of his hold. "Kas is dead ... I cannot now break this dream! We can never go back."

The expression smoothed from his face, even his eyes seemed turned inward. He knew now, and he would not, could not forgive what she had done. They were lost in a dream ... there would be no return to Ty-Kry where he ruled a sky tower kingdom.

"This is so, you are sure?" his question came evenly, in a voice as expressionless as his face.

"It is so," she replied desolately. She had hated Kas for what he had tried to do, his plot to see Starrex dead within some dream she herself had spun. But she should have preserved him, if she could, that they might return.

"So be it!"

Kilwar was smiling, his face lighting as she had never seen Starrex appear.

"Do you not remember, my Tam-sin? In that Ty-Kry I was but half a man, tied to a body which would no longer obey my commands. As Harrel I was half a man in another way, for there was a simplicity of thought in that one which I could not live with for long. But here," his head lifted proudly, "here I have what I sought! Do I think the past is better than the present? Not so! I am lord in LochNar and I have my lady. If Kas is dead, then let us accept that as a fact and turn our faces to the future. Look," gently he lifted her higher, took her up and bore her to the cabin window.

There was the sunlight topping the waves without. A dark body leaped from the water, hung a moment in the air, its snouted face turned in her direction and Tam-sin had no doubt that the loxsa had seen and recognized her.

"Tam-sin, this is another day. We have won from the night of mists into the day which is given us to use ... that we shall do. Do you regret the past?"

"No!"

Nor did she. Dreamer she had been, but whether this was a dream without substance in which they were now entirely entrapped she no longer cared. Perhaps her real body lay in Ty-Kry's tower, but she refused to believe that that was real ... not now. She was Tam-sin and this was Kilwar not Starrex; and they were both free to follow, not the devious path of a planned dream, but life itself. She laughed joyfully until Kilwar's lips closed upon her own and another kind of happiness followed.

PART THREE

GET OUT
OF MY
DREAM

Get Out of My Dream

Every world had its own rites, laws and customs. Itlothis Sb Nath considered herself, in position of a Per-Search agent, well adjusted to such barriers and delays in carrying out her assignments. But inwardly she admitted that she had never faced just this problem before.

Though she was not seated in an easirest which would automatically afford her slim body maximum comfort, she hoped she gave the woman facing her the impression she was entirely relaxed and certain of herself during their interview. That this ... this Foostmam was stubborn was nothing new. Itlothis had been trained to handle both human and pseudohuman antagonism. But the situation itself baffled her and must not be allowed to continue so.

She continued to smile as she stated her case slowly and clearly for perhaps the twentieth time in two days. Patience was one of the best virtues for an agent, providing both armor and weapon.

"Gentle Fem, you have seen my orders. You will admit those are imperative. You say that Oslan Sb Atto is one of your present clients. My instructions contain authority to speak with him. This is a matter of time, he must be speedily alerted to the situation at his home estate. That is of utmost future importance, not only to him, but to others. We do not interfere on another world unless the Over-Council approves."

There was no change in the other's expression. By the Twenty Hairs of Ing! Itlothis might as well be addressing a recorder, or even the time-eroded wall behind the Foostmam.

"This one you seek," the woman's voice was monotonous, as if she were entranced, but her eyes were alert, alive, cunningly intelligent, "lies in the dream rooms. I have told you the truth, Gentle Fem. One does not disturb a dreamer. It would be dangerous for both your planetman and the dreamer herself. He contracted for a week's dreaming, provided his own recorded background tapes for the instruction of the dreamer. Today is only the second day . . ."

Itlothis curbed a strong desire to pound the table between them, snarl with irritation. She had heard the same words, or those enough like them to seem the same, for six times now. Even two more days' delay and she could not answer for success in her mission. Oslan Sb Atto *had* to be awakened, told of the situation on Benold, then shipped out on the first available star ship.

"Surely he has to wake to eat," she said.

"The dreamer and her client are nourished intravenously in such cases," the Foostmam replied. Itlothis did not know whether she detected a note of triumph in that or not. However, she was not prepared to so easily accept defeat.

Now she leaned forward to touch fingertip to the green disk among those she had spread out on the table. Her polished nail clicked on that ultimate in credentials which any agent could ever hope to carry. Even if that disk had been produced off world by an agency not native to this planet, an agency which held to the pretense of never interfering in local rule, yet the sight of it should open every door in this city of Ty-Kry.

"Gentle Fem, be sure I would not ask you to undertake any act which would endanger your dreamer or her client. But I understand there is a way which such dreaming *can* be interrupted . . . if another enters the dream knowingly to deliver a message of importance to the client."

For the first time a shade of expression flitted across the gaunt face of this hard-featured woman, who might well have played model for some of the archaic statues Itlothis had noted at this older end of the city where the sky towers of the newer growth did not sprout.

"Who? . . ." she began and then folded her lips tightly together.

Within Itlothis felt a spark of excitement. She had found the key!

"Who told me that?" she finished the other's half-uttered question smoothly. "Does it matter? It is often necessary for me to learn such things. But this can be done, can it not?"

Very reluctantly the other gave the smallest nod.

"Of course," Itlothis continued, "I have made a report to the Council representative of what I wish to do. He will send the chief medico on his staff, that we may so fulfill regulations with a trained observer."

The Foostmam was again impassive. If she accepted that hint as a threat or a warning, she gave no sign that Itlothis's implied mistrust caused her any dismay.

"This method is not always successful," was her only comment. "Annota is our best A dreamer. I cannot now match her skill. There are unemployed only . . ." She must have touched some signal for there flashed on the wall to her right a brilliant panel bearing symbols unreadable to the off-world agent. For a long moment the Foostmam studied those. "You can have Eleudd. She is young but shows promise, and once before she was used as an invasion dreamer."

"Good enough." Itlothis arose. "I shall summon the medico and we will have this dream invasion. Your cooperation is appreciated, Foostmam." But not, she added silently, your delay in according it.

She was so well pleased at gaining her point that it was not until the medico arrived, and they entered the dream chamber, did Itlothis realize that she was facing a weirder adventure than she had in any previous assignment. It was one thing to trace a quarry through more than one world across the inhabited galaxy, as she had done for a number of planet years. But to seek one in a dream was something new. She did not think she quite liked the idea, but to fail now was unthinkable.

The dreamers of Ty-Kry were very well known. Operating out of the very ancient hive presided over by the Foostmam, they could create imaginary worlds, adventures, which they were able to share with anyone able to pay their high fees. Some of the dreamers were permanently leased out to a household of the multi-credit class inhabiting the upper reaches of the sky towers, where their services were for the amusement of a single individual or house-clan. Others remained at the Hive, their clients coming to them.

While entwined mentally with a dreamer, that client entered a world seeming utterly real. And an action dreamer of A rating was now fashionably expensive. Itlothis surveyed the room in which her quarry now lay lost in his dream.

There were two couches (the Foostmam was overseeing the preparation of two more which would crowd the room to capacity). On one lay a girl, thin, pallid of skin, half her head hidden in a helmet of metal which was connected by wires to another such covering Oslan's head where he rested on the adjoining couch. There was also an apparatus standing between their resting places hung with bottles feeding liquid into the veins of their arms.

Itlothis could see little of Oslan's face, for the helmet covered it to nose level. But she identified him. This was the man she had hunted. And she longed to put an end to her frustration at once by jerking off that dream cap, bringing him back. Only the certain knowledge that such an action was highly dangerous made her control her fingers.

The Foostmam's attendants had set up one couch beside the dreamer and a tech made careful linkages of wires between that of the cap now worn by the girl, and the one waiting to be donned. While a second couch was placed beyond Oslan's, another cap adjusted to match his.

That uneasiness was growing in Itlothis, akin now to fear. She hated beyond all else to be under another's will in this fashion. On the other hand, the need for bringing Oslan back was imperative. And she had the medico to play guard.

Though she showed no outward reluctance as she followed the orders of the Foostmam, settled herself on the waiting divan and allowed the helmet to be fitted on, yet Itlothis had a last few moments of panic when she wanted to throw off that headgear, light and comfortably padded within that it was, to run from this room . . .

They had no way of telling into what kind of an adventure Oslan had been introduced. No two dreams were ever alike and the dreamer herself did not often foresee what pattern her creations would follow once she began the weaving of her fantasies. Also the Foostmam had been careful to point out that Oslan had supplied the research tapes and not relied on those from the Hive collection. Thus Itlothis could not know what kind of a world she might now face.

She could never afterward be sure how one *did* enter the dream world. Was there a moment of complete unconsciousness akin to normal sleep before one opened one's eyes upon . . . this?

Itlothis only knew that she was suddenly standing on the rough top of a cliff where rocks were wind-worn into strange shapes among which a flow of air whistled in queer and mournful moaning. There was another sound also, the drum of what she recognized as surf, from below.

But, she *knew* this place! She was at Yulgreave, on her own home world! She need only turn away from the sea's face to see the ancient, very ancient ruins of Yul in all their haunted somberness. Her mind was giddy. She had been prepared for some strange, weird dream world, then she had been abruptly returned to the planet of her own birth! Why . . . how? . . .

Itlothis looked for Yul, to make sure of her situation.

But . . .

No ruins!

Instead heavy and massive towers arose unbroken, as if they had grown out of the cliff's own substance, as a tree grows from the earth, not as if they had been laid stone upon stone by man or manlike creatures. The ancient fortress in all its strength was far more imposing in every way than the ruins she knew . . . larger, extending farther than the remaining evidences of her own age suggested.

And, remembering what her own time deemed Yul to be, Itlothis shrank back until her shoulders scraped against one of the cliff pinnacles. She did not want to see Yul whole, yet she found she could not turn away her eyes, the dark rise of tower and wall drew her.

Yul, Yul had been in ruins when the first of her own species had come to Benold's world a thousand planet years ago. There were other scattered traces of some very ancient civilization to be seen. But the least destroyed was Yul. Yet, eager as her own kind had always been to explore the mysteries of those who had proceeded them in rulership of any colonized world, the settlers on Benold did not willingly seek out Yul. There was that about the crumbling walls which made them uneasy, weighed so upon the spirit of any intruder that sooner or later he withdrew in haste.

So, though it was viewed from a distance, as Itlothis viewed it now, and tri-dees of it were common, those were all taken from without. Why had Oslan wanted to see Yul as it might once have been?

The puzzle of that overrode much of her initial aversion. That this dream had a real purpose she guessed. It was not merely a form of pleasant escape. The girl moved away from the crag against which she had sheltered and began to reconsider her mission.

Oslan Sb Atto, he was heir to the vast Atto holdings, after the custom of Benold. Thus when Atto Sb Naton had died six planet months ago it had been very necessary that his heir take up Clan-Chief duties as soon as possible. His brother, Lars Sb Atto, had hired Itlothis's agency to bring back with the utmost dispatch the heir who had cruised off world. Later, when the continued absence of the Atto heir had taken on political ramifications, the search became a Council matter.

But why had Oslan come to the dreamer's planet, sought out the Hive, and entered a dream set on his own home world in the far past? It was as if he, in turn, might be searching something for importance. Itlothis thought this the truth. What *did* he so hunt?

Well, the sooner she discovered that, the sooner they would both be freed to return to the right Benold and Oslan's duties there. Though Itlothis hated the very thought of what must follow, she began to walk toward Yul, certain, as if Oslan himself had told her, that there lay the core of this tangle.

At least the visible forms of life familiar in her own time had not altered. Overhead swooped the seapars, their crooning cries carrying above the boom of surf, their brilliant orange, blue, and green plumage bright even on this day when the sun was cloud-veiled. Among the rocks grew small plants, almost as gray-brown as the stones about them, putting out ambitious runners toward the next cupful of soil caught between the crags.

Itlothis kept a wary watch on Yul. Though its walls were now entire, its towers reaching high, unbroken, she could detect no sign that it was any more inhabited than in her own time. No banners were set on those towers, nothing showed in the windows, which were like lidless eyes staring both seaward and toward the rise of sharp hills to the west.

Yul lay on the edge of the Atto holdings. Itlothis had seen it last when going to confer with Lars Sb Atto before leaving

Benold. They had flown hither from Killamarsh, crossing the mass of ruins to reach that inner valley beyond the hills.

In fact, the House of Atto could claim this cliff and the ruins had they so wished. But the ill repute of Yul had made it no man's territory.

Determinedly Itlothis scrambled over the rough way, listening to the cries of the seapars, studying the grim pile of Yul. She had thought, that, plunged into Oslan's dream, she would meet him immediately. But apparently that did not follow. Very well, she must hunt him down, even though the trail led to Yul. For the belief that it did grew firmly in her mind, in spite of her desire to be elsewhere.

As she approached the now unbreached outer wall, the huge blocks of its making added to her uneasiness. There was a gate in that wall, she knew. Oddly enough it did not face the interior of the land, but the sea. And, if she were to reach that, she must follow a perilous route along the verge of the cliff.

There was no road, nor even path. That there had been none such had always baffled the experts among her own people. Why had the only gate not fronted on some road impressive enough to match the walls? Also there was no trace of harbor below, no sign this had ever been part of a port.

Itlothis hesitated, surveying the way before her with a doubt which began to shake her self-confidence. She had initiated this quest believing that all her experience and training prepared her for any action. After all, she was a top agent, one with an unbroken number of successfully concluded cases behind her. But then always she had been operating in a normal world ... normal as to reality, that was. Here she felt more and more cast adrift, all those familiar skills and safeguards challenged.

In any *real* world ... she drew a deep breath. She must make herself accept for the present that this was a real world. If she could not regain her confidence she might be totally lost. After all many of the planets on which she had operated with high efficiency had been weird and strange. Thus, she must not think of this as being a fantasy Benold, but rather one of those strange worlds. If she could hold to that, she must regain command of the situation.

The way ahead was very rough and she did not know whether the strip was under observation from Yul. She kept glancing up at the windows, to see nothing. Yet she could not escape the feeling she was being watched.

Setting her chin firmly, Itlothis crept forward. The space between the edge of the cliff and the wall seemed very narrow, and the thunder of the surf was loud. She set her back to the wall, slipping along sidewise, for she had the feeling she might tumble and fall out and down.

There were many upward jutting rocks and by each she paused. Then she crouched into hiding, her heart beating wildly, her breath shallow. For more than seapars now soared over the waves!

Whatever the thing was, a flying craft perhaps, it came at such speed as to make her wonder. And it was homing on that sea gate toward which she crept. Like an arrow shot from some huge primitive bow it sped into that opening with the same unslacking speed.

Craft . . . or some living monster? Itlothis could not be sure which. She had a confused impression of wings, the body between them shining with metallic brilliance. Man-made . . . or living?

She was startled by a flicker of movement overhead and glanced up. There, well above her, she was certain that someone, or something, had moved into a window opening.

Itlothis leaned far back against the rock which sheltered her. Yes, head and shoulders were framed in the window opening. And, by comparison of size, either the stranger she sighted or the window itself was far out of proportion, for the body was dwarfed by the frame about it.

He, he was climbing out on the sill!

The girl gasped. Was he going to jump? Why?

No, he was moving cautiously, hunkering down to swing over, Now he appeared to find some support for his feet. But how did he *dare?* He was pressed tightly to the wall, inching down, with hands and feet feeling along the stone for grips.

Itlothis was tense with empathy for the strain of that descent. That he was able to find a way seemed to her a miracle. But he moved surely, if slowly, seemingly certain he could find the holds he sought.

The sight drew Itlothis from her shallow hiding place to the foot of the wall immediately below where he hung so perilously. She lifted her own hands to skim that surface, unable by eye to distinguish any break in it. Then her fingers dropped into a kind of niche cut so cleverly that it must have been fashioned for no other purpose than to so afford an invisible ladder for a climber.

She stepped back a little the better to watch the man descending the wall. There was a familiar look about his head, the set of his shoulders. Her eyes trained to value such points identified him.

Oslan!

With a sigh of relief Itlothis waited. Now she need only make contact, explain the need to break his dream. Then they could return to the world of reality. For the Foostmam had admitted that Oslan's desire held the dreamer's efforts in balance, that, whenever he wished, he could awake.

Perhaps he had already completed whatever purpose had brought him to this ancient Yul. But at any rate Itlothis's message was important enough to keep him from lingering any longer.

Having made sure of his identity, she noted he was wearing clothing alien to any she had seen. The covering clung tightly to his body but was elastic, as if fashioned from small scales, one fitted to slightly overlap the next. Only his hands and his feet were bare. The exposed skin was brown enough to match the stone down which he crawled.

His hair made a smooth cap, dark enough to show better. Itlothis knew, though she had not yet seen his face, that he had the well-cut features of his clan; he could be counted handsome if in the tri-dees she had seen there had been any expression to lighten a dull, set countenance.

Still a way above cliff level, he loosed his hold, ending his descent with a leap. He breathed heavily as he landed. Itlothis could guess the cost in effort of that long trip down the wall.

For a moment he remained where he was, gasping, his hands and feet both resting on the ground, his head hanging as he drew air into laboring lungs.

"Clan Head Oslan," Itlothis spoke with official formality.

He flung up his head with a jerk, as if he had been so hailed by some monster out of the sea below. His gaze centered on her as he scrambled to his feet, planting his back against the wall. His hands balled into fists, prepared to front some attack.

She saw his brilliant green eyes narrow. There was certainly no lack of expression in his face now! No, what she faced was raging anger. Then his eyes half closed, his fists fell to his sides, as if he saw in her not the danger he had expected.

"Who are you?" His question came in almost the same monotone as the Foostmam used, his voice might be willed not to display any revealing emotion.

"Per-search Agent Itlothis Sb Nath," she replied briskly. "Clan Chief Oslan, you are needed."

"Clan Chief?" he interrupted her. "Then Naton has died?"

"In Ice Month Two, Clan Chief. You are badly needed on Benold." Itlothis was suddenly struck by the oddity of their present position. They *were* on Benold. A pity the dream world was not the real one. It would save so much valuable time.

"You have not only clan affairs to settle," she continued, "but there is a need for a new treaty over the output of the mines, a Council affair much pressed by time."

Oslan shook his head. Once more a look of mingled alarm and anger crossed his face.

"No way, no way, agent, do you get me back yet!" He moved closer.

In spite of herself, Itlothis, to her annoyance, retreated a step or two.

"Now," he said with a whip-crack note in his voice, "get out of my dream!" It was as with each word he aimed a stun bolt at her.

However, his open opposition brought a quick reaction. Itlothis no longer retreated, standing firm to meet his advance. This was not the first time she had faced an unwilling quarry. And his negative attitude steadied her.

"This is a Council affair," she replied briskly. "If you do not . . ."

He was laughing! His head was flung back, his fists resting on his hips, he laughed, though his amusement was plainly fired with anger.

"The Council and you, Per-search agent, what do you propose to do? Can you now summon an armsman to back you—*here?*"

Itlothis had a momentary vision of yet another couch, another dreamer, if any such could be crowded into the Hive chamber, an armsman ready to be transported. That was utterly impossible. On this case she did, indeed, have only herself.

"You see," he took another step closer, "what good is any

Council authority here? The Council itself lies uncounted years in the future."

"You refuse to understand," Itlothis retained her outward calm. "This is of the utmost importance to you, also. Your brother Lars, the Council, must have your presence on Benold by High Sun Day. I have the necessary authority to get you on the nearest hyper ship . . ."

"You have nothing at all!" Oslan interrupted her for the second time. "This is my dream and only I can break it. Did they tell you that?"

"Yes."

"Well, then you know. And you are my captive here, for all your powers and authorities, unless you willingly agree now to let me send you back."

"Not without you!" Even as she retorted, Itlothis wondered if she were making some fatal choice. However, she had no intention of giving up as easily as he seemed to think her willing to do.

"Do you wish to be cited as relinquishing your clanship?" she added quickly. "In this matter the Council has extraordinary powers and . . ."

"Be quiet!" His head turned slightly toward the walls of Yul. So apparent was his listening that she did also.

Was that deep humming note really a sound, or a vibration carried to them through the rock on which they stood? She could not be sure.

"Back!" Oslan flung out his arm and caught at her, to drag her to him until they both stood pressed to the wall. He was still listening, his face grim, his head at an angle, as he stared up at the outer defenses of Yul.

"What is it?" Itlothis asked in a whisper as the moments lengthened and he did not change position.

"The swarm. Be quiet!"

Highly uninformative, but his tension had communicated to her the necessity for following his order. This was Oslan's dream and he had come out of Yul, therefore he plainly had knowledge she lacked.

There came a burst of light, like that of an alarm flash, aimed at the air over the sea. Another and another, issuing from the cliff-facing gate and shooting over the waves so rapidly Itlothis could not see more than what seemed balls of fierce radiance. Then these were gone, quickly lost far out over the water.

As he stood body against body with her, Itlothis felt the tension ebb from Oslan. He drew a deep breath.

"They are gone! There will be a safe period now."

"Safe for what?"

Oslan looked straight into her eyes. Itlothis did not quite like that searching stare, it was as if he wished to read her thoughts. Though she wanted to break free, she could not. And her failure brought resentment. She did not wait for him to answer her question but repeated her own message as bluntly as she could.

"If you do not break the dream, now, you will lose Atto. The Council will confirm Lars as Chief in order not to waste time."

His smile was tinged with anger as his laughter had been.

"Lars as Chief? Perhaps . . . if there is an Atto left for him to rule over."

"What do you mean?"

"Why do you think I am here? Why do you think I crossed half the star lanes to find a dreamer to put me in Yul's past?"

His stare still held her. Now his hands fell on her shoulders and he shook her, as if that gesture would emphasize his words.

"You think Yul is a ruin, a masterless place in our own world. Men have repeated that since the first of our kind explored Benold. But Yul is not just tumbled walls and a feeling of awe. No, it is the encasement for something very old . . . and dangerous."

He believed this, she read the truth in his voice. But what? Itlothis did not get a chance to ask her questions, words poured out of him now in a torrent of speech.

"I have been in this Yul. I have seen . . ." he closed his eyes as if to shut out some sight. "Our Yul above ground may be three-quarters erased by time. Only that which is the heart of Yul is not dead. It lies sleeping, and it begins to stir. I tell you I have speculated on this for some years, searched out all accounts. A year ago I dared take a scanner within for a reading. I sent the data to the central computer. Do you want to know the verdict, do you?" He shook her again. "Well, it was that the new mine tunnels spreading east had alerted, awakened something. That thing is ready to *hatch*. . . ."

Itlothis realized that he believed so fervently in what had brought him here that she could raise no argument he would listen to, the fantasy possessed him.

"To hatch," she repeated. "Then what is *it*?"

"That which once filled Yul with life. You have just seen its swarm take flight. Well, that is only a thousandth part of what Yul can produce. Those flying things are energy and they feed on energy. If one came near you, your body would crisp into ash. There are other parts to it, also." She again felt him tense. "That which lies in Yul can appear in many forms, all utterly alien and dangerous to us.

"Men, or beings not unlike men, reared Yul, made those other cities we can trace on our Benold. Then . . . *that* came. Whether it sprouted from some experiment which went wrong, or broke through from another dimension, another world . . . there is no record.

"Only those who found it made it a god, fed it with life energy until it was greater, the absolute lord of the planet. Then it blasted away the men it no longer needed, or thought it no longer needed.

"But when there was no more life energy, it began to fail. Instead of spanning the planet, it was forced back to this continent, then into Yul alone. It knew fear then and prepared a nest. There it went into hibernation . . . to sleep away the years."

"But the mine-search rays awoke it. Those fed it new energy. It grows again. Benold has new food for it. And . . ."

"You must warn the Council! Wake us."

He shook his head. "You do not understand. This monster may not be destroyed in our time. It can feed upon the minds of those who face it, empty their bodies of life force. There is no shield. Only in the past can it be defeated. If its nest is sealed against it, then it will starve and die. Benold will be free."

Itlothis was shaken. Oslan must be mad! Surely he knew this was a dream! What could they accomplish in a dream? Perhaps if she humored him a little . . .

"I gathered all the reports," he continued. "I brought those to this dreamer. They can use such research to back a dream. Clients are often interested in the past. I had her concentrate on my readings."

"But this is a dream!" Itlothis protested. "We are not really on Benold in the far past! You cannot do what. . . ."

This time the shake he gave her was savage. "Can I not? Watch and see! There are dimensions upon dimensions, worlds upon worlds. Belief can add to their reality. *I* say that this is the Benold which foreshadows the Benold that is now." Oslan swung away from her to face the wall. "It has sent out its feeders, it will be concentrating only on them. This is my time!"

He reached above for a hold, began to climb.

Itlothis moved too late to prevent him. She could not leave this madman here. If she went with him, agreed outwardly that what he said was true, might she lead him to break the dream? Ever since she had entered this fantasy she had felt at a disadvantage, shaken out of her calm competence. She now could only cling to the hope that she could influence Oslan in the future if she kept with him.

She sat down on the rock, pulled off her boots. With her fingers and toes free, she searched for the wall hollows, started up the wall of Yul.

Luckily she possessed a head for heights. Even so she knew better than to look down. And she feared and hated what she was doing. But, determinedly, she drew herself up. Oslan was already at the window. Now he reached over to aid her. And they pushed from the wide sill down into a shadow-cornered room.

"Best you did come," Oslan remarked. "Otherwise *that* might sense your presence. You must be quiet for you cannot begin to imagine what your folly in entering my dream might cost you."

Itlothis choked down her anger. This was a madman. He could not yet be influenced by any argument, no matter how subtle. So she offered no protest, but crept after him along the wall, for he shunned the center portion of the chamber.

The stone walled, ceilinged, floored room was bare. What light came issued from the window behind them. Oslan did not head to the door Itlothis could sight on the other side. Instead, he halted halfway down the wall, and felt above him at the full stretch of his arms, as if seeking another place to climb.

However, he did not swing up as she half expected him to do, to no purpose, since the ceiling, though well above their heads, appeared entirely solid. There sounded a grating noise. Three massive blocks before which he stood thudded back, to display a very dark opening.

How had Oslan known that to be here? Of course, in a dream, an imagined wall passage was entirely possible. Only the seeming reality of this shadowed room continued to war with logic. How *could* a dream appear so real?

"In!" he whispered. When she did not move at once he jerked her into the hidden way. She tried to break free as the blocks moved to seal them in a dark which was more horrible because now she was conscious of an intangible sense of wrongness, that which dwelt in the Yul she knew.

"Here is a stair," his grip on her wrist was mercilessly tight. "I will go first, keep hand on the wall beside you."

Now he loosed her. Itlothis heard only the muted sounds of his moving. There was no way back, she had to follow orders. Setting her teeth, more afraid than she had ever been in life, Itlothis cautiously slid one foot forward, feeling for the drop at the end of the first step.

Their descent was a nightmare which left her weak of body, drenched with sweat. That there was any air to fill their lungs was a minor marvel. Still always the stair continued.

Oslan had not spoken since they left the room above. Itlothis dared not break silence. For about her was the feeling that they now moved, in a caution born of intense fear, past some great danger which must not be alerted to their presence within its reach.

A hand on her arm brought a little cry from her.

"Quiet!"

His grasp drew her beside him. There her bare feet sank into a soft cushion, as if centuries of dust carpeted this hidden way. Once more Oslan was on the move, towing her with him. In the utter darkness she was content to cling to him as she dared not think or face what might happen if she were to lose contact.

Finally, he dropped his hold and whispered again: "Let me go, I must open a door here."

Trembling, Itlothis obeyed. An oblong of grayish light appeared ahead. After the complete dark of their journey this was bright. Across it moved a dark bulk of what must be Oslan. She hurried to follow. They stood in what was nearly twin to the room far above, save that its ceiling was much lower and one full wall to the left was missing. Thus, they could look out into a much larger space. That was not empty. What light there was, and Itlothis could not locate the source of that wan glow, made clear a massive park of wheeled vehicles jammed closely together.

Oslan paused, his head turned a little to the right as if he listened. Then he beckoned to her, already on his way toward the outer area.

There was only a narrow space left open around the wall through which they could move. Oslan hurried at the best pace he could keep in such cramped quarters. Now and then he paused to inspect one of the strange machines. Each time, seemingly unsatisfied, he pushed on again.

At last they reached another open wall and there he halted abruptly, his nostrils expanding as if he caught a warning scent. She had seen a vast hound do so on settling to hunt.

Here was another of the strange vehicles directly before them and Oslan made for its control cabin. When Itlothis would have gone after him he waved her back. A little mutinous, she watched him climb into the driver's seat, study a control board.

The rigid line of his shoulders eased. He nodded as if in answer to his own thoughts, then beckoned again. Itlothis wriggled through to join him. The seat on which she crawled was padded, but both short and narrow, so his body pressed tight to hers. Oslan hardly waited for her to settle before he brought the palm of his hand down on a control button.

There was an answering vibration, a purr, as the vehicle came to life, moved forward, down the open way it faced. Itlothis waited no longer for an explanation.

"What are you going to do?"

"Seal the nest place."

"Can you?"

"I will not know until I try. But there is no other way."

There was no use in trying to get any sense out of him while he was so sunk in his obession. She must let him follow his fantasy to the end. Then, perhaps, he would break the dream.

"How do you know how to run this?" she asked.

"This is my second such visit to Yul. I came at an earlier time in the first part of my dream, while there were still men serving *Its* needs."

He had been two days deep in the dream when she had located him and she supposed a dream fantasy could leap years if necessary. That did have some logic of its own.

The vehicle trundled forward. Now the passage began to branch, but Oslan paid no attention to the side ways, keeping straight ahead. Until a rock wall blocked them. At that barrier he turned into the passage at the left.

This new way was much narrower. Itlothis began to wonder if sooner or later they might not find themselves securely caught between the walls. From time to time Oslan did stop briefly. When he did so he stood upon the seat, reaching his hands over his head to run fingertips along the ceiling.

The third time he did this he gave a soft exclamation. When he sat down he did not start the vehicle again. Instead he crouched closer over the control panel, peering at the buttons there.

"Get out!" he ordered without looking up. "Go back, run!"

Such was the force of that command she obeyed without question. Only she noticed, as she jumped to the floor, his hands were flying over the buttons in a complicated pattern.

Itlothis ran, back along the corridor. Behind her she heard the vehicle grinding on. As she turned, pausing, she saw Oslan was speeding toward her, the machine moving away on its own. Satisfied he had not deserted her she began to run again.

He caught up, grasped her arm, urging her to greater efforts. The sound of the vehicle receded. They gained the mouth of the main tunnel. Oslan pulled her into that, not lessening his furious pace as he pounded back the way they had come. The fear which boiled in him, though she did not know its source, fed into her, making her struggle ahead as if death strode in their wake.

They had reached the cavern holding the machines when the floor, the walls, shook. There came a roar of sound to deafen her. After that, darkness . . .

Something hunting through the dark . . . a rage which was like a blow. Itlothis hid from that rage, from the questing of the giant anger. Shaking from fear of that seeking, she opened her eyes. Inches away from her face was another's which she could see only dimly in this light. She wet her lips, when she spoke her voice sounded very thin and far away:

"Clan Chief Oslan . . ."

She had come here hunting him. Now someone, some *thing*, was hunting her!

His eyelids flickered, opened. He stared at her, his face wearing the same shadow of fear as possessed her. She saw his lips move, his answer was a thread of sound.

"*It* knows! *It* seeks!"

His mad obession. But perhaps she could use that to save them. She caught his head between her hands, forcing him to continue to look at her. Pray All Power he still had a spark of sanity to respond. Slowly, with pauses between words, summoning all her will, she gave the order:

"Break the dream!"

Did any consciousness show in his eyes, or had that same irrational and horrible fear which beset her now, driven him into the far depths of his fantasy where she could not reach? Again Itlothis repeated those words with all the calm command she could summon.

"Break the dream!"

The fear racked her. That which searched was coming nearer. To lapse herself into madness, the horror was worse than any pain. He must! He . . .

There was . . .

Itlothis blinked.

Light, much more light than had been in that cavern below Yul. She stared up at a gray ceiling. Here was no scent of dust, nor of ages.

She was back!

Hands had drawn away the dream helmet. She sat up, still hardly believing that she, they, had won. She turned quickly to that other divan. The attendants had removed his helmet, his hands arose unsteadily to his head, but his eyes were open.

Now he saw her. His gaze widened. "Then you *were* real!"

"Yes." Had he really imagined that she was only a part of his dream? Itlothis was oddly discomfited by that thought. She had taken all those risks in his service and he thought she had only been part of his fantasy.

Oslan sat up, looked about as if he could not quite believe he had returned. Then he laughed, not angrily as he had in Yul, but it triumph.

"We did it!" He slammed his fist down on the couch. "The nest *was* walled off, that was what made *it* so wild. Yul is dead!"

He had carried the fantasy back with him, the obsession still possessed him. Itlothis felt a little sick. But Oslan Sb Atto was still her client. She could not, dared not, identify with him. She had performed her mission successfully, his family must deal with him now.

Itlothis turned to the medico. "The Clan Chief is confused."

"I am anything but confused!" Oslan's voice rang out behind her. "Wait and see, Gentle Fem, just wait and see!"

Though she was apprehensive during the hyper jump back to Benold, Oslan did not mention his dream again. Nor did he attempt to be much in her company, keeping mostly in his cabin. However, when they reached the spaceport on their home planet, he took command with an authority which overrode hers.

Before she could report formally he swept her aboard a private flyer bearing the Atto insignia. His action made her more uneasy than angry. She had dared to hope as time passed that he had thrown off the affect of the dream. Now she could see he was still possessed by it even though this was not the Benold the dreamer had envisioned.

As he turned the flyer north he shot a glance at her.

"You believe me ready for reprogramming, do you not, Itlothis?"

She refused to answer. They would be followed. She had managed to send off a signal before they raised from the port.

"You want proof I am sane? Very well, I shall give you that!"

He pushed the flyer to top speed. Atto lay ahead, but also Yul! What was he going to do?

In less than an hour planet time, Itlothis had her answer. The small craft dipped over the ruins. Only this was not the same Yul she had seen on her first flight to Atto. Here only a portion of the outer walls still stood. Inside those was a vast hollow in which lay only a few shattered blocks.

Oslan cut power, landed the craft in the very center of the hollow. He was quickly free of the cabin, then reached in to urge her out with him. Nor did he loose his hold on her as he asked:

"See?"

The one word echoed back hollowly from the still standing outer walls.

"What . . ." Itlothis must admit that this was a new Yul. But to believe that action taken in a dream on a planet light years away could cause such destruction. . . .

"The charge reached the nest!" he said excitedly. "I set the energy on the crawler to excess. When the power touched the danger mark it blew. Then there was no safe place left for *It* to sleep in, only this!"

She had, Itlothis supposed, to accept the evidence of her eyes. But what she saw went against all reason as she knew it. Yet whatever blast had occurred here had not been only weeks ago, the signs of the catastrophe were ages old! *Had* they been sent eons back in time? Itlothis began to feel that *this* was a dream, some nightmare hallucination.

But Oslan was continuing:

"Feel it? *That* has gone. There is no other life here now!"

She stood within his hold. Once in her childhood, when she was first being trained for the service, she had been brought to Yul. Then only just within the outer wall, beyond which few could go, and none dared stay long. She remembered that venture vividly. Oslan was right! Here was no longer that brooding menace. Just the cry of seabirds, the distant beat of waves. Yul was dead, long ago deserted by life.

"But it was a *dream!*" she protested dazedly. "Just a dream!"

Oslan slowly shook his head. "It was real. Now Yul is free. We are here to prove that. I told you once, 'Get out of my dream,' I was wrong; it was meant to be your dream also. Now this is our reality ... an empty Yul, a free world. And, in time, perhaps something else."

His arms about her tightened. Not in anger or fear. Itlothis, meeting that brilliant green stare holding hers, knew that dreams, some dreams, never quite released their dreamers.

PART FOUR

NIGHTMARE

Nightmare

I

"But I know nothing of this sector." The youngest man in the room squirmed slightly in his easirest, as if that half-reclining seat, intended for maximum comfort was now giving more than minimum unease.

"Which is precisely why you are necessary for the operation," came a cold-tinged reply from one of the three facing him, the Trystian whose feather crest held the slight fading of age.

"A Terrian of a wealthy clan, touring this sector," the man to the Trystian's left elaborated, "could visit Ty-Kry, order a dreamer's services without comment or questions being asked in the wrong places. It is well known that our multi-credit class are ever avid to try new experiences. Your background would be impeccable, of course."

Burr Neklass shrugged. He had never had any quarrel with that department of the service. Any background they supplied could be combed and recombed with impunity for the one using it. He would be provided with a life history dating back to the moment of his birth and it would be a flawless one. That was not the base of his present uneasiness.

Being who and what he was, he now came out frankly with that basic argument.

"I am not an Esper."

"You were chosen for that very reason," Hyon returned. "Anyone testing Esper, and do not consider for a second that they will not investigate you thoroughly, would have no chance."

"So I'm just bait." Again Burr hunched his shoulders against the easirest. "And it appears very expendable bait."

Grigor Bnon, the only true human on that inner council, smiled. It seemed to Burr there was an implied taunt in the curl of his lips as he did so. Bnon had a reputation, which it was said he delighted in, of being utterly *un*-human when it came to assignments.

"Very good bait," he said softly now. "According to the record you are just the type meant to this trap, whatever it is or however it works."

"Thank you so much, Commander!" Burr snapped. "And what if I say 'no'?"

Bnon shrugged. "There is always that, of course. And it is your privilege."

"And you want me to do it," Burr returned silently. "You have been waiting a long time to catch me a hair's space off orders, either way, 'yes' or 'no,' you'll have me." There was a sour taste in his mouth which could have come from biting hard on that realization.

"So I go in without any backman, then what if I turn up dead? Will you know any more than you do right now? You haven't been able to monitor these dreams in any way ..." His sentence had a slight lift which made it half-question. If they could monitor, get him out before the final fatal minute, that would put a different face upon the whole operation.

"Not in the way you think," the third of those facing him spoke for the first time. Outwardly he was so humanoid that Burr might have accepted him for a Terran-descended colonist. Only his strange pupilless eyes and the fine down which covered the visible portions of his skin named him alien. "But there will be a backup for you. To have another man killed uselessly would avail us nothing at all."

"I am grateful to hear that," Burr put what irony he could in his reply to Corps Master Illan.

Illan appeared not to hear him. "We shall provide the dreamer you know; I have been informed that you were fully briefed, that these dreamers are either hired or purchased from the Hive. On the death of any purchaser, the dreamer must be returned, half of her price being repaid to the clan-family of her owner. If she is rehired, then it is for an agreed-upon time only.

"Osdeve, Lord of Ulay, purchased a ten-point dreamer two years ago. He was in the last stages of kaffer fever. Two days ago he died. This dreamer, Uahach, must now be returned to the Hive. It is the general custom that once an out-dreamer so returns, she is not resold for at least a year, since each owner or hirer programs the dreamer to his taste and she must have a rest before such reprogramming.

"However, the Foostmam of the Hive is not one to suffer idle minds. She will allow Hive dreaming for Uahach, providing that the one who purchases the girl's time is willing to accept any dream and does not require a certain briefing.

"You will be a tourist, wanting simply to try a dream as part of your travel experiences. Therefore, Uahach would answer your purpose as well as any other. You have heard of her and can ask for her with an excellent reason . . ."

Hyon paused for breath and Burr shot in his question.

"How did I hear of her if I have never been in Ty-Kry before?"

"Osdeve was off planet three years ago. He visited Melytis. As the person you will be on Ty-Kry you made his acquaintance there. In fact he spoke so much of dreaming that you came to Ty-Kry lured by his stories."

Burr was frowning a little. He had no doubts about their meeting in Melytis, that would be so expertly documented that it would stand now for the truth. But he was puzzled concerning another point.

"This Uahach, how can you be sure of her?"

"She is an agent . . . or will be by the time she returns to the Hive," Bnon explained. "With some plasta buildup she'll be Uahach; she *is* an Esper and has been undergoing dream study for some time. We had her long before the assignment computer selected you."

And this unknown "she," Burr accepted, was taking even a far greater risk than they expected him to accept. Dreamers were born, though they underwent vigorous training to achieve the status of A or E, ready to guide someone through their imagined worlds.

"Yes, she is one of us," Hyon once more took over. "And her being unattached at this moment is what brought us together. We had to wait for just such a circumstance. Five deaths and no answers!" For the first time the Trystian showed outward emotion. "There is too leading a pattern: two diplomats, an engineer who had made recently a discovery, which left him so wealthy that he was about to set up his own research laboratory, two men of great possessions whose dream deaths brought about almost galaxy-wide confusion. Someone is troubling waters in order to collect the flotsam of such storms."

"Maybe they all had weak hearts ... I hear that action dreams can be tough to take," Burr suggested, though he did not believe his own words.

Bnon snorted. "You do not Hive-dream if you do not present a certificate of health to the Foostmam on your first visit. They may not follow up what happens to the owner of a dreamer, but one-time dream excursions within the Hive are well supervised so that this sort of thing does not happen. They want no accusation of killing off their clients. It would be ruinous for their business."

"Yet it has happened," Burr pointed out. "Five times."

"Five times within the space of one planet year," agreed Hyon.

"But if these deaths are arranged, aren't they playing it reckless?" Burr mused, more to himself than the other three. "I should think they would be waiting for the authorities to do some investigating."

"The planet authorities," Hyon returned, "have done what they could. But they cannot shut down the Hive, nor are they even allowed to screen the dreamers, that could be fatal. And Ty-Kry is dreamer-oriented. The dead were all from off planet and such as would not cause any local stir. In fact, Villand and Wyvid were both traveling incognito and not officially. But the authorities were enough concerned to call us in, a step which is revolutionary as far as they are concerned, as the locals resent to a high degree off-world contacts. They made the proviso when they did that we were *not* to appear there officially either, and they will give no open help to any investigation we might start."

Burr grinned without mirth. "Do they know about your planted dreamer?"

"No. And they are not to know either. The Hive has a monopoly on its product. To learn that a dreamer might be created by artificial means would turn the whole planet hostile. There is a religious significance to the existence of these girls and that we dare not meddle with."

"But what would make me so important they would try their game a sixth time?" Burr wanted to know.

"Burr Neklass has become owner of an asteroid which is nearly pure Bylotite," Hyon answered.

Burr's eyebrows lifted in unbelief. *"Is* there any such thing?" he asked wonderingly.

"It exists, yes. And it is under the guardianship of the Patrol. All rights are now on record in your name. You have no near family, and ..." Hyon paused as if to give extra emphasis to what he would say next, "one of your partners in Neklass Enterprises has been approached, very cautiously but with enough seriousness to be understood, to discover whether, at your death, the Bylotite will be included in your general estate. I do not doubt that there is already on record, perhaps not on Ty-Kry as there would be too pointed, a will ready to turn this estate over to whoever makes the highest bid for your life."

"Fine, you do have me well hammered in, don't you?" Burr scowled. "So, I'm good bait for murder. All right, when do I lay myself all ready and waiting on the Hive altar?"

"You will be briefed at once," Hyon said. "Then you will take your own space cruiser to Ty-Kry. There you will proceed to make yourself very visible as a man of great wealth who wants to try the unusual. I think there will be no difficulty in your finding the Hive welcoming and you will then ask for Uahach ..."

"And get down to a good death dream," Burr finished for him. "Thank you, one and all, for this exciting assignment. I shall remember you in my dreams!"

II

Her figure hidden in a dull gray sack of a robe, her hair cut so close to her head that it seemed less than half a finger in length so that the dream helmet would fit more easily, the slight figure sliding out of the carrying chair could have been any age from pre-teen to elderly. Her face was blank of any expression as she moved with the air of one still inhabiting those dreams which were her trade. The guard flung open the door and she stepped into the noiseless, curtained secrecy of the Hive.

As she moved down the central hall her eyes kept their fixed stare, but inwardly she was recognizing that which she had never seen before, but which the intensity of a mind-to-mind briefing had made plain to her. She was not Ludia Tanguly any longer, but Uahach an A dreamer with a ten-point rating. And it had been two years, a little more, since she had left the Hive to which she now returned. Luckily they had been able to so dip into the dreamer's mind that her double was familiar with all she saw, knew well the routine for returning.

Uahach turned toward a door to her right and stood, impassive, waiting for the spy ray to announce her. When the barrier split in two, she entered.

The room was small, containing only two chairs, not easirests but of the archaic hard-seated kind. It would seem that the Foostmam made no concessions of comfort for those who sought an interview. A memory control stood between the chairs, within easy reach of the ruler of the Hive. And there was a blank screen on the wall to one side. While the Foostmam herself sat waiting Uahach's arrival. She gave no verbal greeting, only raised a hand to signify that the dreamer might sit in the second chair.

"You have not come very speedily," the woman observed. "Your late lord died four days ago." Her tone was monotonous. If she meant her words as a question, they did not carry that inflection. And if she offered a reproof for tardiness, that, too, could only be guessed at.

"I was not released by my Lord's heir until an hour since. I then vision-messaged at once," Uahach's own voice held the same absence of meaningful accent. She had let her hands fall limply in her lap, sitting as one who had been under orders all her life.

"True. It was necessary for the Hive to remind the Lord Ylph that our contract was only with his predecessor. His reluctance to release you has been duly noted in the records. Perhaps he had thought to bargain ... because of your rating and the satisfaction your Lord took in your dreams. We, however, do not bargain. And you are returned. Your dream records have been fed into the archives. For the present you are on inactive status. The Lord Osdeve required much research; it may even be necessary for you to undergo an erase." Now there was a faint shadow of some emotion in the Foostmam's eyes. "The records must be studied to the full, I do not wish to order an unnecessary erase."

Uahach remained outwardly impassive, but inside her instinct for self-defense awoke. Had the Corps Master foreseen that? To undergo an erase would negate everything she was programmed to do. If that happened she would become Uahach in truth.

"There is this ..." the Foostmam's thin mouth snapped out each word as if she cut it free with a knife. "We are getting more and more of a new type of client, off-worlders who seek sensations strange to them. The lore you studied for Lord Osdeve was largely action adventure. And you might be a Hive dreamer for a length of time, serving these newcomers. They would not find what you had to offer too familiar."

"I am a Ten Point," Uahach said.

"And so above Hive service?" The Foostmam nodded. "It is agreed. Yet you must be rebriefed before you are again hired for outside. Be assured that you shall not be downgraded in the least."

"I shall be guided by you in this as in all else," the girl gave the conventional answer. So Bnon had been right, already the first move of her game had been made.

"You are a true dreamer," the Foostmam replied with her

conventional dismissal words. "I have given you the Chamber of the Mantled Suxsux. Dial what you may need. Your credit is unlimited."

Uahach arose and raised one hand to touch her forehead, the Foostmam replying with a prefunctory copy of that gesture. To be told that her Hive credit was unlimited meant that she was still rated a very valuable piece of merchandise. As she moved along the hall, ascended the twenty steps to the next floor she was already planning what she must do now. And since the Foostmam had suggested that she was to be hired in Hive service she had every right to start learning all she could.

The library of tapes owned by the Hive was the most spectacular collection of general information gathered anyplace in the galaxy except at Patrol Headquarters. Travelers' tales from thousands of worlds, history, strange stories, anything which could enrich the worlds the dreamers created for their clients, was at the call of those within the Hive. But was there any method of locating the special tapes either of the suspected dreamers had called upon? That was one fact they had not been able to ferret out for her. She knew the names of those dreamers, Isa and Dynamis. Both were action dreamers, neither one supposedly of ten-point rank, and both never hired outside the Hive. Uahach's memories, which had been sifted as well as the Patrol science could manage, had supplied a hazy picture of Isa. Dynamis was totally unknown. She was young, one of the Late Dreamers, whose talent developed enough to be measured only when she entered adolescence and not in early childhood when most of them were found and brought in for training.

Isa had survived the two dreams which had killed her clients ... but just barely. She was, by all accounts the planet law enforcers passed along, now a near vegetable. Dynamis had had better luck. Though it had been necessary for her to undergo, the Foostmam had sworn, a lengthy period of reeducation.

The dreaming itself was not too complicated an affair, though it was particular to this world. Linked by a machine which capped both dreamer and client, the dreamer entered into a hallucinatory state in which the client partook of vigorous action, some type of which he selected in advance. He could so return into the past, explore other worlds, venture into the speculative future. If a lengthy dream was desired, both dreamer and client could spend as long as a week so engaged, fed intravenously. And at any point the client could demand to break the dream.

Yet five men had dreamed themselves into death, and had not awakened. Once, perhaps twice, a faulty machine, a weakened heart, or some natural fatality could have occurred, but five were far too many.

The Foostmam had had, as Uahach well knew, every machine tested before the authorities. She demanded, and in this she was backed by those same authorities, certificates of health from every would-be client. And those were the result of examinations which could not be faked. The law in Ty-Kry had no wish to continue a scandal which was growing far too fast for comfort. The dreamers, long in use by the natives, had recently become a prime tourist attraction, the worth of which the rulers of the planet fully recognized.

Yet, in spite of all such safeguards, one dreamer was brainwashed into idiocy and five men were dead. Five men whose deaths could be turned to the credit of others off world. Suspicion was heavy, now there must be proof.

She came to the door bearing the painted design of the fabled creature the Foostmam had mentioned, and knew the chamber to be one of coveted single rooms within this warren. She was, indeed, being shown that her value to the Hive had in no way diminished.

Though the room was considered luxurious by any dreamer who had not been quartered in one of the sky towers of the Lords, it was a small one with few attractions. There was a couch formed of piled cushions covered in dull greens and grays; nothing must distract the attention of a dreamer, lure her attention from her work. Against one wall was a reading screen with a slitted block before it into which any tapes she desired could be fitted. On the opposite wall was a small board with a row of buttons; she could there order the bland, nearly tasteless food high in protein and nourishment which was the usual meal of her kind.

A curtain hung before a small private bathroom. That, too, was gray, as was the thick carpet on the floor. Uahach sat down on the divan, wondering if the Foostmam had some hidden method of viewing the chambers of her charges. That point certainly could not be overlooked, and she must never be off her guard.

There was a thick silence here, not a single sound came

from without, though the Hive was crowded. Again the
dreamer must be able to study undisturbed by anything outside her own cubicle. Probably they did not find silence op-
pressive. To them dreaming was life and the world outside
those they themselves created did not exist except as a
shadowy and uninteresting place.

She went to dial for a drink, accepting the small cup of hot
liquid gratefully. Her mouth felt parched and she was aware
of that usual reaction to coming danger. The familiar dryness
of her tongue and lips, the moisture of her palms were warnings for her to exert the techniques in which she had long
been schooled.

Waiting was always difficult. If one could plunge straight
into the indicated action, one lost oneself in that. But to have
to sit and wait ... How long before the other player Hyon
was putting on the board arrived? She would not even know
who he was, nor how much she could depend on him. And
she did not like working in the dark. This was far outside of
any operation of which she had before been a part. And she
found she enjoyed it less with every passing minute.

III

"So I ask for this Uahach."

The Foostmam's hands rested on the edge of her memory
control board. She favored Burr with an unwinking stare so
devoid of any personality, he began to wonder if the ruler of
the Hive was now caught in some dream herself. Then she
spoke, without any warning inflection in her voice.

"You say that the Lord Osdeve spoke of her. Yes, she was
on lease to him. But you must understand, Lord, she is still
unbriefed in a new series, for she has only returned to the
Hive two days ago. You would not be able to choose your
subject matter. ..."

Burr opened his belt pouch, produced a silvery credit plate.

"I'm not asking for a series to be arranged just for me. In fact, I am only curious to see how this dreaming of Ty-Kry works. Any briefing she had had for Lord Osdeve would be all right as far as I am concerned. It is merely that I would like to try it as an experiment, you understand."

The Foostmam's stare had shifted for several breaths to the credit plate. Burr himself had never handled such before: unlimited credit, a promise to be accepted on any planet where the Council had an Embassy.

"For a single dreaming time," the Foostmam said, "the price is higher, since the dreamer has no security factor for the future."

Burr shrugged. "Price does not matter. But I want Uahach. Osdeve had plenty to say about her dreaming when I saw him last."

The Foostmam again favored him with that blank expression. But her hand went to one of the buttons on the small control board and pressed two. A pattern, not a face, flashed on the vision screen. She eyed it and then her hand closed over the credit plate.

"She has not yet gone through debriefing. Very well, if you will accept Osdeve's series, it can be done. You have your certificate of health and stability?"

He produced a second piece of perforated plasta. She accepted that to push into a slit on the control board. There was a relay of clicks and the pattern on the screen changed.

"What is the danger in dreaming?" he decided to come openly to the point. As an off-worlder, unfamiliar with the processes of the Hive, Burr believed that he could ask such a question as a matter of routine.

"A ten point A dreamer," the Foostmam returned, "can produce so vivid a dream that its reality entirely grips the client. In such cases any strain on the heart or the mind can prove to be a very serious thing. Therefore, we naturally wish to know that this will not happen. We will also have a Medic standing by. But the final choice anywhere in the dream to leave is always for the Client to exercise. If you dislike the dream you will it to end. Since you will be mind-linked with the dreamer, your will instantly records with her and she releases you."

"The danger then must be slight," Burr prodded.

"It has been so." Apparently the Foostmam was not going

to say anything about the recent fatalities in the Hive. "When do you wish to call upon Uahach's services?"

"How about right now?" Burr pressed. "The rest of this Five Days I guest with Lord Erlvin and I believe he has made arrangements I cannot alter."

The Foostmam held his credit plaque between thumb and forefinger. She was again fixed of eyes, but Burr was sure she was no longer studying him, rather thinking deeply.

"Uahach is free, that is true. But there must be our own preparations to be made. At the present all our interior dream rooms are occupied. But if you will choose to return past nooning it can be arranged."

"Good enough." Burr reached forward and plucked the credit plate from her fingers. She had continued to hold that as if reluctant to lay it down. He wondered fleetingly just how many such plaques she had ever seen. Galaxy wide complete credit vouchers could not be too common.

He nooned in the best of Ty-Kry's restaurants. And he ate sparingly, selecting from a list which had been supplied him along with the plaque which had so entranced the mistress of the Hive. All that could possibly be done to ensure his own safety (outside of actually canceling the operation entirely) was accomplished. But he did face the unknown, and a threatening unknown.

When he returned to the Hive he was shown directly to a room occupied nearly to the full extent of its area by two couches. Between them stood the machine of linkage and there was already a girl stretched on the right-hand couch, her face masked past nose level by a helmet. Its twin awaited him. The dreamer was breathing in slow, regular breaths and Burr wondered if she were already asleep.

Two attendants, one of whom wore the insignia of a Medic greeted him and, within moments, Burr was installed on the other couch, blindfolded by the padded helmet. He drew a very deep breath of his own. There was no pulling back now; this was it!

He blacked out with a queasy feeling of whirling out and out through space itself. Then there came a burst of light as if he lay under the warmth of a sun, helmetless and in the open.

Burr sat up slowly, surveying the country about him. He had not expected this ... this freedom of body, the absolute reality of all he could see. Experimentally he pulled at a tuft of gray-green grass. It resisted and then gave way, so that roots and reddish soil parted company. He . . . this . . . was so *real!*

Around his present position small hills or mounds arose to make a wall about a cup of lower land in which he crouched. On the top of each was embedded a standing stone, weather-worn, but certainly never so regularly placed by any natural means. The country bore no resemblance to any he had ever seen before.

Burr got slowly to his feet. An A dream promised straight action adventure. This landscape had a certain grim and threatening appearance, but as far as he could see, he was alone in it and there was an absence of any life signs. No bird wheeled overhead, no insect buzzed or flew. This was being on a deserted stage before the curtain arose and the play began.

The nearest of the rounded hills attracted him. From its summit surely he would be able to see more than he could in this hollow. And toward that block-crowned summit he climbed.

The tall mound was covered with grass of the same gray-green shade as the tuft he had pulled. And it was both steep and slippery, so he stumbled and had to clutch at the grass to keep from slipping back into the spot where he had entered this hallucinatory world.

Once on the crest he turned slowly, facing outward, trying to get an idea of the country. The hills with their pillars continued on into what he guessed was the north in an unending series. But to the south there were only a few before they gave way to a wide open land in which were embedded a number of stones, tumbled together in a manner which suggested they were very ancient remains of some building or buildings, long reduced to a rubble, either by time itself or some ancient disaster.

There was a deep, quiet brooding over this stark world. Yet from somewhere came a vibration which could be felt rather than heard. It was almost as if the land itself were breathing, slowly, heavily.

Burr had a desire to shout, to make some sound which would rip away that quiet. He mistrusted all he saw with more than the mistrust which warnings had set in him. This was . . . dangerous, in a way he could not grasp.

His hand went to his belt, or where his belt should have

rested, instinctively hunting a stunner such as any prudent man wore in strange territory. But his fingers swept across bare skin and for the first time he looked down at his own body.

He was no longer wearing the rather fantastic suit which had been designed for Burr Neklass, multi-credit man. Instead his body was darker of skin where it was clearly visible. He did have on a pair of breeches of a steel-colored material, seemingly elastic and fitting nearly as tightly as that same skin. On his feet were coverings feeling as soft as if fashioned of cloth, but soled with thickness of a dull red material, while the upper part of the shoes(?) were stitched with glittering red threat to mark each hidden toe plainly.

Above the waist he had two belt straps, not for about his waist, but reaching one over the right shoulder and one the left. Where those crossed on his breast they were united with a palm-sized plate of silver metal in which were set colored stones ranging in shade from a deep red to a brilliant orange. About each upper arm was a wide band of the same silver, one bearing all red stones, the other yellow to orange. It was to Burr the dress of some off-world barbarian, in spite of the obviously fine workmanship, and certainly one he had never seen before.

Movement among the tumbled blocks of the ruins sent him ducking prudently to shelter behind the monolith which stood beside him on the hilltop. For the first time he realized his folly in making so open an appearance there. Something was flitting from cover to cover among the stones, moving so fast he could catch only a confused glimpse of it. He could not even be sure it was humanoid.

There were plainly no weapons furnished him in this dress. Now as he knelt behind the stone, Burr gazed around him for some possible way of arming himself. Finally he pried loose a small rock which he held in his hand.

A usual client of any dreamer was prepared for the nature of the dream, since he had indeed ordered it. But Burr must accept the programming which Osdeve had ordered and what had been implanted in the pseudo-Uahach.

Therefore he did not know what to expect, except trouble. And perhaps that was flitting toward him even now.

IV

There was more than one ... Burr drew a deep breath, his grip on the stone so tight that the rough surface scored his fingertips. One hid behind two blocks still piled one on top of the other, a second moved, with the same fluid speed, more to his right, gone to cover before he had more than an impression of raw color, an acid blue which flashed swiftly among the stones.

That they hunted him, he somehow knew. Perhaps Osdeve enjoyed this type of thrill ... chase, choosing, because of the infirmities of his final years, a physical-combat type of dream.

Burr glanced over his shoulder at the procession of mound-hills filing on to the far horizon. He could retreat perhaps, play what he was sure would be a deadly kind of hide-and-seek, through that countryside. But that would only prolong whatever action lay in this dream. No, he would stay where he was until he was sure that the danger ahead was too much for him to handle.

Perhaps they had lost sight of him and their impatience was enough to bring them out. For they were moving again, this time farther into the open. There, some distance from each other, yet in an even line, three oddities stood statue still, as if by freezing they could also conceal their presence.

For an off-world traveler Burr had long lost the ability to be surprised by any alien difference from his own norm. But these were unusual enough to rivet his attention.

It was hard to judge sizes from this distance, but he believed that all three of them were taller than himself. And they were birds, or at least birdlike in form. Their bodies, perched on long, thin legs, were covered with a vivid blue or green feathering (there was one green and two blues) which fluffed into plumes for tails. Their heads were unusually large, bearing tall crests of feathers, large eyes, and murderous appearing bills with points like Harkiman short swords. These outsize heads were connected to the bodies by long and very supple necks which were bare of the feathering, showing instead an expanse of scaled skin.

There was nothing reassuring about them. Rather Burr *knew*, just as he had been sure he was the quarry of a hunt, that they were deadly enemies to his own kind.

Now they were no longer so still. The green one dropped its head, a fraction, straightened its neck. Thus it pointed directly in Burr's direction. The man began to suspect that perhaps his lingering here had been the wrong choice after all. Yet the speed with which the bird things had transversed the ruins made him sure that any race between them would end fatally for him.

Was this how those others had died? Had they been hunted, perhaps not by those feathered monstrosities before him, but by other enemies? He remembered the warning of the Foostmam: he could wake . . .

The green bird took a flying leap which lifted it from among the blocks, moved it as if it were a chess piece in action to the crown of a nearer hill, slightly lower than that on which Burr had taken refuge. No use trying to play hero, this was a time to wake.

Instead of his directive being answered by an instant cancellation of the hunt menacing him, there was a quiver of light through the air. Point deep in the earth beside his sheltering monolith stood a spear, its haft still vibrating a little from the force of the throw which had hurled it there.

Instinctively Burr's hand went out to tighten on that haft. And the same time he was startled by a shout from the north. The head of the green bird snapped around, its intent gaze now in that direction. Burr wrenched the spear out of the ground. But overriding all else in his mind at that moment was that the cancellation demand had *not* worked!

So, he balanced the spear in one hand. This was it! He could well have been abandoned here. And the pseudo-Uahach who got him into this could not get him out. His stubborn refusal to be downed took over. Someone had thrown him a weapon, though it appeared a very paltry one taken in connection with the size and swiftness of the enemy. And someone had drawn the bird's attention . . .

Burr edged around, trying to keep an eye both on the birds

as well as discover who had come to his rescue, if only momentarily. At the same moment the green bird gave vent to the first sound he had heard it make, a shrill, ear-tormenting scream. It sprang directly into the air from the stand it had taken on the other mound.

And, though it seemed wingless and unable to fly, that prodigious leap carried it directly to another mound, this even with the one on which Burr crouched, but still a short distance away. It no longer watched him, rather continued to look to the north.

Though he felt he dared not glance away from its two companions still among the ruins, he had to know who, or what, the thing was now moving to attack.

The body of the bird tensed, its long legs just a little bent. Burr was sure it was about to launch a third spectacular leap. If so, it was a fraction late in coming to that determination. Something whirled through the air. The weighted ends of a long cord snapped about the legs just under the bird's body, the force of their passage wrapping the limbs tightly together. The bird crashed with a fury of squawking, its head bobbing up and down as it tore at that prisoning cord with its wicked bill. As it writhed on the ground a second weighted cord whirled, wrapping about its neck with force enough to completely overset it and bind its head partly to its body.

Burr slued around to watch for its companions. They had vanished, though they might be using the cover of the mounds themselves to come to the aid of their half-bound fellow.

"Come!"

That was no scream from the bird, it was a clearly distinguishable word in everyday Basic. Burr turned again. Two mounds away a figure stood waving him on. The newcomer was cloaked, a hood pulled well down so he could distinguish little more than it had at least a general humanoid shape. And since there was nothing else to do, he obeyed, running down one slope and up the next at the best speed he could manage, while the corded bird continued to screech.

He was gasping as he fought up the last incline. A hand shot out from under the edge of the cloak, caught his arm and jerked him on, so that both of them were able to dart behind the monolith on this mound.

"That whip-round will not hold the qwaker long." Burr was looking eye to eye with a girl. She pushed back her hood, showing hair pulled tight into a clasp high near the crown of her head, flowing freely from that down to her shoulders. And that hair was a dark blue. As with Burr the skin she bared as she shrugged the cloak back on her shoulders to free her arms was dark brown. And under her slanting blue brows her eyes shone like fiery sparks of orange flame.

Burr balanced the spear thoughtfully. "I would not say this would be too effective either," he commented dryly. "What now, do we run?"

He had no idea from whence this female had sprung. She seemed to have saved his life for the moment at least. Now she was shaking her head so that upheld plume of hair swished back and forth whispering against her hooded shoulders.

"That is what they wish. They can move faster than any man. No, we change . . ."

"Change what," he repeated.

"Change our dream site. Give me your hand!" Her fingers closed about his in a grip which had no gentleness in it. With the other hand she made a sweeping gesture.

The world reeled and Burr closed his eyes to fight nausea, for this instability was outside of any state of consciousness he knew. When he made himself look once more he was standing on a beach of yellowish sand against which washed, with turgid slowness, a vast body of water which might even be a languid sea. But his hand was still clasped in hers and he caught what might be a sigh of relief. Then she dropped her hold and moved a little away.

"So . . ." she said as if to herself, "so far that they cannot alter."

"What is all this?" Burr asserted himself to demand, and his voice came out almost embarrassingly loud above the slight whisper of the wavelets.

"Listen," she turned a little to fix him with a very direct gaze, "they have us locked somehow. When you tried to break, I could not make it. Do you understand? They have us both locked in this dream, and it is only partly out of Uahach's memories. The ruins were hers . . . and the qwakers. They actually exist, or did exist, on Altair IV. But they are not hostile. Now . . ."

"Uahach's memory," Burr caught the part that he understood the first. "Then you are . . ."

She laughed harshly. "I am your backup, the dreamer. But

I am now caught in my own snare. You gave the signal to wake, I would have obeyed. But there was a barrier. However, they did not, as least yet, manage to inhibit movement within this dream. We are now here," she gestured to the beach, "instead of dodging qwakers back on those hills. I do not know if they can control us within the dream, or just keep us here. But we dare not count on any safety."

Burr tightened hold on the spear haft. He understood her well enough. They were caught in this exceedingly real dream and at present there was no escape. "Can you keep doing this . . . move us around if they threaten us?"

She shrugged. "Some. I can call on Uahach's memory in a little. But if they force me to reach the end of those, then . . ." she shook her head. "Beyond her memory I have no pattern to follow. I knew of this sea in this particular dream. There are perhaps four other sites we can switch to."

"And after that," he finished for her, "we will be really trapped?"

Slowly she nodded, and echoed him. "Really trapped."

V

Burr examined the point of the spear which he still held. The metal was three-ridged, though dull of color. He had been schooled in the use of such barbarian arms as the sword, dagger, and primitive weapons which fired projectiles. But he had never attempted to use such as this before.

"You know this dream," he said slowly, "what is the pattern Uahach set in it for Osdeve? Can you see that ahead enough so that we will know what might come up next?"

"So far it is the same, as to background, even to the qwakers. However there are subtle alterations. The qwakers were meant to be hunted, not to hunt. Osdeve enjoyed such hunts. Here . . ." she hesitated. "Be warned—he was dreamed here to meet with Sea Rovers and join them on an expedition against the ancient sea Lords of the Isles. There were three such episodes within the dream: a hunting of the birds, the sea voyage, and at last the venture to take him to the Tower of Kiln-nam-u. Each has potential danger if the dream does not proceed as it should. Now there is a pressure which I do not understand . . ."

She spoke slowly, a slight frown marking her forehead. "You understand that you are now a different personality. Your name is Gurret and you are the Warrior of the Right."

Burr scowled. "How much of this . . ." he began.

"The dreamers create a form of reality," she struck in before he could complete his question. "You are a part of this world, which is an ancient time on Altair IV, yet not quite that either, since each dreamer adds her own touches. I am Kaitilih, a War Woman of the Left. Traditionally we would have been enemies. But it seems that Uahach altered that point also. By her plan we are united on a quest whereby, in the manner of legends on each world, we must find certain things. Having these in hand we are to return to the Three Towers and there . . ." She smiled faintly, "I gather from dreamer memories our reward would be spectacular. Of course, even though there was a strong element of risk in this dream, Osdeve was at no time in great danger, just enough to satisfy his need for the action he craved. But now, with the alterations, I cannot foresee what may lie ahead within the general frame of the original dream."

"If we are warriors," Burr returned, "why no real weapons?"

"Because this quest was meant to be a testing. I carried the spear, the whirling cords, but neither was used. It was set on you to go bare-handed."

"You snapped us out of that attack. Can you dream up a stunner, or something better than this?" Burr banished the spear.

Slowly she shook her head. "I can add nothing of my own, only use the material provided from Uahach's memory. You know I am not a trained dreamer. And . . ." she turned her head to look up and down the deserted beach, "there is pressure on me. There is someone else who meddles and changes so subtly that I cannot trace that interference to its source. Just as the hunt in the hills was reversed. I believe we can look for other reverses to come."

"Fine!" Burr snapped. "Best if we stuck it out right here while you try to break the dream."

"We cannot halt the flow of action," the dreamer replied. "We have to play the pattern through to the end."

Burr knew she was speaking what she believed to be the truth. So roles were reversed so far in the dream. Might they then take it that that would continue?

"Two more pieces of action then. What should they be?"

"You are to light a beacon of the drift," Kaitilih, as she had named herself, motioned toward the bone colored, sea-cured wood which was caught among the shore rocks. "This should be done at twilight. Then a boat will come in from a raider named the Erne. You have already, or Gurret has, contacted the Captain of the Erne, promising him rich loot at the Sea Keep of Eastern Vur. All you want from Vur is the Cup of Blood Death kept in hiding there. There will be great peril, but the Erne will be lucky, getting in and out without dire mishaps. With Cup in your possession you can then bargain with that which holds the Tower of Kiln-nam-u—"

Burr laughed harshly. "This is like some tale for a child's reading screen! Do you mean that Osdeve actually wanted to live out this wild nonsense?"

"It is not a story, but a legend with a core of truth," the girl corrected him. "Much research was done to provide the very old bones of a hero tale with the proper background and contemporary details. Part of it is history. There *was* a Gurret who was the first Supreme Arms Lord of half his world. And he gained that position because he pursued such a quest. The dreamers are adept in returning to the past, not only of their own world, but any other planet whose history appeared in their study tapes."

"But if it *was* ... *is*, history, then how can it be altered? I gather I was supposed to do something else upon awaking than run from those qwakers as I did."

"Yes. You were to capture two who would then make you free of their nest place. There in the debris you would find a very old cylinder of metal in which lay a map of Vur ..."

"It's unreasonable!" Burr interrupted. "I can't believe that any adult would be serious about this ... even if it is supposed to be history!"

"I assure you Osdeve was. As a man who had lost much use of his own body he craved this outlet as a drug addict craves the powders which will give him entrance to another world for a space. This was Osdeve's last dream before he died and it was the most elaborate and complicated one Uahach was ever called upon to plot, for he had good warning that he was very close to the end."

"I thought that anyone in poor condition was not allowed to dream," Burr countered.

"An off-worlder, yes. But a native of Ty-Kry is not bound by such rules. Some have chosen to die in dreams."

"But that . . . I thought that was impossible. It was because men died that we are here."

"Then the situation was entirely different. Those victims were off-worlders, known to be in good health, and they had not signed any dismissals. Also the dreams they had selected were not dangerous ones."

Burr shook his head. "But a man can be dreamed to death?"

"If that is his recorded desire. And it must be recorded and certified by the Lords in Council, also the First Person of his name clan. It is not permitted to any off-worlder."

"All right," Burr knew that she was doubtless well schooled in this dreaming business. "But this dream has been already altered. I did not get that map or whatever that Gurret is supposed to have. What if I don't build the signal fire and the raider does not come? Will that break the dream?"

"I don't know. Perhaps you will be forced to take the next step."

Burr dropped down on the sand, balanced the spear across his knees as he sat cross-legged. "That I do not believe."

She seated herself a little away, her head bared to the sea wind which tugged at the length of her hair. "Good enough. We can so test the strength of what stands against us." Her reply was calm.

Some moments later he broke the silence between them with a question:

"You still cannot wake?"

"No. And there is this also," she hesitated as if considering the wisdom of telling him, then she added: "I am no longer in command."

"What does that mean?"

"Just what I have said. Before I was aware of what lay before you . . . us. Now," she lifted a handful of sand and let it shift through her fingers, "I cannot be sure of the future. It is . . . blurred . . . is the best word I can find to describe it. As if you might take one picture and lay another over it so that two different scenes strive to cancel out each other."

"Then there is another dreamer?" Burr asked.

"I cannot be sure. Only that the dream I knew is being overlaid with another and . . ."

She was gone. Burr stared at the place on the beach where she had been sitting. There was still a vague depression in the sand. But Uahach, or Kaitilih (whoever she was) had vanished before his steady gaze, winked out in an instant!

He got to his feet, still staring, and reached forth with the butt of the spear to touch with caution that slight mark in the sand. No one . . . nothing there!

That this was of her own doing he doubted. The other pattern she had sensed over the dream which had been Osdeve's . . . had that strengthened to obliterate her, take over his own future?

She had saved him from the qwakers. It might be that he was *not* to be saved from the next ordeal of the ancient legend. But she had said he must light the beacon to bring in the ship, and that he could refrain from doing.

In fact, he was going to get away from here right now! Though he could not travel Uahach's instant roadway, he could move away from what was suddenly a treacherous shore inland, give himself time to find some way he could defeat the unknown dreamer, since he had not the slightest hope, he thought, of his signal to wake being answered . . . except by refusal.

VI

Burr faced sharply away from the sea. Before him the land was wooded by small, dense appearing clumps of what was either very tall brush, or stunted trees. The leafage was thick and dark in coloring, making each copse appear like a blot.

There was something sinister about that landscape. Whereas the mound country had seemed eerie and alien, this gave him the impression of being actively threatening in a manner he could not define.

Also he had to struggle against a very definite and growing compulsion *not* to head inland. Perhaps the new dream pattern was trying to force him to light the shore beacon, follow the original dream into the raid on Vur. Now Burr set himself to a grim battle of wills, fighting his way on.

The same tough grass which had clothed the mounds covered the ground, and the long, sharp edged ribbons of that tangled about his feet, jerked him nearly off balance, as if it were moved to make this journey as difficult as possible. He only knew that he *was* advancing against the desire which fought him, and for the moment that was all he could hope for.

Such was the foreboding atmosphere of the region ahead that he expected any moment to see some peril leap or slink out of the tree blots avid to do battle.

Choking for breath Uahach-Kaitilih-Ludia (who *was* she in truth?) swayed back against a support she could feel but not see clearly, and tried to regain full consciousness. She was no longer on the seashore. Nor had she been summarily returned to her couch in the Hive. No, she was back again on the mound where she had entered the dream. Beyond her she saw the man crouched against the monolith, the qwakers about to leap for his perch. Her hand had already gone to her belt to free the throwing cord.

Only . . . this was wrong!

Her thoughts were hard to order into clarity. She must save the man.

But it seemed to her that the whole scene before her quivered. It had none of the in-depth reality of the first time.

Her will sharpened and her mind awoke fully. No instinctive action . . . This was not her dream, but that other's. She was being presented not with the man who was her companion in their adventuring, but a dream simulation.

The qwaker leaped, its bill flashed down, transfixed the chest of the man whose fending blow had been easily deflected. She heard his sobbing cry, the triumphant screech of the qwaker. But she was fighting her own battle, the one to tear the false dream to pieces.

Now the whole scene rippled, fought desperately to remain, tore, like rending cloth, from top to bottom. In that instant she caught a single glimpse of a shadow form far removed from her own place, but operating on what must be another plane. She saw the enemy, but she could neither identify that lurker, nor even discover where was its normal position.

Dying man and qwaker vanished, the mound melted into a mist which thickened about her, so that she breathed faster and faster in frantic gulps of air. For it seemed that she was being enclosed in a monstrous blanket of damp. If she did not fight ... bring her own natural Esper powers as well as all she had learned from Uahach to the highest pitch she would meet death here.

This was a dream, an illusion. And a spinner of dreams could not be caught in another's dream, not without her full consent. Therefore, she could not be killed unless she accepted the illusion. She forced herself to breathe deeply and slowly, to fight the evidence of her eyes. She was not enmeshed in the enemy's dream, but a part of the one whose pattern lay deep in her own mind! That only was truth!

The mist rolled back. She knew a moment of triumph which she would not yield to. This happening was beyond the knowledge she had acquired from Uahach, beyond any records she had had access to. Only it was plain that, in spite of the enemy's efforts, a hallucination could not be held once she knew it for what it was. She was so armed, but what of Burr?

They had been separated deliberately, and she believed that he could well be governed by the other dreamer, strong as his will might be. He had no Esper talent or he would not have been chosen for the part he was playing, he lacked her only weapon.

There was only one hope for them both, she must find Burr. Only together did either of them have a chance.

The mist had rolled back a little, but not enough for her to see the country now about her. She could only be sure that her instant defense, her refusal to be caught in the reaction of the mound duel, had broken the pattern the other had set. She had only one way to find Burr, that was, by concentration of will. They had been on the shore ... she shut her eyes and concentrated on the shore even as she had on that first move which had so swiftly snapped them from one point of the altered dream to the next. Shutting her mind to every outward

sight, every inward fear, she pictured the shore as she had
seen it last, and fiercely willed herself to be there again.

There was that sense of weightlessness, of sharp pain. She
looked about her. Yes, here was the sand, the turgid wash of
tideless ocean, the rocks . . . But one portion of the beach was
exactly like the next. And there was no Burr.

She had half expected to see him busied erecting the
beacon. For she was sure that the other dreamer still tried to
move within the general framework of the original dream.
But there was no sight of him.

Swinging around she faced inland. There was nothing
pleasant about the landscape. She was chilled by the sight of
those trees the outlines of which against the lighter grass had
hints of strange shapes. As if the trees could dissolve their
nature at will and assume other and far deadlier forms.

Nothing there . . .

Yet she could feel . . . What did she feel? A very vague
tugging as if a cord as light as a thread spun out from her
body and was anchored to some object out of sight but
among those threatening trees. That must be Burr and he had
left the shore, was striving in his own way to break the threat
of the dream by moving directly against the future she had
sketched out for him.

That he had been able to do so surprised her. She had been
sure that any dream will strong enough to snap her back at
the beginning of all action would have had no difficulty in
moving Burr to the new pattern. He had made himself vulnerable by playing the role of client, so accepting the original
dreaming.

Perhaps it was the struggle she had fought her way through
which had served him indirectly, removing a greater part of
that unknown other's will from him. Thus he had had a
chance to change course.

At any rate they must come together or they would have
no chance at all now. For client and dreamer were bound in-
dissolubly together and entered and exited so or not at all.
While all she had to follow was that very tenuous sense of a
tugging. Resolutely she began to walk inland.

The sky was darkening. She believed that night was not far
off. In the true dream they had spent that night on board the
Erne. But this was the new pattern and what dangers could
be fashioned to attack any wayfarer in the dark? The rising

wind was chill, she drew her cloak more closely about her, but she kept on, hoping that her guide would not fail.

It was getting dark. Burr had avoided the scattered copses of trees, making detours to skirt even the shadows they threw upon the ground. He was very tired, not of the walk itself, but rather from the constant struggle against the will which would enforce his return to set the beacon. That came now in surges of strength which were more disquieting than the first steady pressure, for there were intervals between, as if to encourage him to hope that he had won, then a blow sharper and more insistent. And that other seemed untiring, so that Burr wondered how long it would be before he did turn, and start back to pile the drift, light the beacon, and bring down upon him some fate he was only too sure awaited him in the altered dream. Since the qwakers had nearly finished him, he thought he could well expect no friendly Sea Rovers, but perhaps men equipped with steel and a strong desire to have his life.

Still he kept on his feet and moving, in spite of those blows. Then he raised his head and looked more closely at a copse to his left. That was altering in outline . . . There was something very wrong about it.

VII

A figure arose from the half crouch which had made it so resemble the other stands of stunted trees. It was larger than human but the outline was so disguised that Burr was not sure whether he faced some large beast or a sentient being. In the swiftly descending twilight it was only a black bulk. And, oddly enough, as he neared it that bulk appeared to draw in upon itself, shrinking in size so that at length it was no taller than he.

Burr gripped the spear tightly. The thing, once it had
strode into his path, made no other move. But he had no
doubt that it represented an enemy force. At least it was not
a qwaker. But what other dangers might walk these lands he
did not care to guess. Though he had faced perils without
number before, there was that in this adventure which was
unlike any operation of which he had been a part. Those had
been in a real world wherein he could assess in part the dangers. But this was a country born of will and mind . . . whose
will and mind? By her own account not entirely that of the
psuedo-Uahach.

Yet now he did not try to evade meeting with the thing
awaiting him. It was better to look fear directly in the face
rather than let his imagination supply him with details.

All at once the figure moved, shrugging away folds of a
dead black cloak. There was enough light remaining to show
him clearly face and head.

She was back!

A welcoming hail was already on his lips when he slowed
to a stop. Though every detail of her features and her movement of head were the same as he had seen before, yet . . .

The girl's hand appeared, waved to him imperiously. Burr
remained where he was. Only now the pressure which had
been against him ever since he had left the shore had veered.
Now it would urge him forward to join this Uahach. And
that very alteration in the unseen will warned him off.

"Come." She spoke the same word which had been her first
greeting to him. Once more she beckoned and there was a
frown, which might have been fostered by impatience, on her
face.

He planted the spear butt down in the ground, tighted both
hands upon it, as if by this he could anchor himself against
obeying that summons.

"Who are you?" he asked.

"I am Kaitilih." Her voice held the same timber, was no
different in his memory from the tone she had used as they
sat together on the shore. It was only that persistent forward
urge which warned, and in this place he would heed any
warning, no matter how small.

"You are not!"

"I am Kaitilih . . . come." It was as if she had not even
heard his denial. "Night falls and in it there prowls that
which will imperil us. We must find a shelter . . . Come!" Her

command was reinforced by a sudden surge of compulsion, so strong it nearly tore him from his spear anchorage, to send him stumbling on.

"You are not she," he repeated; though what if she was? Burr was uncertain, could only depend upon that revulsion stirring within him for a guide.

"I am Kaitilih!" Now she raised both hands to pull back her hood. "Look upon me, fool, and see!"

Burr steadied. Her mistake that. For a moment she had slipped out of her dream disguise. That was *not* the girl from the shore.

"You are not Kaitilih," he was convinced now.

She stared at him, all emotion smoothed from her face. Then she reacted so quickly that he was only half prepared. Her right hand swung up to hurl something at him. He was aware only of a flash of light, but his trained reflexes had not been lost even in the dream world. For he hit the ground, rolled, and was up again with the practiced swift and fluid motion of an expert unarmed fighter.

Something struck behind him and from that sprang a burst of fire. Burr leaped, not at her, but to one side again, as again her hand moved. This time, with the flash, came a sensation of burning close enough to touch him.

Then her face convulsed into an ugly mask, she spat in his direction. Her cloak whirled up as if the material had a life of its own or was controlled by her will alone. It wrapped tightly about her, transforming her into a dark pillar, hiding once more her head in shapeless folds.

That column of darkness began to sink into the ground, swiftly disappearing. At Burr's side a patch of grass was charred and small red embers glowed there. But she was gone.

An acrid odor arose on the night air. However, save for the shadows of the trees, he seemed to be alone.

"Gurret?"

Spear ready he wheeled about. There was another shadow advancing toward him.

"Gurret," there was recognition in that. But he was not deceived. She thought to play the game a second time, did she?

Once more Burr saw her face clearly. Even in this twilight her features had a kind of radiance which made them plain. He readied himself to again avoid attack.

"It is no use," he said, "you are not Kaitilih."

"No," she agreed, "but I am she who dreams."

Burr eyed her warily. There was indeed a subtle difference (one he could not put name to even in his mind) between this girl and the one who had vanished as if the earth had opened under her feet.

"If you are . . . the dreamer, give me proof."

"What proof can I offer?"

"Tell me . . . where did you go . . . and why?"

She did not try to come near to him. "Where did I go? Back to the beginning of the dream. Why? I know not that, save that the one who seeks to change our venture would have me believe that you were dead."

"She nearly achieved that purpose. If a man can be brought down by a dream weapon." He used the point of the spear to stir the charred grass.

The warning which had been so alert in him when he had fronted that other one was lulled. "How did you return?"

"By my will." Uahach seemed confident of that. "What was not real fled when I willed it."

Burr shook his head. "Shadows and dreams . . . how can a man fight them? At least your double had a weapon which could do this." Once more he plodded the scorched earth and ashes of grass. Then he told her of that other who had taken her form.

"The other dreamer," Uahach returned. "You did not follow the pattern, now . . ." She drew a deep breath. "That having been broken the other can substitute her own."

"So we will not know what to expect?" he caught the significance of her uneasiness.

"Perhaps so. There is one last thing we may try . . . to go on to nearer the end of the dream, try to hasten its conclusion. Before she gathers her forces and builds up a greater command of the dream design we might break free from there."

"Can you do this?"

"I do not know. At least she could not hold me with her illusion when she returned me to the mounds. Perhaps she cannot hold the two of us if we will the end. It is not easy to retain any pattern, though I do not know if it has ever occurred that the client strove to alter it for himself. I am your dreamer, thus tied to you . . . if we two work together we may be too strong . . ."

"You think we can . . . go ahead?" Burr demanded.

"We can try." But he thought there was a shade of hesitancy in that reply.

"And what is your choice?"

"The Tower of Kiln-nam-U."

She held out her hand, even as the other had done. And the likeness of their gestures was so alike, that, for a breath or two, he was almost hesitant to approach and take it ... lest he indeed had been deceived for a second time. But here there was none of that pressure, the choice clearly remained his.

He took the two strides to her side and felt her grasp close about his fingers. The touch of her flesh was a little chill, and he sensed through that contact, slight as it was, the whole tension of her body, the concentration building in her.

"Think," she said with sharpness, "of a tower by the sea, the same sea we looked upon ... think of it!"

He did not know the tricks and shifts of an Esper mind, but if it would help he could at least think of a tower. And he summoned as best he could a mental picture of one ... archaic by the standards of his own world, but at least matching in part the ruins he had seen from the mounds. Burr closed his eyes better to build that mental picture. and then was no longer aware of her touch, rather of something which burned high with an almost consuming force, as if great energy struck full on the flesh-and-bone link between them.

VIII

So this was the Tower and Uahach's efforts had brought them to the end of the dream. Burr stared at the edifice before him. For a long moment the mental concept he had built in his mind lay like a misty illusion over the reality. Then that was gone and he faced the place native to the dream world.

It was set so that rising pinnacles of a cliff sheltered two of its walls on the sea side, those forming a right-angled corner into which ancient masonry had been carefully fitted in a way so that not even time itself could level it. For there was about this erection such a heavy feeling of age as to lie almost a visible shadow.

For a space which Burr counted as possibly two ordinary stories in height there was no break in the stone, the blocks showed no openings. Above that space existed a triangle of wedge-shaped windows set in a diamond design, giving upon utter blackness, for no bit of the sunlight penetrated those deep holes.

That was another startling shift. They had left night behind them on whatever journey their united will had energized. It was, he thought, now near midday.

The stone from which the Tower was built was a dull red in color unlike the rock of the cliffs which half sheltered it, which were a yellow brown. While caught in the crudely smoothed surface of the blocks were sparks of glittering crystals which reflected the sun, so that the edifice appeared necklaced with gems.

"Kiln-nam-u," Uahach dropped her hold upon his hand. "So much have we won."

"And what was Osdeve set to do here?" Burr wanted to know.

"He was to anoint that block." His companion pointed to one of the stones, reaching near to Burr's shoulder in height, seemingly a well set part of the foundation of the Tower. "With water from the Cup of Blood. Then would issue forth the Thing which has always dwelt within and with it he bargained . . . for the Rod of Ar . . . that he might rule."

"Since we don't have this cup," commented Burr, "can't we just break the dream now?"

When she did not answer he glanced from the Tower to her.

Her face was set, her eyes not seeking his, nor even the tower itself, but rather as if she looked beyond or through all which lay before them.

"I . . . can . . . not . . ." Her words, separated by forced breaths (she might have been at the end of a long, hard flight), came in harsh whispers.

"If we have reached near the end of the dream ... and cannot break it? ..."

"Then we shall be forced into the other's chosen pattern, here and now," she gave him the bitter truth.

Burr accepted her reply as being correct. All right, so they could not break the dream (the dream Osdeve had set up) but must follow another ...

"You know all Uahach knows. You must have if they briefed you." He continued. "Is this ever done?"

Now her head did turn a fraction so her wide eyes met his.

"To my knowledge, which is Uahach's in truth, such a transference is unknown. She is a ten-point dreamer ... the Hive knows no higher class on its test scale ..."

"Yet there must be one, or we would not be caught. Have you any way of locating the source?"

The faint shadow of shock which had been in her eyes faded. She wore an intent expression, but not that of one wrapt in concentration.

"I could try. They ... she ... must reach us here sooner or later. The dream must come to a definite end or the medic at the Hive will know there is trouble. They ... the Foostmam, if she is a part of what we seek, would never dare not to allow him to intervene. We certainly lie in proper dream sleep now ... back there. Therefore, since our dream is timed, whoever would spin the new pattern must move fast. We have cut out the midportion of Osdeve's adventure, brought it close to the end. I can do no more than wait for the next move, and that will be theirs."

Burr did not like it. Patience was a tool he had had to cultivate in his own operations. But those had dealt with the real world and he had then had a measure of control over the future. He had waited out attacks before, but always the opponent had then been working within a framework he himself could understand. This nebulous kind of battle irked him.

"Is there any way we can arrange a defense in advance?" he pressed her.

She did not reply, instead her hand came up to signal warning. A second later he staggered under a blow which was not really physical, although it felt as if some giant fist slammed between his shoulder blades giving him a massive thrust forward toward the Tower. At the same time Uahach's hands went to her head and she cried out in pain.

On ... that force wanted to push Burr on, to slam him

bodily against the block of stone. But he had his wits about him now and he dug in with the spear again to anchor him. His body swayed back and forth under the unseen blows, but he held fast, his mouth set in a grim line.

His companion fell to her knees, her hands still over her ears, tears edged from her eyes. She moaned, that sound oddly echoed by the rocks about them. It was apparent that, even as he, she fought against some compulsion which was nearly too great to withstand.

The Tower blurred before Burr's eyes. Or was it that the block Uahach had earlier indicated moved? On, whatever strove to control him now wanted to hurl him on, into a dark slit opening there. If it was a door, its outline was a very uneven one, following the natural cracks between the stones.

Burr stood fast. He was not going to obey. Uahach said they had reached near the end of the proper dream; therefore, he would not accept any new pattern. He summoned all the stubbornness of will which he had ever shown, used that as an armor against this beating.

The girl was slowly rising to her feet. Her face, wet with tears, still showing pain lines, had also set (though he did not realize the likeness) into a determination matching his own.

That irregularly framed hole at the base of the Tower was completely open. Uahach said that in the proper dream the Thing, as she called it, had come forth to bargain with Osdeve. Well, Burr did not have the mysterious Cup of Blood it wanted. And whatever rode him now wanted him to go in, not wait here.

As in the wedge windows above, the sun did not enter that opening, even though it made the Tower plain to the eye to the every edge of the jaggered doorway. The darkness lying beyond the threshold of that had a tangible quality which held out all natural light.

Was the Thing coming now? And now would it react to the fact Burr did not have what Osdeve had used to summon it? He wavered forward one bitterly contested step as the compulsion dealt an even more severe blow.

It wanted him in. Therefore that was where he was *not* going!

For the first time during their struggle Uahach spoke. "That other dreamer must fight hard to hold us both." She had regained much of her air of command as well as mastery

over herself. "When I raise my hand, try to move back ...
try with all your might!"

She was again watching the Tower with a fixed stare, her
body stiff. Then her hand arose. Burr threw himself back,
putting into that action every bit of stubborn strength he
possessed.

A cord might have snapped. Burr lost his feet, struck the
ground with a force which half stunned him, then rolled. The
girl stood straight, a defiant pillar between him and the hole
he had no doubt was a trap. But he felt a release which left
him weak.

Uahach's figure wavered. Once more she sank to her knees,
as if pressed so by a punishing weight. Before he thought
Burr dropped the spear. And, getting to his feet, leaped to
cover the distance between them. His grip closed tight and
steady on her shoulders, holding her so as she went limp.

IX

What filled the atmosphere about them was a malignant
and petulant anger. Burr could not have told why he was so
sure of that disembodied emotion, he only knew that he was.
And from that sullen rage he gained a fraction of confidence.
The other had not expected such a forceful defense from the
two of them, for the moment it was defeated. But only for
the moment ... of that Burr was also sure. There was a sudden end to the manifestation of the unknown's will, even the
anger winked out.

Uahach drew a deep breath, nearly a sob.

"She is gone," her voice was ragged, drained.

"Will she try that again?" Burr asked.

"Who knows? At least she still has power enough to keep
us here."

"You are sure?"

"Do you think I have not already tested?" the girl flashed at him. "Yes, we are fixed here, in Osdeve's dream. What new pattern may have been devised I cannot guess."

Burr looked to that irregular gap in the Tower wall. He had half expected it to close now that the pressure on him to enter had been withdrawn. However, it remained not only open but with an ominous kind of threat lying within its thick blackness. He wanted to go and thrust the spearpoint deeply into that. But another part of him shrank from advancing any closer to the enigmatic fortress.

"Is there any way," he continued to explore possible avenues of escape or means of defense, "for you to continue improvising from the end of Osdeve's own dream?"

She shook her head. "I am not a true dreamer. Since I am Esper I could pick up just Uahach's experiences, relive those. But these dreamers of Ty-Kry are born with different talents, and those talents are fostered by training from the moment their abilities are recognized. Many of them actually have very little real life apart from their dreams. I know only what my briefing, which was thorough just as to Uahach's past, could give me."

"There is no way then." But Burr refused defeat. He was not to wait here tamely for what the unknown could bring into being as a threat against them.

"I do not know . . ."

At first her words hardly pierced through the milling thought in his own mind. But when their meaning did reach him, Burr turned on her swiftly, his controlled anger at the whole situation making his demand explosive in force.

"You may not know, but you are speculating . . . about what?"

"There is this, and it will be highly dangerous. She will make a move soon, you must have felt her rage when she could not force us to her desire. If we let whatever menace she sends against us develop fully, then there is just a chance I can connect with the thread of her dream weaving. But the dream then must be hers . . . not mine, nor a hybrid one which is half and half."

"So you may be able to find the connecting thread . . . what then?"

"Just this, if I can fasten to it firmly, we can force our way out. These dreamers are fully programmed in one important factor . . . they must break the dream on the client's order. I could not do that for you because this unlooked-for situation had arisen. The dream was secondhand and it was already overlaid, before I tried, by a blanketing force from another and very powerful dreamer."

What she said made sense to Burr, after a fashion. But he did not like it at all.

"How far must the new dream go before you have a chance to do this?"

She did not meet his gaze. "I am afraid far enough to make the situation highly dangerous. You will have to face whatever peril she introduces, and hold it, until I have located the dream thread and can anchor us to it."

There was a kind of desperate logic in that and Burr could understand what she suggested, even though it was far outside his experience. That the result of such action would be perilous he had no doubts at all. But neither had he any other choice that he could see.

"We wait then . . . until she moves." That was not a question but a decision on his part. Then he did add a question, "Can you guess who 'she' is? The Foostmam?"

"No. She trains dreamers but she is not known to be a dreamer herself. You understand, many dreamers are almost completely locked away from reality; they must be tended as one tends an infant. Those who so protect and care for them are not dreamers for that very reason. There are two dreamers in the Hive who had their clients die. One was herself maimed in the dream world so that she lives, but just that . . . her dreaming mind is either dead or so shocked it cannot be reached.

"The other dreamer is unusual in that her potential was never realized until she reached adolescence. This *has* been known to happen, but very rarely. Any family which has produced a dreamer in the past knows the signs to watch for in early childhood and are eager to find one of their clan house with the ability. It means a large sum of credits for them. So a late developer has been found now and again, but it is an uncommon happening."

"You think this is the one?"

Uahach shrugged. "How can I tell? Two men died in dreams she spun for them and she was not shocked herself. Those are the only facts I can give you."

"Have you seen her? Talked to her?" Burr pressed.

"No. The Hive keeps all their dreamers of higher rank separated. A dreamer not in service is expected to build up her dreaming ability by the garnering of information, using the stored tapes to gather material for her dreams. It is a very lonely life for those who wake."

"Each of those dead men provided reason to wish them dead," Burr commented. "Either their wealth or their offices made them vulnerable. So if someone could tamper with a dreamer, perhaps even provide the proper background tapes . . ."

The girl was already nodding. "Yes, it could be done. Each one of us hides in his or her inner mind some personal and private fear. If the nature of that fear was known and it could be materialized to the highest wave . . ."

"They could well die, or wake raving! But that information would have to be supplied by someone close enough."

"What of your fears?" she asked.

"They provided me with a tight background for identity," Burr mused. "But hardly recorded anything such as that."

He paced up and down beginning to wonder. Could a dreamer herself shift out of a man's mind his greater fear and then materialize it?

As he turned to face the girl once more he saw she had changed position, her eyes fixed on the dark hole which remained open in the Tower. The tense rigidity was back in her figure. He needed no more warning than that.

There was something coming, their enemy once more moved. But so far all Burr could see was that deep darkness within. Breathing a little quickly he came to stand shoulder to shoulder with Uahach. He wanted to ask if she could give any hint as to what to expect, but feared to break her concentration. She had already made it plain to him that he must stand up to anything which awaited them long enough for her to reach the dream line lying behind it.

There was a curdling crawl of the black shadow. Some of it licked forward like a black questing tongue, striking out into the light and air in a pointed ribbon of darkness.

Instinctively Burr retreated, drawing his companion with him.

There was something about that evidence of strange life which churned his stomach, made his flesh roughen as if he stood in the midst of an icy blast.

The point end arose from the ground, weaved from side to side, as might the head of some reptile. Now there were bulges there. These popped with an audible sound to display red coals of eyes.

Burr could not identify the thing and, though the sight made him sick in an odd way he could not define, he fought to subdue his fear. Perhaps, since the unknown dreamer did not have any briefing as to his private fears she was producing now a fragment of her own most morbid imagining.

The black ribbon flowed forward slowly. Its head had stopped weaving, those coal eyes were centered on Burr. If the head was narrow, the bloated body coming into view through the hole door was slug fat, with a quivering hump forming most of it.

"No!"

The girl beside him cried out, raised her hands as if to push the crawling monster back into hiding. Her face was a mask of disgust and terror, the fear taking over.

X

Burr guessed what had happened. The enemy had not struck at him, but rather at Uahach, perhaps because already the opposition was aware that in such a battle as they faced the girl was the stronger opponent.

A fetid odor wafted from the crawler, thick and loathsome enough to make Burr gag. He had put out his left hand to grip the girl's shoulder, and could feel the shudders running through her. Though this crawling monstrosity was unknown to him, it was not to her.

"Hold on!" He gave her a shake. "It is a dream ... remember ... a dream!"

She could not still her shivering, but he saw her head move. It was plain that she was in no condition at this moment to do what must be done ... trace that thread of communication with the other dreamer.

Burr raised his hand from the roundness of her shoulder, grabbed for the throat buckle of the bulky cloak she wore. His fingers freed the latch and he gathered the long folds of material swiftly into his grip.

"Stand back!"

Setting the spear between his knees he took the cloak into both hands. The material was very closely woven, yet silky to the touch. He shook out the length and then, with what skill he could summon, he sent the outer edge snapping up in the air, spinning the goods out and down.

The folds settled over the crawler, masking the creature from view and, before the thing could free itself, Burr sprang forward to stab down again and again at that bulk heaving under the cloth. In his head, not his ears, shrilled a thin screaming which shook him, but not enough to make him retreat. There were growing splotches on the cloak, evil-smelling liquid oozing through the slits the spearpoint made.

Yet it would seem that the thing could not be killed for there was no end to the movement under the torn and befouled cloak. Burr stabbed ... stabbed. Could *not* the Thing be killed?

Once more he sensed the rise of strange fierce anger in the very air about him. But at last the monster no longer moved. Burr drew back warily from the bundle of stinking cloth, his spear ready for a second assault.

Uahach breathed in deep gasps, but when her eyes met his this time there was recognition in them.

"Were you able to get anything?" He thought that a very vain hope. She had been too shaken by the emergence of the crawler.

But she nodded. "Something ... not enough. I must try again. That ... I did not expect *that*." Still shivering she pointed to what lay hidden from their eyes.

"That was your fear."

She shook her head. "Not mine ... hers ... Uahach's! It seems they implanted more than her memories in me."

For a moment there was silence between them. That attack had been cunningly organized ... not to get directly at Burr, but rather remove the support of his true dreamer. If he had been killed it would have served a double purpose. But now he was convinced that the girl with him had as much to fear as he did. And when she spoke, Burr knew that she realized that in turn.

"To shake me," she spoke in a voice hardly above a whisper. "With me held, then you can be easily taken, or so she thinks!"

"What will she send next?" He knew the folly of asking that even as he voiced the question. Esper talented this pseudodreamer might be, but to be able to outsee the enemy dreamer was too much to expect of anyone.

There was a noise, not issuing from the dark bowels of the Tower but rather from the rock cliffs. Burr slued around, and his breath caught in his throat.

Perhaps the enemy did not have the proper knowledge of his personal fears, but what had been conjured up now, what was scrabbling over the waste of rocks would awaken sick fear in any one in whose veins even a trace of Terran blood now flowed.

Each planet has its own perils. But there was one overriding one which had led in the past to two desperate measures, the actual deliberate burn-off by force of whole worlds which had been infected, lest a horrible death spawned on the surface somehow be carried on to blight more of the galaxy.

This ... this *Thing* which lurched with purpose toward them ... Burr had seen its like in the tri-dees of warning each agent must memorize in first training. The mewling creature must once have been human, or humanoid enough to interbreed with Terrans. For their species alone in the galaxy was susceptible to what it harbored within it. And it was an added curse of that rotting disease that those victims who harbored it were driven in turn to infect their fellows. Touch, a whiff of breath from their half-dissolved throats ... a myriad different things could transmit the virus ... a virus which had a deadly life of its own, feeding not only on the victim's body, but on his liquifying mind, so that it learned from its carrier where and when it could be most likely to pick a fresh victim.

The creature, dead as a man knows death, yet stumbling on, powered by the will of the thing which had killed it so horribly, lurched toward them. All Burr's instincts lay toward flight, even though he knew it would do no good. Once the thing was set on their trail it would tirelessly follow. Since it was already dead, no weapon save a burner beam could destroy it. And it was a menace to both of them. So it would seem that the dreamer was now determined to slay them together in a single supreme effort.

Burr kept telling himself that this was a dream, that only his own acceptance of such action as being reality could give the thing the power of killing. But his indoctrination against the disease went so deep that the logic of that argument was far too feeble.

The sea ... the sea was behind it and here the cliff was high. If there was only some way of hurling it back over that rise they could gain time, for it would take long for that broken, eaten body to climb such a barrier and be after them.

Burr, gritting his teeth, took a couple of strides forward and snatched up the cloak which hid the battered monster, paying no attention to the noisome mass beneath.

"You have another weighted cord?" he said over his shoulder.

She did not answer and when he looked around he could see his companion was caught again in a trance state. Apparently this time unaffected by the loathsome thing tottering inexorably toward them, she was striving to trace the nightmare creature back to its creator.

Dragging the torn, stained cloak, Burr leaped to her side. She did indeed have one of the weighted cords in a hook on her belt. He jerked it free, nearly dragging her from her balance by that sudden grab. Her attention did not shift to him, but he did have the cord in his hands.

Burr swung around to face the shambling horror. The weighted cord was a weapon new to him, but it was all he had. To let the thing come near enough to spear would avail him nothing for that body, until its legs rotted away under it, would pursue, it would even crawl as long as its bone-arms lasted.

He whirled the cord about his head as he had seen the girl do. This was such a slim chance, but the only one. He loosed the thong ... to see it pass out through the air. It caught about the thing a little lower than hip-high, just at a moment when the thing teetered on a rock from which it could leap out and land close to them.

However, instead it fell under the impetus of the weighted cord. Instantly Burr moved, flinging the cloak over the floundering thing much as he had done over the slug-creature. It fought the folds of cloth. A limb which was half bone protruded through from one stained slit. But Burr was ready.

Twisting the spear he jabbed fiercely with its butt at the fighting thing. Twice his weapon thudded home, rolling it back toward the edge of the cliff. With a mighty effort, for it had somehow gotten to its knees again, he sent the spear in a third blow, into which he put all of the strength he could muster, straight into the middle of the muffled shape.

This time he hurled it well back. For a second or so he was afraid not far enough. Then, as it fought to rise, to balance, it teetered farther back and was gone ... down into the sea beneath.

XI

"It is gone for a moment." He could have shouted that in his relief.

But when he looked to Uahach again he saw she had not turned her head a fraction; she could not have witnessed his small victory. Her lips moved though ...

"Come."

She had not spoken that word aloud, he had only read it with his glance. Her left hand made a vague motion away from her body as if seeking something to grasp. Burr plunged forward and gripped her fingers within his. Had she done it ... found the link with the enemy? ... Could he dare to believe? ...

The world of the Tower was blotted out by a burst of utter darkness, if one could imagine dark snapping instantly into being. Burr could not even feel if he was still hand-linked to the girl, that he had any anchor at all. There came a sensation of rushing through that darkness ...

Was this how a dream ended? His lost feeling awoke new fear. Suppose they were now caught within this place of not-being ... held forever here. Twice there were flashes of sight, a misty uprise of tower and rocks. Burr had the sensation of being drawn in two directions. And there came a pain in that which was not of body, but struck rather at some innermost core.

The dark held steady now. And the sensation of passage through this space was more intense. Then came a break in the blackness. What lay there, clothed in mist, was not rock or tower, rather a body stretched out on some support which did not come into visibility at all. And he was drawn to the side of that body.

This was a dreamer, her head half masked in the helmet which reinforced and held the dream intact.

And now Burr was aware of a strong emotion. Not the anger which had struck at him before ... no, this was the need for action, imperative and demanding. It came not from the dreamer, but from somewhere about him.

He watched a hand materialize out of nothing, its fingers crooked as if it would claw at the helmet of the sleeper. And at the same moment there was a wordless demand ...

"Now! Give me ... now!"

In him arose, without his conscious volition an answer to that cry. He must give form and substance to that clutching hand with every particle of energy he could summon. There was a swift outrush of such strength as he did not even know that he could produce until he felt it drain from him.

The hand grew denser, more real. Still he was being drained, as it began to descend with infinite slowness, moving in small jerks as if fighting its way against some defensive covering, down toward the body of the dreamer.

He could not continue to give, yet he must! For unless that hand completed its mission he would be lost indeed. Burr did not know how he could be so sure of that, he only knew that he was certain of it as if it had been part of his briefing.

Slowly the hand moved ... so slowly. He was so weakened by the drain it caused that he felt now only a tatter of man which any wind might bear away.

The crooked fingers straightened a little. They no longer resembled claws. The forefinger turned, pointed to the breast of the sleeper.

Burr held on. This was such a battle as nothing in his past had prepared him to wage. It all depended upon that finger ... the touch ... but that must come soon, very soon!

Still in jerks as if the energy which powered it flowed and ebbed the hand continued to descend. Then, the forefinger touched the misty figure of the dreamer, which had not taken on any substance at all during the long space of time, or so it had seemed to Burr, since he had come to its side.

The dreamer writhed. The finger could have been a point of steel well aimed. Then the mouth showing beneath the rim of the helmet grimaced, lips moving as if spewing forth some curse. Yet Burr could neither hear nor read words.

Again dark snapped down and he was . . . lost . . .

Something stung with a sharp stab of pain. And that pain had not been in his innermost self . . . no, he had felt that in his body. The virus ridden horror? His imagination painted a picture of that climbing doggedly up the cliff, coming to embrace him—to . . .

Gasping, he opened his eyes. A man wearing the badge of a medic leaned over him, watching him with a steady, measuring gaze. Burr blinked and blinked again. He felt dazed, unable to put name to this place at first.

"You'll do . . ."

Even those words spoken in Basic sounded queer and far away.

His whole body was stiff as he raised his hand jerkily. The helmet was gone. He was back! Recognition came now with a warm rush. He levered himself up on the divan.

"Uahach?" Burr got out the name in a shaken voice.

"She'll do," the Medic reassured him. "Close thing there though . . ."

"The other one!" Burr remembered. "The other dreamer. . . ."

He saw the Medic's eyes narrow. The man was attached to the Council HQ here, he would have been briefed before this experiment.

"She . . ." a voice as weak as his own brought Burr's head around.

Dreamer's helmet had been shed. A thin girl with cropped hair of dull brown, her wan features sharp as those of a famine victim, sat on the side of the other divan. Her slender arms were folded over her middle and she was so different from the fighting Kaitilih he had known in that other place that it was almost impossible to equate this wan and drab other being with his companion.

"Come . . ." Uahach attempted to rise to her feet, wavered and fell back. The Medic turned quickly.

"Lie still!" he ordered.

"No!" her answer came as emphatically. "We must ... go ... to ... *her* ... now!"

Burr wavered to his feet. He was as weak as if he had come out of the nightmare of the tower world sorely wounded.

"She's right," he said. "It has to be finished."

He was glad when another man, wearing a guard's side arm stepped into his line of vision, put out a hand to steady him. While the Medic, though looking as if he highly disapproved of the whole affair, was aiding Uahach up.

"Where is she?" It was Burr who asked that.

"Lost ... there...." Uahach's faint answer did not quite make sense.

As the Medic supported her from the room, the Foostmam stood just outside the door, facing them with an expressionless face. She made no move to step aside, barring their way.

"By order of your own lords," the Medic snapped, "give us free passage."

"The Hive cannot be forced!" the woman retorted sharply.

"In this case, yes." The Medic gave a jerk of his head which brought another guard into sight. "Step aside, or be put aside."

A spasm of pure hate contracted her features. "You take too much on you, off-worlder. The Hive cannot be so used."

"As you have used it for murder?" Burr asked.

She swung around to face him, her face once more expressionless.

"That is not the truth. I have already been proven, by your own methods of questioning, blameless."

"But you harbor a dreamer who is not ..." the Medic retorted. "Now we go to face her. And later there shall be inquiries as to her briefing, Foostmam. Perhaps you shall discover those who may give the Hive a darker repute than it now has."

"The Hive is innocent. Dreamers cannot kill...." Her armor of defense remained undented.

"I can testify," Burr said, "that they can try ..."

His weakness was ebbing, he was able to stand now without the support of the guard.

Uahach had said nothing during their exchange. Her face was set, her body once more rigid as it had been when she had thrown all her power into the search for their unknown enemy. The Medic glanced at her and then nodded.

"Step aside!"

This time the Foostmam shrugged and obeyed. They proceeded down the hall, around into a second corridor. The ruler of the Hive must have followed them for now her voice was raised in a new protest.

"There are no dreaming rooms here. . . . You must not enter the private chambers!"

The Medic did not even answer her. His arm around Uahach kept her on her feet. Burr guessed that the draining of the girl's Esper power to effect their return had been far more serious than his own ordeal. Yet she moved forward now as if driven by the need to find the source of the energy which had attempted to lock them into the dream world.

She swayed to a stop before a door at the far end of the corridor, putting out her hand to rest fingertips on the closed portal.

"Inside . . ." Her voice had gained no strength.

XII

At a gesture from the Medic the guard who had loomed over the Foostmam set his palm on the seal of the door. For a moment or so it would seem that had been locked against any outside interference. Then it began to roll aside, slowly and grudgingly.

From inside came a noise, a kind of mewling such as a sick animal might make. The Medic, staring over Uahach's head, showed such shock that Burr moved up beside him. Instantly the man pushed Uahach back, flung out an arm to bar Burr's advance.

"Close that, damn you!" he ordered. And the guard, wearing the same expression of shock and horror, slammed the barrier to. But not before Burr had had a single glimpse of what half lay across the divan within, was making an effort to rise, its blind, eroded face turned questioningly toward those it wanted as prey.

It was not as far gone as the horror which had hunted them on the cliff. But there was no mistaking the signs of the same dread disease. Burr made a quick move to support Uahach as the Medic rounded on the guards with a series of orders.

And it was Burr who led the girl back to the dreaming chamber. As he settled her on the divan and sat beside her, his arm about her shoulders, she spoke slowly:

"It ... recoiled. What she dreamed against us became a part of her."

"How could that happen?" Burr asked. He tried not to remember what he had seen in that room, what must now be destroyed without mercy and as swiftly as possible.

"I don't know," Uahach returned. "But I think that she was not a true dreamer, not one such as they have always known on Ty-Kry. And she has been using her powers deliberately to kill. They said that she was a late developer ... perhaps she was something else, a mutant of the dreamer stock. But I believe she was striving to send that crawling death against us even as we broke into wakefulness. Then, somehow, the force returned upon its sender. They called her Dynamis. We must find out now from whence she came, and who stands, or stood behind her."

"Not our job," Burr told her. "Let the regular hounds take over that coursing now."

Uahach sighed. "We must report . . ."

"That much I agree upon. But let the Organization take over then. We are entitled, I am sure, to hazard leave."

"And, by the way," he added a moment later. "What is your real name? I refuse to settle for either Kaitilih, as good a fighter as she was, or Uahach, a dreamer . . ."

She shivered. "I am *not* a dreamer! It was as if with that statement she thrust aside all which had menaced them, up to and including that last burst of horror found in the Hive chamber.

Burr smiled. "That you are not! They say that Avalon is an excellent leave planet. But I'd like a name to enter on the request token."

"I am Ludia Tanguly," she answered. And her voice was

firm. "Yes, indeed I *am* Ludia Tanguly!" It was as if she must affirm that identity and make sure that nothing remained of Uahach.

Burr nodded. "Very well, Ludia Tanguly, it is now our duty to get to HQ, to give recorded statements and then . . ."

She straightened up within the half circle of his arm as if new strength flowed back into her. "And then . . . *I* shall think about your suggestion," she ended firmly.

ANDRE NORTON
in DAW BOOKS editions

☐ **MERLIN'S MIRROR.** A brand-new novel, written for DAW, of science-lore versus Arthurian legendry.
(#UY1175—$1.25)

☐ **SPELL OF THE WITCH WORLD.** A DAW exclusive, continuing the famous Witch World stories, and not available elsewhere.
(#UY1179—$1.25)

☐ **THE CRYSTAL GRYPHON.** The latest in the beloved Witch World novels, it is an outstanding other-world adventure.
(#UY1187—$1.25)

☐ **HERE ABIDE MONSTERS.** Trapped in a parallel world, just off Earth's own map and right out of legend.
(#UY1134—$1.25)

☐ **GARAN THE ETERNAL.** An epic adventure in lost worlds and unmeasured time—never before in paperbacks.
(#UY1186—$1.25)

☐ **THE BOOK OF ANDRE NORTON.** Novelettes, short stories, articles, and a bibliography make this a treat for Norton's millions of readers.
(#UY1198—$1.25)

DAW BOOKS are represented by the publishers of Signet and Mentor Books, THE NEW AMERICAN LIBRARY, INC.
